The Devil's Ridge

By Andre Bergeron

Mars Media Publishers

This book is dedicated to L. D. Clepper, for his tireless efforts and enthusiasm.

Thanks to my parents, brothers, wife, and friends who have read many versions of this story as it has matured from concept to published novel.

Designed by Roderick Brons | Textcase, Nassaulaan 25, 1213 BA Hilversum, Holland
Contact: info@textcase.nl or visit www.textcase.nl

Manufactured in the United States of America

First Edition

ISBN-13: 978-1-60136-016-8
ISBN-10: 1-60136-016-9

Library of Congress Control Number: 2007935905

For information regarding special sales or for any and all matters related to the purchase of the book or its rights, please contact Mars Media Publishers at marspublishers@gmail.com or write to us at PO Box 119, Franklin Park, NJ 08823 USA

Please visit www.thedevilsridge.com

Contents

* * *

Harmon Willoughby raced up the steep incline on his forest green sheriff's department ATV. He was followed by two trusted deputies on their own vehicles. The three officers had left Steve Akers' farm a day after having rescued Mark Dunston and flown him to the hospital. They were heading into the dark Kentucky woods along nearly the same path used by Jesse and his companions days earlier. Sheriff Willoughby and his men were each armed with shotguns and sidearms and carried evidence collection packs on their ATVs. They were not looking for more survivors. They were venturing into the woods for one purpose – cleanup.

* * *

PART I

Mist shot out of Brad Brown's mouth as he breathed rapidly in the cool autumn air. Brad struggled to catch his breath as he settled down next to his father. The two crouched behind the trunk of a massive fallen spruce tree and gazed out over the top of the lichen-covered log. The light drizzle falling was fogging up Brad's glasses and his father's binoculars.

Brad took off his glasses and wiped them on his wool coat. His breathing was already returning to normal. The past week of acclimatizing to the elevated peaks he and his dad had been trekking through in the northeast corner of Utah's Uinta Mountain Range had allowed him to slowly get used to breathing the thin high-altitude air.

This was Brad's first out-of-state hunting trip with his father. They had left their home in the suburbs outside of Detroit and flown into Salt Lake City the previous Saturday. Brad took a couple of days off from school right before the Thanksgiving holiday so he would not miss too many lessons from his fifth grade class.

It had been a grueling week climbing and hiking in the Uintas. Brad struggled the first few days to get used to the high altitude and the foreign terrain. The loose, red rock they scrambled over sometimes was accented in places with a lone cactus and at other times was covered in dense stands of evergreens.

Brad had not even seen the elk spotted by his father, but he was excited to be on the trail of something after days of fruitless searching. The large animal had been moving through the valley below and Brad's father anticipated that it would soon ascend the next ridge over. Brad stood up a little and peered over the horizontal tree trunk in hopes of seeing movement in the trees below. He had to take his glasses off again to wipe away the rain and condensation.

A loud call burst out from the valley floor and Brad looked up at his father in surprise. He had heard countless versions of an elk bugle on the tapes he had been forced to listen to in the weeks building up to the trip. He was pretty sure that the noise now echoing off the surrounding ridges did not match the calls that had come from his tape player at home.

"Dad?" he asked, hoping for a response from his father.

Brad's father did not answer, but was instead focused on intently scanning the tree line below. Then, he stood up from the crouched position behind the fallen, weathered spruce. He leaned forward to get a better look at the valley.

"That's no elk," he whispered. "If it is, I'm a goddamn Chinaman."

Brad had only heard his father curse on very rare occasions. The expletive and the strange expression on his father's face caused Brad some concern.

"Dad?" he asked again.

His father finally broke off his survey of the opposite ridge. "Here Brad," he said, handing him the binoculars, "see if you can see that animal walking along the bottom of that next hill. It seems to be moving through those trees. I caught a brief look at it through the binoculars, but let's see if I can spot it through my rifle scope."

As Brad scanned the opposite hill, he worked his gaze from the top of the ridge to the bottom, looking for anything to stand out against the wet red rock and the green of the pines and spruces. His father had crouched back down and was using the fallen tree trunk as a steadying rest for the rifle and scope. The weathered Remington 700 rifle was chambered in 30.06 caliber – sufficient for game from whitetail deer to moose. The expensive riflescope sitting on top of the action had a variable lens that could be adjusted for magnification much greater than the old binoculars Brad held.

Brad could tell that his own heartbeat had sped up as he tried to calm his hands and hold the binoculars still enough to focus clearly on the scene in front of him. Meanwhile, his father mumbled softly to himself as he stared through the more powerful riflescope. "I can just about see the individual branches on those fir trees down there. Anything as big as what I saw a minute ago will be easy to spot at high power on this scope. Now Brad, if that animal moves out into the open again, I want you to …"

He stopped speaking immediately and, fumbling, clumsily set his rifle down. "There's no way – no way in the world," he stammered.

Brad grabbed the loose rifle resting on top of the spruce trunk and held the scope to his eye. He could not see anything but a blurry black mass on the opposite ridge. He had to put the rifle down and change the focus to match his, rather than his father's, vision. When he looked back at the area, he just caught a brief glimpse of a hairy black hide moving behind a dense clump of trees.

"What was it, dad?" he asked. He had attempted to ask his question with bravery and excitement, but instead a tone of fear crept into it. "Was it a big elk?"

"Let's go, son," Brad's father replied. "Grab your pack and let's get down to the bottom of that other ridge. I think we can cut it off before it gets above the tree line."

Brad still did not know what "it" was, and he was concerned that the look of bewilderment on his father's face had changed to one of fierce determination. He tried to tell himself, though, that perhaps a trophy elk would be waiting at their destination and his father's strange manner would turn to one of satisfaction and ease with a successful conclusion to the hunt.

As they clambered down the hillside, Brad did his best to keep up with his father, who was not paying much attention to the breakneck speed he was traveling. Brad slipped on some loose rock, but grabbed a fir tree to steady himself. He looked at the digital watch on his wrist. It was already four o'clock in the afternoon. He knew from the previous days' hunts that they had just over an hour of daylight left and that the cool autumn air would then become bone-chilling in the sun's absence. In fact, it seemed like it was already getting colder. As they reached the valley below, they stood in a small clearing formed by a mountain stream. Brad realized then that the drizzle that had been falling earlier was turning into freezing rain and sleet, and then to snow.

"Dad," he said with alarm, "it's snowing."

"It'll blow over Brad, now come on. If we keep moving we'll meet that thing halfway up this ridge."

His father slung the rifle over his back and crossed the stream with a leap. Brad tried to stay close, but once they started going up the ridge, he could not match the pace of his determined father. He protested several times and grew more worried when occasionally he would lose sight of his father climbing up the incline. Brad finally caught up when his father had stopped to inspect some tracks. The snow had increased and there was already a quarter inch covering the rocky soil of the upslope.

"He's going straight up the goddamn mountain," his father said, half in anger and half in awe. "We can catch up to him in that clearing up ahead."

Before Brad could muster a futile objection, his father was already back to his feverish pursuit. Brad could no longer keep pace and resigned himself to following his father's footprints in the snow. Brad finally got near to the top of the ridge and found his father crouching at the entrance to a thick stand of pines.

"He's in there," his father said through labored breaths.

Brad was breathing heavily too and his legs ached from the climb.

"Can't we rest now, dad?" he whined.

"You stay here, then," his father responded. "I'm going into this patch of trees here. Don't go anywhere so I know where to find you."

Brad watched helplessly as his father entered the dense stand of trees. They were all young pines about six to seven feet tall, their identical height and age the result of a fire that had swept through this area a few years before.

The snow had stopped and a hushed stillness had descended over the ridges and valleys. Brad could see for at least a few miles from his vantage point. The dusting of snow gave the surrounding terrain a uniform appearance. The scene in front of him would have been appropriate for a postcard, but Brad's unease crept back up to dominate his attention. He switched his gaze onto the stand of trees behind him, hoping to catch a glimpse of his father.

In the stillness and quiet of the late afternoon, Brad felt sure he might be able to at least hear his father moving about through the evergreen limbs and branches. He leaned forward at the entrance of the thicket and strained to listen. He could not hear a thing except for an occasional breeze of wind moving the needled branches near him, and his own breathing – which was finally starting to settle down after the strenuous hike.

Brad's breath stopped, though, when a thunderous roaring shriek boomed out over the tops of surrounding pines. The noise blasted through the thicket and even seemed to shake snow off some of the tree limbs. The shrillness of the noise reminded Brad of an ambulance siren from back home, but it had a deep bass quality to it that seemed to rumble the very ground Brad stood on.

Not more than a second or two after the terrifying sound caught Brad off guard, he heard the distinct crack of his father's rifle – normally a loud blast itself. It seemed puny and insignificant following the horrific noise that had just boomed across the ridge top. Brad waited a few minutes, expecting to hear his father's voice calling to him to enter the thicket and see whatever manner of quarry he had just taken.

No reassuring call ever came, though, and soon Brad began to pick his way slowly through the dense evergreen boughs. He could barely make out a rough trail of footprints from his father as the late afternoon light began to wane. He struggled through the interwoven branches and finally saw a dark object ahead. He cautiously crept forward and then realized what he had been looking at – his father, lying motionless on the ground.

"Dad, Dad!" he yelled as he rushed up to the lifeless body. He began crying instantly as he shook his father's cold body. After a moment or two of hysterics, it dawned on Brad that his father was dead and the question of how that had come about arose. Brad studied his father. The rifle was still in his clutches, he had no scratches or bruises, and he seemed to be intact and otherwise fine.

Brad did not know what had killed his father, but he thought of the ominous roaring howl he had heard earlier. And now, seeing his father dead on the cold snowy ground, he realized that he was truly frightened. Brad did not just feel scared the way he had when separated from his parents in the grocery store, or when he had heard ghost stories at bedtime. He felt something different and deeper, and it was coupled with a gnawing solitude – knowing that there was not another human being for perhaps miles and miles around him. These feelings unnerved him to his very core.

Brad sat on the snowy, rocky ground, leaning against his father for security and for shelter from the cold breeze that whipped through the stand of evergreens from time to time. The one thing he remembered from the preparations for this hunting trip was something his father had said many times and the guide at the lodge had repeated. "If you ever get lost up in the mountains, stay put. It's much easier for rescuers to find you if you stay in one place than if you're moving around getting yourself more lost."

Evening and darkness were creeping up the ridgeline and Brad started wondering if he could stay put in this situation. He was trying not to think about the corpse of his father right behind him. He knew he would cry too much if he dwelt on it right then. He had bigger issues at the time. With each passing minute, it grew darker and colder. Brad's fears were starting to get the better of him as his imagination tried to supply an explanation for what had happened on the ridge.

Then, suddenly, his racing mind stopped. It stopped so abruptly that even Brad noticed it. He was immediately much more aware of his surroundings.

He was hearing everything more clearly – the wind brushing through the evergreen needles, and … Brad then realized something was wrong, that the occasional breeze is all he heard. The forest thicket had gotten eerily quiet and still.

Snap. It was just a twig, but in the stark silence and with Brad's heightened attention, it was loud enough. Brad spun around to face the dark woods behind him. *Creak.* Brad could make out a whole tree bending to one side under the pressure of some unseen force. *Crack.* Someone or something had just swung a log against the side of a thick pine tree with enough force to break the log in half. Brad could hear a piece of it hurling through the other pine branches and rolling to a rest deep into the darkness.

The steps kept up all night. Something was pacing through the trees – a dark shadow sometimes discernible. Against the starry sky Brad could barely see its outline above the tree tops before it would disappear again. Brad did not close his eyes the entire night. The terrorizing fear he felt actually was the only thing that kept him alive through a night of temperatures that dropped into the high twenties. Besides his own hunting clothes, Brad had taken off his father's hunting coat and wool toboggan to put on for extra layers. He hunkered down next to his father's body, relentlessly watching the woods around him.

Brad awoke with a jerk the next morning. His head had been resting on the now-stiff stomach of his father's body. He must have just fallen asleep as he remembered watching the first signs of dawn spreading across the night sky. Then he heard a welcome sound.

"Here he is, I've found him."

It was the guide from the lodge who, along with a small band of search and rescue personnel had begun combing the local mountains before daybreak. The guide had known where Brad and his father had set out from the day before and the tracking dogs had picked up their trail easily.

"We would've found you twenty minutes ago if the dogs hadn't gone so haywire when we got to the woods here," the guide told a half-frozen Brad as he approached. "Sometimes they pick up some critter's smell that makes 'em act skittish and spooky, like they don't really want to find what's at the end of that scent trail. Good thing you got your old man's hunting jacket on, though – you can see that blaze orange color a mile away."

The grizzled guide made his way over to Brad and helped him to his feet. The guide looked down at Brad's father. "Sorry 'bout your father there, son. Wouldn't be the first fella we've lost high up in these mountains. Let's get you back to the lodge and warmed up and then we'll call your ma."

* * *

PART II

Hot, moist air crept out of Brad Brown's mouth in short, controlled breaths. Though it was evening, the day's oppressive heat still lingered, and Brad's shirt was already soaked with sweat. Brad shivered a bit when a sudden breeze blew through the area and across his sweat-covered body. The anxiety and excitement of the moment sent chills up and down his spine and made his teeth chatter lightly. He tried to control himself, though, because in this situation, errors could be deadly.

He could see movement beyond the trees in front of him. A large bush moved and hundreds of leaves quivered – very slightly – but noticeably enough to Brad, who intensely focused on the foliage just thirty yards ahead. In the hot, heavy evening air, a smell crept up to Brad. It was not the dampness or the plants. It was an animal. This smell sent Brad's senses to high alert. A predator was nearby.

Brad clicked the safety on the old Remington rifle – his father's. He was ready to shoot the large animal creeping through the underbrush. A bead of sweat trickled from his forehead. Annoyed, he wiped it away with his sleeve, and instantly returned his concentration to the forested area in front of him. Brad adjusted a focus knob on the side of his rifle scope and soon the foreground became much clearer through the amber lenses. He scanned the tree line with the scope, slowly looking for more signs of movement.

A few tall blades of bush grass faintly swayed just ten yards in front of him. Somehow, the animal had covered twenty yards of ground heading right in Brad's direction – totally silently and almost invisibly. Brad's heart pounded in his chest and his breathing sped up even more. He tried to calm himself down, but there was not any time.

A beastly roar burst from the tall grasses in front of Brad and the animal rushed his position, leaping with a fanged mouth wide open. Brad squeezed off his first shot, manipulated the bolt back and forth, and fired a second round all in a fraction of a second, while the animal was still in the air hurtling towards him. Both shots hit dead on. At this close of range, he could see the bullets impact with hair and blood flying as the huge beast fell to the ground at his feet.

A thin trail of smoke slowly curled upwards from the barrel of Brad's

Remington rifle. The deafening sounds of the lion's roar and the gunshots gave way to a period of stark silence. Brad looked down at the magnificent beast before him. He had wanted to hunt the biggest predator on the continent, and the brute at his feet pushed the heavy end of five hundred pounds or more. Brad poked the giant animal with his rifle barrel to make sure it was dead, then bent over to feel its mane and check out its formidable teeth.

The silence after the gunshots was broken by Brad's guide, Willem Conradie, rushing through the crunchy brush and bushes to check on his client. Willem stood a robust six feet tall, and his bushy, reddish-orange beard made him look older than his thirty-seven years. He was a South African hunting guide who arranged exotic hunts and safaris all over the African continent for wealthy customers. Willem had spotted this particular male two nights earlier near the perimeter of their lush wilderness camp. The guide had combed the bush looking for its tracks and sign, and had this animal's daily patterns down to a routine.

Willem now looked at the big cat, bent over it and stroked its mane and hide. "He's a nice one Mr. Brown. You did a good job mate. Me and Tomás were just a few yards behind you, ready to finish him off if you had any trouble. But you did a fine job of him. Right Tomás?"

"That's right Mr. Willem," Tomás Nhacumba responded as he silently moved through the grasses and scrub brush to get a closer look. He was a native of Mozambique and often teamed up with Willem Conradie to take clients out in this area. His coal-black skin blended in with the darkening sky and surroundings so that the most prominently visible feature was the loose white T-shirt that clung to his now-sticky body. "I was about to fire a shot when this big fellow leaped in the air. I would have too, but Mr. Brown hit him square on. He's a big one, isn't he?"

"Well, thanks guys," Brad responded quietly, and then did not say another word. A period of strange silence passed over the group.

The bushy red-haired Afrikaner glanced over at the tall, skinny Mozambique native with puzzlement. Willem finally reached for his field-dressing kit and said, "Me and Tomás need to get working on this old boy, mate. Take this flashlight here and we'll meet you back at the truck right along."

Brad grabbed the flashlight and headed off into the darkness. Behind him he could hear Tomás and Willem pick right up with their chatter as they began working away and talking loudly in a language foreign to his ears. He reached the modified Toyota Landcruiser SUV in just a few minutes.

Brad slung the Remington 700 into the cargo area of the SUV, then opened the front passenger door. Sitting on his seat rested a blindingly-polished silver tray with an expensive-looking envelope. Brad opened the envelope and took out the heavy card inside. It said, "Congratulations, From Conradie African Safaris!" in typed letters, and then in handwritten ink, "Well done, Brad, we knew you would get your lion in fine fashion." It was signed by Willem and also had Tomás' name written underneath.

Brad reached over to the center console, where a handsome wooden humidor held a few samples of his favorite cigars, and a bottle of champagne chilled in an electronic device. Brad lit one of the cigars, took a few puffs and leaned back into the comfortable, leather bucket seat. He gazed through the windshield at the dizzying display of stars emerging in front of him in the African sky. The twenty-seven year old should have been overwhelmingly satisfied by the awesome sensory delights surrounding him, but not even a smile cracked his lips. He just puffed away on the cigar and stared at the twinkling stars in front of him.

* * *

The jolty, bone-jarring ride home did not bother Brad. The Landcruiser absorbed quite a few of the blows, and the soft leather seats helped cushion the impact as the three men sped along dusty trails and dirt roads. Soon the twinkling brilliance of the stars was replaced by torch lamps and electrical flood lights that blazed from the colossal hunting lodge looming before the travelers on an elevated platform. Willem, Tomás, and Brad pulled up to the high fence that surrounded the entire compound. Willem spoke something fast into a speaker mounted next to the gate. Gears whirred and the massive gate began to roll back, allowing them entrance. Willem pulled forward, and then up the steep hill that led to the main lodge.

Kelly Graham opened the door to her suite when she heard the hunting party approaching in their SUV. She was amazed at how cool the night had gotten after the sun dipped below the African horizon. She saw the lights of the SUV coming up the hill from the gate entrance and waved. She was not sure if Brad had seen her wave, but she wanted to seem excited for him.

Kelly really hoped that Brad had had success that night. She thought he had been awfully quiet and kind of grouchy recently, even though they were on this African safari. Perhaps if he had gotten his trophy lion, she thought, not only would he be in a better mood, but maybe they would also be able to go home now.

Willem and Tomás saw Kelly coming toward the vehicle and hopped out to greet her. They were both used to their clients bringing a spouse on safari. Some men even had their wife or significant other accompany them on the hunt. Brad, however, had wanted to be alone.

"Hello Miss Kelly," Tomás said as she came down the steps. "Come see the big lion your Brad has shot tonight."

Kelly smiled at them as she came down the steps and up to the SUV. Brad eased out of the front seat and Kelly rushed up to him, showing that she was proud of his accomplishment. Brad was uncomfortable with the praise he was getting from his fellow hunters, but Willem and Tomás insisted that he show Kelly the magnificent lion before they had to take it way for some more processing.

Kelly stared at the lion in mild disbelief. The huge creature was stretched out limply on the back tailgate, held in place with several ratchet straps. Its massive paws draped off the back. The long, pink tongue hung out of one corner of the lion's mouth, and its giant canines shown prominently. All she could manage to say was, "That's the biggest cat I've ever seen."

Willem and Tomás got a hearty laugh out of that. They wished the two a good night as they climbed back in the SUV and drove around to the back of the lodge compound to unload the lion and prepare it for further butchering and taxidermy work. Kelly grabbed Brad's arm and they headed up to their room.

Inside, Brad flopped down onto the king-sized bed without saying much. He bunched up some pillows under his head and grabbed a book that he had been reading off and on. Kelly jumped on the bed and made her way over to Brad. She snuggled up to him and rested her head on his chest and shoulder. Brad did not seem to notice. He kept staring at the pages in his open book. Kelly unbuttoned some of his shirt and began rubbing his chest with her free hand and played with his chest hair. She moved her hand lower to his stomach, then further down. She reached to unbuckle his belt, expecting that this would finally get a response.

"Not now," Brad said icily.

Kelly snapped. "Brad, what's wrong with you? In fact, what's been wrong with you this whole trip? You've either been a jerk or out in left field this whole time, and especially the last few days."

Brad shifted on the bed, uncomfortable with Kelly's stare.

"Look Kelly," he began timidly, "I'm sorry about how I've been acting. This has been a weird experience for me, and apparently I've made it a bad experience for you."

"No, Brad," Kelly interrupted, "this has been a good experience for the most part, like almost all of our adventures. But it makes me confused and irritated to see you in such a foul mood. Is it something I've done?" Kelly gave up on her defensive standing posture and sat down on the corner of the bed.

Brad reached over and grabbed her hand. "Sweetheart, you've been great – a real trouper. I know you don't love coming on these hunts. I appreciate your willingness to do so. It's just, well, it's the hunting experience that's let me down … and left me wondering about some things."

Kelly didn't understand. "What are you talking about, Brad? I would've thought that the hunting's been all you could've asked for and then some. I mean, you shot a huge lion today. That thing was massive. Wasn't that the type of trophy you were after?"

Brad shrugged in response and took a long breath as if he were trying to figure out how to best answer Kelly. "That's not really the issue," he mumbled.

"Does this have something to do with your therapy sessions – with what happened to you as a kid? If so – and I thought you were way over that a long time ago – I just don't see the connection."

"You just don't get 'over' something like that Kelly," Brad answered. "But, I am trying to. I would like nothing more than to be 'way over' the fear that still wakes me up on an almost nightly basis. I know I've bored you countless times with the dreams I have just about every week. I still get short of breath and sort of dizzy when I remember the terror that I felt on that mountain lying next to my dead father, waiting and watching as the very darkness of the night seemed to surround me."

Brad stood up off the bed and continued. "Am I 'over' it? Not by a long shot. I know I *should* be. Most normal people would. But that same fear and anxiety's still got me by the balls. I wake up with it and I go to bed with it, and the only thing I've found that helps is confronting that type of situation head on."

"Like you thought this would be?" Kelly asked, trying to follow Brad's point. He nodded and was silent for a moment. Kelly took the opportunity to pry further. "I mean, I'm not trying to be insensitive, but like a lot of people's parents die. A lot of people have scary or traumatic things happen when they're kids. Right?"

"Don't you think not a day goes by when I don't wonder why I can't just be like all those people? Why almost two decades later these emotions still have such a grip on me instead of fading into childhood memories? Why do you think I've been going to therapy all those years? To figure out why I can't shake this when most people can."

"And this helps?" Kelly offered as she gestured to the surroundings with her hand.

"Yeah, it does," Brad replied, easing up a bit.

"But it's not quite what you're looking for is it? I can see now that a lion wasn't enough for you. You want something else. Something *more*."

Kelly could tell that she had just zeroed in on exactly what Brad wanted. She flopped back down onto the bed and sunk her head into her pillow. She rolled her eyes and let out a sigh. "Brad, we've been together for a long time now and I've seen you struggle with your inner demons. I've also seen what has looked like progress. But where is this all going? Where does it end?"

"Look Kelly," Brad said as he moved closer to her on the bed, "I don't have an answer right now. But I promise I'll come up with one. And just talking about it helps – a lot."

Kelly did not respond immediately. She lay on the bed staring up at the ceiling, wondering how much longer they would have to talk about this sort of thing. She did not want to be in the wilds of Mozambique any longer. She was not sure she was prepared to continue helping her boyfriend tackle his psychological problems when it involved such peculiar schemes. She wanted to get back home and to a sense of normalcy.

* * *

Brad Brown had moved into his parents' old house when he turned twenty-one. His mother was still alive and well, but had remarried a few years after Brad's father's death. She and Brad's stepfather moved out of the house when Brad returned from college. He only stayed there off and on because he was so frequently out of town.

Brad flipped absentmindedly through a mixture of magazines and hunting brochures while Kelly watched a cooking show on the big-screen plasma TV. Brad eventually tossed one of the magazines across the room with enough force to knock off-kilter a hanging picture of Brad posing with a black bear in the Canadian wilderness.

Kelly looked up from her show. She knew Brad was trying to find a new type of hunt to go on. That was all he could talk about during the flight home from Mozambique a week earlier. He had been racking his brain for a solid week now, with no positive results. His frustration was beginning to spread to Kelly who wanted to talk about something other than hunting for more than a minute or two.

Kelly knew that Brad's father had passed away during a hunting trip and that Brad had stayed the night by his deceased father's side alone in the wilderness. While she thought this was surely a scarring incident, Kelly just did not understand why Brad had not moved on past this event.

For his part, Brad had never told anyone about what really happened in the mountains of northeastern Utah. The hunting guide who found Brad had alluded to the presence of a mysterious animal in the area when his dogs picked up a set of strange tracks coming down the mountain. Even then, Brad had not wanted to inquire about the glimpses of something he and his father had seen, or the gloomy, dark presence that had stalked him throughout the night at the top of the snow-covered mountain.

He was getting closer and closer to talking about it with his therapist, and each hunting trip seemed to take him back to those terrifying hours. It was a slow process, and Brad knew that Kelly was growing tired of being involved in it. After almost seven years of dating, he was still not comfortable discussing with Kelly the details of this very secret and private incident in his life.

*　*　*

Kelly shifted around in the oversized leather chair after Brad had tossed the magazine against the wall in frustration. "If those magazines aren't doing you any good, why don't you try searching the Internet? I've found some pretty hard-to-find clothes on the Web before that you would've never even seen in the stores or in a catalogue."

Brad considered Kelly's advice for a while. He mulled it over in his head long enough for her to lose interest and return to watching her cooking show and dozing in the comfortable chair. Brad was normally reluctant to take a suggestion from Kelly, especially when it was regarding something so obvious and important. He mentally kicked himself for not having thought of the Internet long ago. He scolded himself again because the best bet he had for success was coming from a shopping tip from his girlfriend.

Brad immediately went over to the desktop computer resting on the heavy mahogany desk. He clicked the icon for Internet service and pulled up a search engine. Then he sat there for a while. Brad leaned back in his chair and stared out into the room, trying to think of a good search term. He chuckled to himself at the symbolism of the moment – he truly did not know what he was searching for.

He typed a few keywords and tried different searches, but with no particular luck. Brad could hear Kelly snoring lightly as she had obviously dozed off in the big leather chair. Eventually he keyed in "dangerous animals," but this primarily yielded results concentrating on sharks, spiders, snakes, bears, and big cats – all of which were certainly dangerous, but not what Brad was looking for. Brad altered his search terms and added "scary" to "dangerous animals" and entered a search for "scary dangerous animals." This produced a lot of the same results, plus a few websites about bats, a few with sci-fi/horror movie reviews and one about giant squids.

The giant squid website interested Brad, not because he wanted to hunt sea creatures, but just because it was a little different than the results he had been looking at and he needed some variety at this point. He clicked on the link and was taken to a website chronicling discoveries of giant squids and other "cryptozoological" creatures. At the top of the page was a collage of several strange creatures. Brad clicked the monster-collage graphic and link, and found himself on a cryptozoological index page, with a variety of links to pages focusing on each type of creature. He had no interest in the Loch Ness Monster, sea serpents, or the mystery big cats of England, but his interest was raised by the list of bigfoot Web sites.

One of the links led to the Bigfoot Researchers Organization. Brad liked the layout of the site and read the Frequently Asked Questions page thoroughly. He was impressed with the scientific analysis that had been done on evidence relating to the bigfoot phenomenon. Brad followed a link to a map of the United States, with each state clickable to see sightings from that state, in a county-by-county fashion. Brad was amazed at the number of reports, especially for the frequency of sightings all over the country. There were even sightings filed for areas in Canada, where the creature is known more commonly as Sasquatch, from its Native American name.

Brad began reading these reports. There were hundreds, if not thousands of eyewitness accounts. These stories ranged from hearing loud, terrifying screams and howls associated with the creature to first-hand daylight encounters with a seven-to-eight-foot-tall massive hairy creature. Some of the reports were straightforward documentations of the occurrences, while others read like horror stories. It was obvious that many people had been clearly scared by something they had seen in the woods. Brad became engrossed in reading these reports. He did not notice time slipping by.

"Are you still awake? What are you doing?" Kelly had awakened and groggily questioned Brad. She was surprised to see him still sitting at the computer, barely lit by the glow of the screen while the rest of the room had gotten fairly dark.

Brad minimized the Internet screen he was looking at and got up from his seat. He took Kelly upstairs to the bedroom and showed her to bed, promising that he would be up shortly. She was still half-asleep and did not pursue her curiosity any further. Brad walked back down stairs, grabbed a cigarette from a pack in the kitchen and headed out to the back deck to smoke. The cool, early night air of spring felt invigorating to Brad as he breathed it in and exhaled his cigarette smoke. He finished his cigarette and went back inside to read some more.

Still on the BRO Web site, Brad focused on the map of sightings. He was also interested to see a marker with sightings in Utah near the Uinta mountain range. Brad clicked on it and read a few brief details of sightings in the mid and late 1970s. A cold chill crept up his spine as he looked at the locations and terrain descriptions while thinking of his own mysterious and tragic experience in the high Uintas. He shuddered as a dull realization crept in that perhaps he was looking at the possible explanation for what he and his father witnessed in those rugged mountains.

Brad clicked to another part of the site with some crude drawings and some sound files. When Brad selected the sound files to listen to, he almost fell out of his chair as the eerie howling scream being played on his computer brought back the vivid memory of what he had heard as a frightened child on that lonely, snowy mountain. Brad's mind raced and he even began sweating, with goose bumps popping up on his arms and neck.

He was besieged again by the feeling of fear suffered through countless nightmares over the years. He realized this and felt silly for feeling this way in the safety and comfort of his own den. Brad noted that this flood of emotions has been elicited by a single sound.

As he continued exploring the Web site, Brad's mind wandered to envisioning an expedition or a hunt for a Sasquatch. He was still having trouble believing such a creature could exist and be unknown to modern science. He did not even know if this kind of animal is what he and his father had confronted on the snowy slopes of the Uinta Mountains. And yet, he thought about the possibilities of such a venture. He could not imagine a more direct way to confront the fears that had tormented him since his childhood.

Brad stayed up for several more hours reading additional reports and encounters, hypotheses and theories, message boards, chat rooms, and just about anything related to the bigfoot/Sasquatch phenomenon. He eventually crawled in bed for a few hours, but did not get much sleep lying in bed with his mind racing.

*　*　*

The next morning, Brad could not wait to tell Kelly about his late-night revelations. She woke up before him and was fixing a bowl of cereal when Brad met her in the kitchen. He explained the whole thing to her, barely taking breaths as he spoke. Kelly thought it was strange, though, and wondered if this was not a sign that Brad's emotional problems had gotten the better of him. She had always considered the tabloid headlines and ridiculous photos as hoaxes or tall tales. She was genuinely surprised at Brad's excitement and a little taken aback that he had already thrown himself headlong into this project without concern over how ridiculous it sounded. She told him that he was not usually the type of person to get involved in something so silly.

Brad did not take the comments well. Kelly had just deflated all of the enthusiasm and excitement that he had built up the night before by completely dismissing the idea. Kelly took a long sip of coffee and said, "If you want to spend your money and time on what will probably just be an over-glorified camping trip, that's fine. But don't expect me to say it's a good idea, and don't expect me to go with you on this one. I can handle exotic trips to fancy hunting lodges to so you can work out your demons by hunting real animals, but when it comes to make-believe…"

Brad was getting ready to angrily respond when the doorbell rang. He stormed out of the kitchen to answer the door. Roy Bakerson stood on the stone front porch, caught off guard by the manner in which Brad suddenly opened the front door.

"Whoa, easy big fella," Roy teased. "You look a little frazzled there buddy. I hope you haven't forgotten our ten o'clock tee time. We've been talking about golfing today for like a week now." Roy threw a fake punch at Brad's shoulder. "Don't shaft me on this one. I need somebody to help polish off that cooler full of beer." Roy gestured toward his silver Mercedes and smiled.

Brad studied his college buddy for a minute and looked back inside at Kelly standing in the kitchen. He really did not want to continue his conversation with Kelly and did not feel like being around her at the time either. So, without much of an explanation, he yelled to her, "I'm going golfing with Roy. See you tonight." Before Brad could close the door behind him, Roy leaned in just long enough to catch Kelly's glare as she looked from around a corner.

"Hi Kell', good to see you," he said. Kelly smiled when she saw Roy, and was about to say something to him, but Brad yanked Roy out of the doorway and onto the porch.

* * *

Back in the house, Kelly fumed. She and Brad had been together for almost seven years since they first started dating in college. Yet, they were still *just* dating. Kelly truly loved Brad, or at least felt like she had at one time. She also enjoyed the lifestyle he was able to provide. His newest idea for hunting monsters, though, was one in a long line of schemes to deal with his inner torment that Kelly had put up with all along. She was not sure she could tolerate this wild proposal. They had recently been growing apart and Kelly believed that they would need to take the next step in their relationship or start considering alternatives. Her list of alternatives did not include fairy tale creatures and childish schemes to go monster hunting.

Kelly had also been thrown off by Roy's arrival at the front door. She had met Roy in college when she transferred her senior year. He was the first person she met before being introduced to Brad. She had actually hit it off better with Roy at first because of their similar interests. Though she eventually started dating Brad, Kelly and Roy had stayed close.

Recently, they had been seeing each other frequently for lunch dates and other outings, often when Brad was out of town for business or on one of his hunting trips. Brad was aware of the get-togethers and never expressed any concern over the two meeting up while he was away. It was, after all, just a friendship, though Kelly had begun to detect a difference in her relationship with Roy the last time they went out to see a movie. There had been some awkwardness at the end of the night when Roy dropped her off at home.

Kelly went back into the kitchen, sat down at the breakfast table and took a deep breath. The emotional roller coaster of Brad's wild scheme and storming off coupled with seeing Roy at the door had shaken Kelly up. She lit one of Brad's cigarettes and smoked it right there in the kitchen. Relaxed a little, she decided she would go shopping for the rest of the day and mull over her future with Brad, and with Roy.

* * *

Out on the links, after being quiet for most of the ride to the course, Brad was working up the nerve to tell Roy his plan. He horribly sliced his tee shot on the third hole, and it took him multiple attempts to get out of the woods on the right of the fairway. By the time he caught up with Roy on the green, it was obvious that his game was off. They had been joined by their occasional golfing partner, Mark Dunston, and it was early enough in the morning that just three golfers were allowed to play.

Brad and Roy did not mind playing with Mark, who was an excellent golfer. However, they did not regularly socialize with him outside of golf. He tended to complain a lot about his fiancée, Vanessa. In fact, it was not unusual for him to get several calls from her during a single golf game. The whole situation was humorous to Brad and Roy, and they gave Mark a hard time about being so "whipped."

This particular day had not been different. In between Mark offering advice on different clubs and varied approaches to each hole, he had to field two separate calls from Vanessa. Brad continued to play miserably and tried to place the blame on the irritating ring of Mark's cell phone.

However, after some prodding, Brad admitted that he had something else on his mind.

"Look Roy," he began slowly and softly as he attempted to keep the conversation out of Mark's earshot, "this is probably going to sound crazy, but just bear with me till I'm finished."

Roy first gave him an inquisitive look then assured Brad that he would let him continue uninterrupted. Roy had put his clubs away and was now sitting in the golf cart readying himself for Brad's secretive discussion. Mark busied himself in the background checking the scorecard and organizing his golf bag.

Brad continued, "You know that I've always been big into hunting, and have pretty much told you everything about my trips – the excitement, the rush from hunting, all the good details. And I think I've told you from time to time about my therapy and how it's kind of connected to my hunting, in a way. But I need to do something different now. Everything up to this point has, I guess, been like preparation."

"Preparation for what – how could there be anything left out there you haven't taken a shot at yet?" Roy asked, grinning. He could tell that Brad had cooked up some new scheme that would surely be interesting to hear.

"Now don't start laughing or anything," Brad cautioned. "I've spent a lot of time researching this, and I know it sounds crazy, but it just might be the most amazing thing ever if it works." He paused. "I'm going to contact some groups and try to arrange a hunt for North America's most cunning, dangerous, elusive, and – up to now – unknown animal. A bigfoot."

Roy did not laugh as Brad thought he might. Instead, he just looked puzzled. "You mean like the bigfoot in the supermarket tabloids?" Roy asked, unsure if he had heard his friend correctly. "I thought that was just some guy in a suit or something, faking it."

Mark approached the golf cart and chimed in too, "Yeah, uh, didn't I see on the news where they proved bigfoot doesn't even exist?"

Brad was concerned that Mark had overheard the conversation and now seemed to be taking part in it. However, Brad was on the defensive with the questioning he was receiving and found himself wanting to support his idea. He needed to prove it to them, and he still needed to convince himself.

"I'll explain it to you," Brad said hurriedly. He hopped in the golf cart and drove with them down the path. By the eighteenth hole, Roy and Mark were starting to come around to the idea and even expressed some interest in accompanying Brad on the expedition. Brad had only known Mark from their somewhat regular outings on the golf course over the past few years. He did not know much about Mark's background and was hesitant about including him in the plan. However, Mark was insistent, partly because of the very home life that Brad knew little about.

Mark was envious of Roy and Brad, but not for monetary reasons. Mark had a well-paying job as a CPA. Instead, he was jealous of the confidence and sureness his golfing buddies exuded. He occasionally heard Brad's tales of hunting adventures and thought about his own unexciting life. Mark also faced a tough situation with his fiancée Vanessa. He never could seem to be assertive enough in his work life for her. The ribbing he took from Roy and Brad only compounded this misery as it highlighted his own henpecked situation and made him realize how much different they were, or at least, seemed to be.

Thus, listening to Brad's discussion about a two-week expedition had instantly caught Mark's attention. As the three drove back to the clubhouse, Mark continued to express his interest in the hunt, though he knew nothing about its proposed quarry. What he had understood, though, was that it would provide a needed escape, however short, from the hum-drum life he lived. It would also possibly bring him closer to Roy and Brad, who were truly his closest acquaintances.

* * *

Roy had not initially received Brad's scheme with as much enthusiasm as Mark. It was just that this plan seemed even more over-the-top than usual. Brad was prone to risk-taking and aggressive – though calculated – enterprises, but Roy had trouble seeing past the obvious flaw in the plan. He did not believe in monsters any more than he did in the Easter Bunny, and had put such things behind him in his childhood. However, when Brad mentioned that he was trying to talk Kelly into going, Roy's attitude changed completely. He soon offered to participate with enthusiasm.

* * *

As the weeks wore on, Kelly Graham's patience began wearing thin with Brad. Brad was absorbed with spending hours upon hours sitting in front of his computer, surfing the Internet. If not at the desk, he was up making calls all over the country. She simply did not understand why he would be so obsessed with this idea. After all, there was not one single shred of evidence to prove that these tabloid monsters existed. She told this frequently to Brad.

Brad, on the other hand, was growing equally impatient with Kelly. The fears that had kept him captive into his adulthood needed to be dealt with and he was convinced that this scheme might be his best bet. Even if such a monstrous creature did not exist, the pursuit and possibility of confronting one was a tempting objective.

Brad was getting closer and closer to singling out a bigfoot group from the Internet that would share his ideas and want to participate in his hunt. On this particular day, Brad was looking at some web pages of groups in the Ohio and Pennsylvania areas.

Brad got up from his computer to stretch his legs and smoke a cigarette on his back deck. He left the Web site he was looking at up on the computer as he planned to return to it in a minute. After his smoke, he came back inside and found Kelly at the computer. The bigfoot page was no longer on the screen, but had been replaced with an Internet travel site.

"What are you doing?" Brad asked incredulously. "That's not the page I was looking at."

"I know. I'm looking at flights to Key West for next spring. Some of my girlfriends have been talking about going there as a nice getaway." Kelly turned to see Brad's scowl. "What? You were just looking at another one of your stupid monster Web sites. I'm sure you can find it again, and I'm sure there's no great loss if you can't." She turned back to the computer screen and began typing.

Brad grabbed the back of the chair and spun her around violently. "You still don't get it, do you? It's not silly, or stupid, or childish. This isn't make-believe. This is a plan of mine that I'm going to follow through on. I've had it with your doubt and ridicule. If you think I'm so stupid, maybe you should just leave." Brad turned his stare away from Kelly's eyes and looked to the left, glaring at a bookshelf.

Kelly was caught off guard. She did think his monster-hunting idea was foolish. She hated how obsessed he had become with it, and how much he had been ignoring her lately. All she could manage was, "Fine."

Brad snapped "Fine," in response. "Maybe you should go get your things."

"Are you throwing me out?" Kelly asked.

"*I'm* not doing anything," Brad replied. "*You're* the one making the decision."

"Fine," Kelly said forcefully, almost at a shout. She got up from the chair and headed for the stairs. Stomping up the stairs she yelled down at him, "Have fun with your childish ideas. I'm *glad* you're not dragging me into it. I'll be happy when I get out of this house and out of your precious way."

She slammed the bedroom door behind her and began collecting some of her things from around the room. She threw open the closet door. An automatic light flickered on in the spacious walk-in closet. Kelly began taking some clothes off hangers and piling them on her free arm. Then she slumped down to the floor as her eyes moistened a little. She accidentally sat down on one of her shoes, pulled it from beneath her and angrily flung it into the corner of the closet. So many shoes, she thought. And so many clothes – nice clothes, not like the kind she used to wear. In fact, she had nicer stuff, and more of it, than ever before in her life.

She looked again at the clothes and shoes she had accumulated. She thought of the nice restaurants she and Brad frequented. Kelly also considered the exotic trips they had taken over the past several months. In all, she and Brad lived a glamorous life.

Brad *was* kind of childish with this hunting obsession, she argued with herself. But then again, he did not exactly have a lot of vices. He did not gamble or drink too much. He had never cheated on her, though she admitted that she could not say the same for her side of the relationship. She thought about the incident behind that admission for a moment, then continued looking around the closet.

Brad never once complained about her shopping extravagances. Kelly rubbed the cashmere sweater resting on her arm, and the silk dress draped underneath it, then surveyed all the other clothes hanging around her. Kelly admitted that Brad was not perfect – far from it. And yet, like the clothes she was surrounded by, she found him to be comfortable. Perhaps, though, their relationship was getting too comfortable, maybe even boring.

And almost as difficult to deal with as Brad's recent harebrained scheme and the lack of progress in their relationship was Kelly's growing closeness to Roy. She and Roy did have one intimate encounter in their past, though that occurred when Kelly and Brad had just started dating. But recently, Roy seemed to be present, available, and interested when Brad did not. Roy also did not seem to be carrying around the same amount of emotional baggage as Brad. It would be a relief not to have to deal with Brad's emotional difficulties for a change.

But perhaps, she reconsidered, it was Brad's emotional problems and vulnerability that she found had once found so endearing. He was not as arrogant or boastful as his wealthy peers. His childhood experience sometimes made Brad seem more humble than he otherwise would have been. Kelly smiled when thinking about some of the many good times they had had early on in the relationship. She decided she would go along with Brad's current plans, or at least not be too confrontational about them, hoping that maybe he would even abandon them eventually. Then he could turn his attention back to her and she would not have to make the type of decision that seemed to loom ahead. Having made up her mind for the time being, Kelly raised herself up off the closet floor and steeled herself to go back downstairs where she knew Brad would be waiting and brooding.

Brad was sitting at the computer, already surfing various Web sites. He did not look up as he heard Kelly come down the steps. "Are you leaving?" he asked, still staring at the computer screen.

"No, I think I'm going to stay, if that's OK. I'm sorry about your Internet page. I thought you were through when I changed it."

"Well, I found it again, so no big deal," Brad responded, trying to sound nonchalant. "Look, if you're going to stay, I just wish you wouldn't give me such a hard time about this. I know hunting a bigfoot must sound like the craziest idea you've ever heard of. Trust me, it still sounds crazy to me when I say it. I know you said you don't want to have anything to do with this, but if you take part, that would mean a lot to me – and to us."

"What do you mean by 'us'?"

"I know things haven't been the greatest recently. But I'm a desperate man who wants to go ahead and do this and get on with my life. The life I'm thinking about has you in it, just you and me – no more wild hunting excursions or therapy sessions. It'd give us a chance to get a lot closer."

"You still haven't explained what you meant when you said it would mean a lot to us," Kelly said.

"I thought I had," Brad replied. "I guess what I meant was, that if you come along with me it will show me how much I mean to you. I know that it would be a big thing to ask you and, well, a great sacrifice deserves a great reward."

Kelly smiled when she imagined what Brad was hinting at. "Like what?" she asked playfully.

"I think you know," he said as he grabbed her and pulled her closer. She smiled even more in his grasp. "Besides," Brad continued, "I would be rescuing you from having to entertain Roy the whole time I'm gone."

Kelly turned white instantly. Fortunately, Brad kept talking without noticing. "I know how boring that can be. Hell, I even told him about my idea a while back. He said he'd be interested in coming, but I'll believe it when I see it."

"Roy's going too?" Kelly asked, with some relief that Brad had not picked up on her earlier reaction.

"Well he's talking about it, but if it makes the difference between you coming or not I'll tell him to stay home."

"No, that's fine," Kelly said as she pulled Brad close to her. "I'll go with you on your camping trip if it means that much to you. And I don't mind if Roy comes – that should make things interesting."

* * *

Jesse McCoy waited in the parking lot of the fast food restaurant across the street from his apartment. He had already eaten, but was lingering to meet Brad Brown from Detroit. Jesse leaned on the hood of his ancient 1983 Ford pickup truck, adjusted his baseball cap, and stuck his hands in his pockets. Heat rippled off the asphalt parking lot in the early August sun. A trickle of sweat rolled down Jesse's back and he impatiently wished that Brad would hurry up.

Jesse was the unofficial head of a bigfoot research group in southeastern Ohio. The group did not have a set membership, but mainly consisted of a few people Jesse had met in town or over the Internet who had had experiences like his own. Five years ago, Jesse had had a life-changing event deep in a creek bottom in the Shawnee State Forest in southeastern Ohio. Located in the Appalachian foothills near the banks of the Ohio River, the 63,000-acre Shawnee State Forest was once the hunting grounds of the Shawnee Indians and its erosion-carved valleys and wooded hills were filled with a variety of plants and animals, including white-tailed deer, wild turkey, raccoon, various songbirds and occasional bobcat and black bear.

Jesse had worked for the park service during his summers while in college. He was working on a degree in forestry and wildlife management and the park service was a natural outlet for further learning experiences. Plus, Jesse had always leaned toward being an introvert, and he relished the opportunity to spend his days outside trimming trees, hauling brush, picking up litter, and maintaining signs, facilities, and trails. The little human contact he did have was from lunch and fishing breaks with his college buddy, Donny Walker. Jesse had convinced Donny to spend the summer between their junior and senior years doing something a little less cerebral for a while. The two often hiked the trails or rode through the park on ATVs, making sure everything was properly maintained.

One afternoon in the late summer, after having worked at the park for several months, Jesse and Donny opted out of their regular work schedule and took off into the park to explore some fishing opportunities. They had searched the week before on topographic maps of the forest and had plotted the coordinates of some likely spots. Jesse found a nice-sized creek deep in the park about one half mile from the nearest trail. Some of the best fishing spots on the small creeks and streams that crisscrossed the park could only be reached with a departure from the maintained trails. Jesse and Donny had to hike down a steep hillside to reach the deep pools and long runs of a small stream that ran along the edge of the Shawnee Back Country Management Area and the Shawnee Wilderness Area. These two sections of the state forest comprised 16,000 acres of even more rugged and isolated topography where human influence did not penetrate very far into the thick stands of hardwoods and evergreens.

Jesse had fished this section of the park before and always enjoyed its solitude. Besides the serenity, the fishing was great and wildlife-viewing always enhanced his outings. Glimpses of deer and turkey were a pretty common occurrence. As the evening wore on, Jesse landed a nice smallmouth bass out of the creek he was fishing. He preferred using a fly rod for the small creeks and streams. It made the fishing more challenging and the fight more fun, especially when he hooked into something big. He had just tied on a deer-hair popper to chug across the surface of the deep pool in front of him, hoping to entice another large bass up to the water's edge. On his backcast, though, he snagged a tree several yards behind him.

Jesse cursed quietly. The woods and constant babble of the stream provided such a peaceful, hushed environment that he never felt like making much noise.

Donny had needed to heed the call of nature, so he had crept off into the woods with a roll of toilet paper. He had been gone for only a few minutes, so Jesse decided he would have to get out of his snagged situation without any assistance. He pulled himself up the hillside surrounding the stream and made his way to the snagged fly, wrapped around a tree limb. The heavy popper had lassoed the tree limb and wrapped around it several times. Jesse patiently worked the fly through the wraps, threading it back and forth until it was almost loose. He was having trouble seeing everything clearly because the sun had dipped below a neighboring ridge and darkness fell quickly underneath the heavy canopy of trees. Jesse realized that he would need to start heading back soon. He got the fly out of the tree and set it down for a second. He needed to work his way back down to the stream bank to get his rod and a few other items of fishing gear. He was getting ready to yell to Donny to get his equipment ready when he suddenly noticed something large and black making its way through the trees on the opposite side of the creek.

Jesse had been excited and scared at first. He had never seen a black bear before, but sightings occurred every now and then in the park, and this would be his first glimpse. The large, shaggy, black-haired creature lumbered into view and Jesse suddenly felt fear. He had goose bumps on his exposed arms and the hair on the back of his neck stood straight out. The creature's back was massive. It was over three feet wide at the shoulders. Just as Jesse was taking in its size, though, what he thought was a black bear suddenly stood up. There, in the creek bottom, an eight foot tall hairy animal stood, sniffing at the breeze. Instead of the snout and large pointed fangs of a bear, Jesse could see a flat, almost human-looking face. The thing made a grunting noise, then reached out and grabbed a nearby tree.

Its long, hairy arm rippled with muscles and Jesse teetered back when he saw the gigantic hand grasp fully around the five-inch diameter sapling trunk, as if it were the handle of a baseball bat in a normal man's hand. This creature did not have a paw, but a hand, with long, strong-looking fingers. The colossal animal standing on the creek bank dwarfed any professional football player or wrestler Jesse had seen on television. Not only was Jesse worried about the massive size of the creature, but a sickly sweet, musty odor was beginning to fill up the creek bottom. It seemed to emanate from the hairy animal and the stench made Jesse even more uncomfortable and scared.

Without thinking of his buddy Donny, Jesse backed up the hillside a few feet and turned to sprint up to the trail as fast as he could. However, the popper fly that he had unsnagged from the tree branch was now caught in Jesse's pants leg. With his first step away from the creek, the fly line became taut, and the drag of the fly reel clicked several times. The creature immediately looked at the rod and reel sitting on the opposite side of the stream and followed the thick fly line up to where Jesse stood, motionless. It saw him anyway. Jesse recognized a change pass over the creature's face, from something akin to nonchalance to a mixture of rage and fear at having discovered an intruder in its territory. Its massive mouth opened, revealing huge, square teeth. Looking right at Jesse, the creature roared. Jesse had never heard anything like it before. It was like a mixture between a woman's scream, a lion's roar, and an ambulance siren – all coming out at once and with so much volume that it seemed to shake the rocky hillside Jesse stood on.

A shock wave of sound passed over him, rattled his insides, and then reverberated in the small creek valley. Jesse's legs turned to jelly. He tried to take another step, but simply sank to the ground. A second later, though, when he heard a heavy splash in the creek, Jesse turned to see the creature heading in his direction. Jesse also saw the white outline of Donny's t-shirt emerging from the woods where he had been using the bathroom. Donny had obviously heard the creature's roar, but in the echoes of the valley, had misidentified where its source originated from. Jesse wanted to yell to him that he was walking right toward the monstrous animal, but Jesse's fight or flight reaction finally kicked in and the surge of adrenaline boosted him to his feet and carried him in a mad scramble up the hill. He finally made it to the trail and continued running.

He did not stop until he was on the ATV. Jesse fumbled with the keys several times as he tried to control his shaky hands. His rapid breathing and quivering limbs prevented him from performing such a fine motor function as inserting the key into the tiny slot next to the throttle. As soon as Jesse finally got the ignition cranked and the engine revved, he jammed the ATV into gear and tore down the rough dirt path away from the terrifying events he had just fled. Jesse's panicked nerves did not even begin to calm down until he was finally back in the safety of his home, with the front door closed and locked behind him.

The next day, Jesse reported in to work barely functioning from a sleepless, anxious night. When Donny did not show up to work, Jesse told park authorities the location of the forested creek bed, but refused to accompany them. They found Donny, lying face-down against a steep hillside – the same one Jesse had managed to scramble up. After police were called in, they determined Donny had died from blunt force trauma to several areas of his body. However, they also reasoned that he very easily could have just fallen while hiking up the hill and hit his head on any number of trees or boulders on the way down. Though this relieved Jesse of any possible criminal charges, he faced immediate and dire administrative action from the park service. As Jesse was still struggling to come to grips with the incident and he found that he simply could not force himself to provide an explanation for what had happened to Donny. Thus, he could not account for how he and his friend ended up in the creek valley or how he made it out and Donny did not. Jesse was promptly fired and threatened with civil litigation.

The episode made the local papers and the story filtered back to college ahead of Jesse. His former friends and acquaintances shied away from him or even accosted him with accusations of involvement in Donny's demise. Jesse could not handle being shunned in addition to the loss of his friend, and the inexplicable cause of all these problems frustrated him even more. He dropped out mid-way through the fall term of his Senior year and never returned to college.

*   *   *

Jesse shivered, even in the warm sunlight, as he remembered his encounter and its aftermath. In one single event, he had lost his job, his friend, an education, and a sense of normalcy and logic about the world. He relaxed his grip and took a deep breath. A few minutes later, Brad Brown pulled into the restaurant parking lot. Jesse recognized the car from a description Brad had sent in one of several emails. The two made quick introductions, hopped in Jesse's pickup truck and left. Jesse was actually a little amazed that Brad had found the restaurant. It was not exactly at the center of the small town. The destination the two headed to next was even farther on the outskirts.

Jesse slowed the truck down as they rounded a sharp curve on the bumpy country road. He pulled off to the side and approached a small gas and service station. The station rested off the side of the road, surrounded by woods behind it, pretty far from the actual town Jesse lived in. Brad was instantly reminded of antiquated service stations he had seen in old television shows and movies. In fact, the pumps and equipment did not look much changed from an earlier era in American history.

Jesse threw the truck in park and jumped out. He reached under the driver's seat before closing the door and fished out a can of Copenhagen snuff. He packed the can a few times, grabbed a large pinch of dip, and inserted it between his lower gum and lip. He walked to the other side of the truck and, as Brad got out, found an empty water bottle in a door pocket that he could use as a spitter.

"Hi Hank," Jesse yelled to an older gentleman sitting in a lawn chair outside the building.

"Hi back at ya," Hank replied in an irritated tone. "The others are in the back. I hope you're the last one showing up today. Seems a feller can't get a decent nap around here."

"Sorry Hank, we'll try to keep it down the rest of the day."

Hank answered with a "hmmph," pulled his hat back over his eyes and appeared to instantly resume his dozing.

Jesse led Brad around the station to the back, where an old grimy door was propped open with a mop handle. A group of men talked quietly inside the room, some sitting in chairs at a small table, others leaning against the ancient vending machines in the room. Their ages ranged from early twenties to late fifties. They seemed rugged with faces showing age and wrinkles from much time spent in the elements. The men were outdoorsmen – hunters, trappers, and fishermen. A few wore camo hats, and one man had a shirt with his name patched on it. Brad felt out of his element amongst these men from a much different social and economic sphere.

Jesse introduced Brad to the men, and there was a quick round of handshaking. As the discussion began, the group informed Brad that their various investigations took place at different hotspots in the region, based on recent reports or frequency of events. Each man told Brad briefly of their own personal encounter, most of which revolved around outdoor activities like hunting, fishing, or camping. Jesse pointed out that no scientist in a lab or academic classroom will ever see a bigfoot – arguing that these creatures do not live in labs or on university campuses. He noted that they live in the woods and that the people who spend the most time in the outdoors naturally have the greatest likelihood of seeing one, whether they want to or not. The men gathered at the meeting all insisted that they would rather their own personal incidents had never taken place at all.

Doyle Barker, an older man with a leathery brown face and grizzled beard, told Brad of the encounter he experienced. He had been deer hunting in the fall two years earlier, in a hardwood creek bottom along the chain of hills and small mountains scattered across the Ohio-West Virginia border. He parked his truck at the edge of a friend's farm, then hiked with his climbing tree-stand, gun, and other gear about a quarter of a mile into the forested area. Aided by a flashlight and headlamp, Doyle attached his tree-stand onto a mature oak, and climbed up to about seventeen or eighteen feet off the ground. He was seated and ready for action by 6:00 A.M., well before sunrise. Doyle saw a few does, a young button buck, and two small six-pointers, but decided to hold off on taking a shot till that evening.

After a warm day, the late afternoon brought a crisp, cool wind. Doyle zipped his insulated camouflage jacket, and tugged his hunter-orange wool cap down over his ears. The sun was just above the horizon, and Doyle knew it would dip lower soon, ending his opportunity to hunt. Just then he saw a wide-racked, stout ten-pointer amble into his shooting range. Doyle drew a bead on it, flicked the safety and was getting ready to pull the trigger when the buck bolted. Doyle cursed, but assured himself that he had been quiet and slow-moving. He reasoned that something else must have spooked the deer. Doyle heard a rustling sound coming up from the creek bottom, heading to the flat spot in front of him. He had thought that perhaps a boss buck had scared off the younger one and would soon present himself.

What Doyle saw, however, almost made him drop his gun. He had been concentrating on the approaching noises, hoping for a monster buck to break through the furthest line of trees. Instead, Doyle thought another hunter had just stumbled into his firing range. The guy was dressed in dark clothing, with no hunter orange or safety clothing on at all. Doyle wanted to see who this idiot was, so he squinted through his scope and increased the magnification power from 3x to 8x. When he did this, he let out a short gasp. The "hunter" was no man at all, but a giant gorilla-like creature, walking upright and covered in hair. When Doyle gasped, the animal looked right in his direction and Doyle could clearly see its facial features, which though massive and frightening, had a slightly human appearance. That is, until he spotlighted the creature with his flashlight. The animal's eyes glowed red, and this eyeshine convinced Doyle that this was no creature he knew.

It let out a series of short grunts, directed toward Doyle. Then a rotten stench filled the area, eventually floating up to Doyle's position in his tree-stand. It made his eyes water and he wanted to vomit. He concentrated on looking through the scope again, but could no longer see the unknown creature. He did not want to stay there a minute longer, but knew that the path to his truck was in the exact direction of where he last saw the bigfoot, as he later decided it was. He stayed put, shivering as the autumn night temperatures dropped quickly.

At midnight, he heard dogs barking and could see flashlights in the distance. His friend the farmer and his older two sons were looking for him. Doyle whistled and flashed his red headlamp a few times. The search party found him, but Doyle was still so shaken from his encounter, and so stiff from the cold, that he could not climb down from his tree-stand. One of the boys ran back to the farm and got a large ladder to help out. When they finally got him down to the ground, the farmer saw the look of fright still on Doyle's face. He laughed, and told Doyle that he had forgotten to warn him about "Ol' Stinky," who occasionally roamed the woods and did a little deer hunting of his own.

Doyle said he has opted out of deer hunting after that incident, missing a pastime that he had loved since he was seven years old. "Something like that," he said as he finished his tale, "shakes you to the very core, not just because it's terrifying, but because you seen something that the rest of the world says doesn't exist."

This last point was agreed on by all present as perhaps the most frustrating – and simultaneously motivating – aspect of the subject at hand. After talking for a little while more, the group disbanded. Brad shook their hands and thanked them for sharing their stories and findings with him.

* * *

Jesse invited Brad to join him at his apartment for a beer before Brad had to drive back to Michigan. They drove to Jesse's apartment and parked across the street at the restaurant parking lot. Brad got some papers out of his own car and the two walked over to Jesse's apartment. As they were walking up the stairs, Brad mentioned, "Those seem like some pretty level-headed guys."

"Yep," Jesse responded as he unlocked his door, "last guys in the world who would make up something like this. After all, it's brought them nothing but ridicule and frustration. But – and this doesn't outweigh the negatives – it has opened their eyes to exploring or even thinking about what all's out there in the world."

They were in Jesse's apartment and he had already gone to the refrigerator to get some beers. "What about you?" Brad asked. "How'd you end up so involved in an issue that only brings 'ridicule and frustration?'"

Jesse's brow furrowed and his mood darkened. He did not say anything for a few moments as he silently opened the cold beers. Brad watched him closely and could tell that Jesse was thinking of something and struggling with a response to what seemed like a simple question.

"That's a story for another time," Jesse said after a long swig of beer.

"Maybe you could tell me at some point."

"Yeah, maybe," Jesse answered shortly.

Brad glanced around the messy, unkempt apartment. Dirty clothes and empty food containers cluttered most spots and cleared floor space seemed to be scarce. Brad's gaze stopped on a small framed photograph sitting on Jesse's computer desk. "A college frat guy, huh? That must've been fun," he said after studying the photograph's content, which showed Jesse and several other young men standing in front of a college fraternity house.

"We're not here to reminisce about my glory days, are we?" Jesse responded. "If I remember correctly, we're here to talk about you." Jesse gestured his beer in Brad's direction. He spoke in a less brooding way as he turned back to the original subject at hand. "What exactly is it you want from me? I gathered from your e-mails that you're interested in bigfoot and want to take part in some expeditions or research outings? That could probably be arranged pretty easily. We go a couple times a year. We can figure out when the closest outing is going to be and pencil you in."

At this point, Jesse launched into a brief description of the group's typical outings in the Southeastern United States. He also mentioned that they had gotten closer and closer to good evidence pointing to the existence of a bigfoot animal. Jesse was well into a speech that he had rehearsed many times.

"… and just like we had hoped, the hair samples we had submitted for DNA testing came back as 'unknown primate.' So take that as you will, but I can't think of much better proof to me." Jesse drained the last his second beer after he finished talking. Brad sat on the sofa silently, absorbing all he had just heard. Brad spoke up.

"I want to hunt one – to kill it. Can you help me?"

Jesse almost spit out the last swallow of beer. He set his empty bottle down and paced for a minute. "I'm sorry, what did you just say?"

"I want to hunt one of these things. I believe that you, like me, had a tragic experience in your past somehow connected to these animals. You have devoted your life to this subject, or at least it seems like it. I'm just now coming to realize that one way to get over what happened is to confront the situation head-on."

Jesse still seemed puzzled. "I'm sorry, I'm still confused about what you're asking of me, or if you're asking me anything. What is it that you want? Did you come here to get more confidence and verification that they exist? If so, I think I've told you enough to get you started."

"That's not it at all," Brad said. "Why don't you get us another beer so we can talk about it. Plus, I need to make a quick phone call."

Jesse took his time going to the kitchen as Brad called Kelly and left a message on her cell phone that he would not be returning to Michigan that night. Jesse came back in with two fresh beers, and a bottle of Kentucky bourbon. "Depending on what you're getting ready to tell me," he explained, "I thought I might need something stiffer."

Jesse settled into a tattered recliner and suggested that Brad start from the top. Brad opened up with the childhood hunting trip that had ended in terror and tragedy and of the cold fear that continued to creep into his life on an almost daily basis. He told Jesse briefly about the therapy sessions he had attended and then discussed his recent hunting trips and how he had started going after increasingly more dangerous animals, but noted that something was still missing. He explained he had discovered the subject of bigfoot during a late-night Internet search and had arrived at bigfoot hunting as a means to confronting his inner fears in a very real and outward way. Brad concluded that he was now simply trying to put together the right components to further his mission.

"Am I the right 'component'?" Jesse asked, amused at the choice of words.

"That depends," Brad answered, "on your willingness to do something never attempted before – at least, never attempted successfully."

Jesse took a sip of beer and mulled over a few thoughts. "Why would I ever go along on an endeavor like you're suggesting, and why would you need me in the first place?"

"I'll try to answer both of those questions at the same time," Brad said as he pulled a piece of paper out of his pocket. "I figured you might ask something like that. First, I'm willing to pay you ten thousand dollars for a week to two week's worth of work – five up front and five at the conclusion of the trip. There will, of course, be bonuses for sightings of these animals and definitely for a successful kill. That's my monetary offer to you, and here's why I think you'll take it. Think about what you told me earlier and then look around you – at this shitty little apartment and the tatters your life has become. Hell, you apparently were a big-time college guy at some point in your life and now this is how you're living. Something happened to derail you and I'm willing to bet it has a lot to do with these creatures."

Brad continued, hardly even taking a breath. "Those are the reasons why I think you'll do this, and they're also some of the reasons why I need you. You've had years of experience researching and investigating these creatures. And from sitting at the meeting earlier, it sounds like you and your group have figured out quite a few things about their activities and behavior. You're up to date on regional sightings. You'd know where to go, what to look for. It's a no-brainer that you'd be a competent, essential addition to the expedition. So what do you say?"

Jesse pulled the stopper out of the bourbon bottle and poured a tall drink. "I wouldn't mind getting out of this town, maybe going back to school or something. What kind of bonus are you talking about for catching a glimpse at one of these critters?"

"Look," Brad responded, sensing that Jesse might be about to accept the offer, "if you take me to one of these animal's front door I can do the rest. You have no idea what I've been struggling with for almost two decades now. Seeing one of these animals would be amazing for me – getting to stand over the dead body of one would be priceless. Think about it for a couple of days and let me know what you would consider fair."

The warmth of the bourbon was creeping across Jesse's belly and spreading fast. He decided he did not want to talk shop anymore, but would rather just sit back and enjoy his bourbon while thinking about the proposal by himself, without any pressure from Brad. He gave Brad directions to a motel a few miles down the road and promised to call him with an answer and details before the end of the week.

As Jesse showed Brad to the door he asked him, "You're used to getting what you want, aren't you?"

Brad fished in his pocket for his keys, then looked back up at Jesse. "Yes I am. But I'm also used to, and willing to, pay the right price for what I want. You take your time, Jesse," Brad said as he turned to leave the apartment porch. "My expedition's going to take place with or without you, but I'd rather have you along. And I think you'd rather be along. Just think about it."

With that, Brad headed down the steps to his car. Jesse closed the door and walked back to his living room. He poured another glass of bourbon, this time adding some ice and a splash of water. He would definitely need some more strong bourbon to mull over Brad's proposal.

* * *

"Mark Dunston, that's the craziest thing I've ever heard of. "You are absolutely not going on such a foolish trip." Vanessa Conner stood over Mark as she lectured him. Mark had given a lot of thought to the conversation he had shared with Brad and Roy out on the golf course. Though he knew he would attract Vanessa's ire, he felt like he had to stand up for himself on this one. He knew he would never be able to live it down if Roy or Brad found out that he had not been able to come simply because his fiancée had not given her permission.

Mark did not respond immediately, so Vanessa continued, "I just cannot understand why you don't arrange something to do with the people from work, instead of this Brad and Roy who I've never even met. You still haven't invited your boss over for dinner like we talked about. And now you want to go with this Brad character on a camping trip in August or September? Mark, that's only a couple of months before the wedding. Do you know how busy we'll be at that point?"

Vanessa kept lecturing Mark, but his mind had wandered off halfway through her nagging. At some point, he came out of his thoughts and heard Vanessa still talking.

"… then my mom and I will be picking out the music for the wedding and you'll be getting tuxes ready for your groomsmen. I mean, that's not even to mention the catering arrangements and coordinating lodging for all of our out-of-town guests. Have you even started making your list yet?"

"Sure I have," he eventually replied, hoping that he had answered her question to a satisfactory degree.

"Look, I hope you've been talking the wedding up at the office. I was thinking about inviting Charlie to some of our showers."

"My boss?" Mark responded as he got up from his seat and tried to calm himself down. He always got worked up when Vanessa launched into her sermons on ambition and goals. He was also upset that the topic had gotten so far off track from the subject of his camping trip with Brad and Roy. "Look, you're always telling me about networking and getting ahead by using my contacts. What better contacts could I have than Brad and Roy. The trust fund Brad's dad left to him would rival my biggest account yet. That one client alone would shoot me up the partnership track. And Roy – well, Roy is the king of the country club. He knows everybody who's anybody. I can't think of two better guys to get in tight with."

"Well, I'm not sure that makes it set any better with me, Mark. I don't know these guys or anything about their families. They're complete strangers to me. Besides, why would grown men go traipsing through the woods like that? Are there going to be guns involved? You know how I feel about guns."

"I know, Honey," Mark said as he hung his head. Appealing to Vanessa's practical side had not worked as well as he had thought it would. "Look, 'Ness, I spend most of my day toiling away trying to get ahead at work. I hardly ever get an opportunity to do something like this."

"Oh Mark, that's not fair." Vanessa sat down and tears began welling up around the corners of her eyes. "Now you're trying to make me feel guilty, like I keep you from having friends and doing fun things." Mark tried not to look at her as he could never resist seeing her cry. He knew he would instantly become a babbling fool and agree to whatever she said just to make her stop crying. Vanessa blew her nose loudly and did not hide her attempts to wipe the tears from her face.

"I've got to go, 'Ness," he said as he grabbed his keys from the coffee table and turned toward the front door – managing not to look directly at her the whole time.

"You're not going to leave me like this are you?" Vanessa pleaded with a trembling voice.

"I've got to go," Mark said again, quickly as he walked through the front door. He stepped out onto the front porch feeling a mixture of guilt and excitement.

*　*　*

Brad made another trip to the small Ohio town where Jesse lived, this time armed with a well-thought-out list of questions and goals regarding the upcoming expedition. He and Jesse hunkered down in Jesse's apartment for a weekend, going over scenarios and trying to come up with the most likely location to have a bigfoot encounter, while also considering logistical factors. After an exhaustive Internet search and a statistical approach to Jesse's own hundreds of sightings reports he had collected over the years, they zeroed in on an area with frequent activity.

Jesse picked an area of Eastern Kentucky in the foothills of the Appalachian Mountains. Their target location was tucked away amidst miles and miles of forest land, sparsely populated rural towns, farm lands, and a mixture of state wildlife refuges, game management areas, and state parks and recreation areas.

They would have to wait about one month before the expedition would begin. Jesse had traced a pattern of reports and sightings dating back for over half a century in a region comprised of a few counties along the foothills. These sightings, almost without exception, occurred at specific times of year, and most consistently in autumn. Jesse suspected that the fall appearances of bigfoot creatures probably coincided with the abundance of a particular crop's presence such as corn. He described to Brad how they would come out of the forests to take advantage of a ready food source just like deer, feral hogs, or any other wildlife would.

Jesse's phone rang and he excused himself and headed to the bedroom. Brad could hear him talking, but could not make out the words. When Jesse came back into the room, he looked a little frazzled.

"Let me guess," Brad offered, "woman troubles?"

"I guess you could say that," Jesse answered as he sat down at the living room table with Brad. He shuffled through their documents and papers for a minute, not saying anything. "It's just this girl I've been running around with lately. Nothing serious."

Brad leaned back in his seat. "Well, I've been in the doghouse lately too. My girlfriend hasn't been very thrilled with me spending a lot of time getting ready for this expedition because she thinks it'll basically just be an outing in the woods."

"Well," Jesse asked, "where does she stand on it now that you're actually going about a month from now? Is she still upset or has she just resigned to the fact that you're going?"

"Oh she's resigned all right," Brad said. "In fact, she's coming with me."

Jesse's eyes almost left their sockets. "Do what now? She's going on the expedition? The one where we're going to track and try to kill a bigfoot? You can't be serious."

"I'm serious as can be. She's gone with me on several of my hunting trips. She gets to keep an eye on me and vice versa. Of course, up till now most of our trips have been to nice lodges and fancy outfitters with luxurious accommodations. We're both going to have to do some adjusting for this trip."

"For crap's sake, Brad. Maybe you're thinking that this is just going to be a camping trip too. You need to get it into your head what we're going to be dealing with if we actually run across one of these creatures."

"Settle down Jesse," Brad said in a patient voice. "You just said yourself that it's going to be tough to get this done. We'll need all the extra hands we can get. I've got two acquaintances who're interested in going too."

"Look," Jesse said, still shaking his head, "I understand that you've had a lot of time in the field. I'm sure you're quite competent at tracking and hunting. Those will be important traits on this expedition, but your girlfriend and your buddies? What skills do they bring to this mission?"

"Hey, they can all take care of themselves," Brad responded defensively. Then, untruthfully he added, "My buddies are just at home in the woods as in their own house. They'll be assets on this, not liabilities."

"Well, when it all boils down to it," Jesse quickly fired back, "I'll do what's needed to keep myself safe. If that means leaving your buddies in the dust, so be it."

As soon as Jesse made this statement, he regretted it. He instantly thought back to his friend Donny Walker, who he had indeed left behind. Jesse grew at once both sad at the memory and furious that Brad's choices might lead to a similar situation.

Brad attempted to calm Jesse's fears and assure him that everything would go as planned. They would meet up again in several weeks as September drew to the midway point, with a few days to get organized, get extra gear, find out some local info, then launch the expedition.

PART III

Brad showed up outside Jesse McCoy's apartment one hour later than planned on that mid-September morning, even though they had a long drive south along highways and back roads to get to their destination in southeastern Kentucky. Brad was driving a new-looking sport utility vehicle and Jesse could not believe his eyes as he stared from his apartment window when Brad pulled up. Out jumped Brad, his girlfriend Kelly, and two guys who Jesse assumed were Mark and Roy. "Jimminy-fucking-Christmas," Jesse softly swore to himself as he watched the large group pile out of the vehicle in the parking lot below. "He brought the whole damn circus."

Jesse carried down his backpack stuffed with clothes and gear for the upcoming trip. Brad made the introductions. Jesse quickly looked over Mark and Roy as he attempted to size them up. Jesse thought that Kelly was attractive with her blond hair and tall, slender build. He could also tell that she was dressed in absolutely brand new clothes and even new hiking boots. To himself, Jesse criticized this rookie mistake – knowing full well that several miles into an all-day hiking trip carrying heavy packs, the well-dressed Kelly would surely be complaining of discomfort and sore feet. But, he admitted to himself, she sure looked good for the time being.

He could not say the same for Mark and Roy. Having only known them for a few minutes, Jesse was already beginning to suspect that Brad had lied to him about their outdoorsy skills. They seemed like they were uncomfortable under his gaze. Jesse determined that Roy had probably not worked a single day in his life. Mark seemed shy and unsure of himself. Jesse struggled trying to figure out the connection between Mark, Roy, and Brad. Jesse could not picture either of Brad's friends involved in any sort of endeavors deep in the wilderness where one would have to rely on one's wits and grit just to get by. Just like with Kelly, though, Jesse tried to tell himself not to be so judgmental, that maybe all his assumptions would be proved wrong once they got in the field.

The drive from Jesse's home in Carroll County, Ohio, to their destination in Pike County, Kentucky, took nearly seven hours. They went straight south on Interstate 77 for several hours, dipped into West Virginia, then into Kentucky until they ended up in a small town outside Rooster Ridge. They took a few wrong turns but eventually reached the Elk Mountain

Lodge. Jesse had found it on the Internet. It was strategically located for their expedition, and there were not many alternate lodging options to choose from.

Brad signed the group in and Jesse looked around the main entrance room of the log-built structure. He picked up a brochure describing the area. Pike and neighboring Floyd County were surrounded by many public lands, wildlife refuges, and the nearby Daniel Boone National Forest. They were among fourteen different counties that comprised over 2.6 million acres of suitable elk habitat for an elk re-introduction program that had been ongoing for several years. In fact, the brochure mentioned that this portion of Kentucky had the largest elk herd east of the Rocky Mountains. The lodge itself had sprung up in recent years to accommodate a growing number of elk hunters and sightseers.

"Planning on seeing some elk during your stay here?" Jesse took his eyes from the brochure and turned to see a young, dark-haired woman standing right next to him. Her large brown eyes stared at him. Jesse stood there looking into her eyes until he realized that she had just asked him a question.

"Yeah, the elk, that's what we're here for," he managed to stammer.

"What, are you photographers or something? I noticed your friends had all kinds of gear with them."

"Just planning on doing some picture-taking," Jesse lied. "We hope to get a glimpse or two of some pretty magnificent creatures," Jesse continued, noting to himself that this was, at least, a true statement.

"They're not so magnificent if they run in front of your car. An eight hundred pound bull can pretty much ruin your day when the rut starts. When the mating season arrives and that testosterone gets flowing, they just throw caution to the wind and forget things like trying to avoid cars. Just like a typical male, isn't it? You guys get one thing on your mind and then Katie-bar-the-door!"

She was smiling at Jesse, who was very uncomfortable at this point. He was not sure how to respond to her statements.

"I'm just giving you a hard time buddy, relax. My name's Laura Calhoun. My aunt owns this place. I work here sometimes at the restaurant and little bar that's attached to it."

"Hi, I'm Jesse McCoy," Jesse said, extending his hand.

"Oh Lord, we haven't had a McCoy around here in years. You aren't planning to start a feud or something are you? Y'all were always known for fighting in these parts."

"Well, uh, I'm actually from Ohio. This is my first time here since I was a little kid on vacation," Jesse said – uncomfortable again.

Laura gave him a little jab on the shoulder. "Relax, Mr. McCoy, you need to lighten up a bit. Most people in these parts got over the feuding long ago. We just play it up when the television cameras come to town."

"Well, all right then. I've never been in a feud before, I'm not sure I'd know where to start," Jesse said with his own attempt at humor.

"See, there you go," Laura congratulated him. "I thought you looked like someone with a funny bone. Well it was nice to meet you Jesse McCoy. I've got to get to my job now or my Aunt'll give me hell later. Good luck with your photos. Come by and see me sometime at the restaurant if y'all are going to be around for a few days."

"We will. I mean, I will. Well, I guess I mean both – I'll come see you and we'll be around." Jesse could not believe how tongue-tied he had become in the short few minutes he had been talking to Laura. She laughed then went through a hallway to the restaurant section of the lodge.

Brad walked up to Jesse after Laura had left. "What was that all about? I didn't know you were such a ladies' man."

"That wasn't about anything," Jesse said defensively. "That was the owner's niece and she was simply welcoming us to the establishment. She was also curious about all the gear you guys have been carrying in."

"What'd you tell her?" Brad asked with concern.

"Well she wanted to know if we were here to photograph the elk. You know, there's huge amounts of land set aside for elk in this and neighboring counties."

Brad slung his bag over his shoulder. "I thought elk only lived out west."

"Yeah, and giant hairy ape creatures only hang out in the Pacific Northwest, right? I have a feeling there's a lot about this area that we'll find surprising."

"As long as it's in a good way," Brad responded. "I'm starving. Let's get this gear stowed then get some dinner in the restaurant. You can introduce us all to your new girlfriend."

Jesse did not appreciate the ribbing he was getting from Brad. After the long car ride with his four new companions, Jesse was ready for some alone time in his own room. Mark and Roy were splitting a room, and Brad and

Kelly had one to share. Jesse insisted on having his own room, and he was glad to have a minute to gather his thoughts away from his new peers.

At dinner that night, Jesse decided he did not care much for Roy. He consistently belittled the bed and breakfast as a sub-par establishment. He even made fun of the interior design aspects of the room they were staying in. He enjoyed mimicking the thick "hillbilly" accent of some of the neighboring diners. When Roy said something about the bartender's outfit, Jesse realized he was talking about Laura Calhoun, and felt himself getting defensive for some reason. Kelly informed the table that she "felt sorry" for the homely-looking girl working behind the small bar.

"Look at her," she said, "stuck in this little place in this little shit-hole of a town. I bet she wouldn't last a minute in some place like Detroit. And that outfit – it's so tacky. You know, if she could get one of those Hollywood makeovers, she might even look reasonable. I bet she's around our age, but look where we are and look where she is. I think people are so interesting."

When Kelly was done with her amateur sociology speech, she had her third glass of wine. Mark had not said much during the meal, though he had laughed at each of Brad or Roy's jokes. Jesse was still not sure how Mark fit into this group. He hoped Mark's quietness was an outward manifestation of inner strength and sureness and not the exact opposite. Jesse knew that they could ill afford to have a timid, cowardly person along on this type of expedition.

Jesse finished his meal early and retired up to his room. He was sure that the group talked about him as soon as he left the table. He wondered what he had gotten into, but then tried to convince himself that it would be bearable. "I can take anything for two weeks," he thought, trying to focus on the large financial reward for being able to tolerate the Michigan crew.

Jesse called his girlfriend back in Carrollton. She was still unhappy with him for leaving to go on this trip. She warned him again of the consequences this might have on their relationship. Jesse reminded her that he did not think that their occasional rendezvous counted as a relationship. His comment did not go over well on the other end of the phone. Jesse got off the phone as quickly as possible and only made a vague promise of when he would call back.

Instead of dwelling on the conversation, Jesse decided to head down to the restaurant bar and get a drink. He admitted that part of his motivation was to speak to Laura Calhoun again. Though he was hoping to see her, he was a little surprised that she was actually still tending bar.

"Boy, you sure work some long hours around here," he said as he settled onto a barstool.

"Gives me something to do, since this is just a one-horse, hillbilly, shitty little town," she said curtly, keeping her eyes on the glass she was washing out. Her playful demeanor from earlier was absent.

"Whoa, hey, what was that about?" Jesse asked.

"Look, your waiter from tonight told me all the things y'all were saying about me and this town. It may not be much to people from fancy big cities, but we like it around here. And if you don't …"

"Laura, calm down. *I* didn't say any of those things. Look, I can't really explain how I ended up with that crew. But as insulting as they were to you tonight, just be glad that it was only tonight. I have to spend the next week or so with 'em."

"Are all Northerners that bad? How do you stand it?" Laura asked with a serious expression.

"No, not everybody north of the Mason-Dixon line talks fast and acts like a jerk. I think these guys were just brought up a lot differently from us. I don't really think it's a result of where they're from geographically."

"Oh really, I've never been out of this county before. I just assumed that's how all Yankees acted." Laura then paused and stared straight at Jesse. It was clear that Jesse was not sure how to respond to Laura's statement in a non-insulting way. A blank look had passed over his face and Laura studied his eyes, knowing that he was racking his brain for a response. A bead of sweat ran down his back, sending chills through his spine. Then Laura burst out laughing.

"Hell, Jesse. I thought I told you earlier you needed to relax. I lived in Boston for several years when I was growing up. I even saw a few games at Fenway. Believe me, I've seen the best and worst of northern folks and it's not much different from the extremes down here."

Jesse was relieved. "Well, I was about to launch into my good-ol-boy routine if necessary," he joked. "Look, can I get a drink? I think I need one now. How about some Jim Beam on the rocks?"

"OK, so to impress me as being a man of the people, you're going to order a Kentucky drink, huh? Well, how about upping the ante and trying a real local flavor."

"Sure," Jesse answered with gusto, willing to prove his mettle. "What've you got?"

"We get a monthly supply of a certain concoction from a moonshiner who lives up on the eastern side of Flag Knob, on the banks of the Brushy Fork. They say it'll put hair on your chest if you need any help in that department. Still want a try?"

Jesse definitely no longer wanted a try, but could not back down from the challenge. "Let me have it." He took a sip of the clear liquid, which almost knocked him on the floor with its strong aroma alone. Jesse decided that the drink itself was not half bad. Though it was pretty powerful and had a harsh taste at first, the aftertaste was not as bad as he expected. The alcohol content was evident. Before his next sip was finished, Jesse could feel the drink's effects over him.

He loosened up a bit and got accustomed to Laura's mischievous sense of humor. He felt like it was a challenge to keep up with her wit. It was a challenge, though, that he greatly enjoyed. He found himself staring more and more into her eyes when she laughed. He discovered that he was having more fun talking to a woman – or anybody for that matter – than he had had in a long time. Eventually Jesse realized that he was well on his way to getting drunk, so he had to excuse himself to head up to bed. Laura teased him about not being able to hold his liquor, but then wished him good night and said that she hoped to see him the next day.

In the time spent with Laura before she had to close down the bar, Jesse had lost himself in her laugh and her easy manner. He felt like he had known her for years. He went to bed with a big smile on his face, completely forgetting his rude companions and the real reason he was at the lodge in the first place.

* * *

The next morning, Jesse could tell that he was not the only one who had been up late drinking. Roy and Mark had gotten into some vodka that Roy had brought along, and their room was dark and silent even at 10:30 in the morning. Kelly had had too much wine, which left Jesse and Brad to explore the town. They had a few objectives – to gather stories and information from the locals, to gather supplies, and to find the best area to launch the expedition.

Before they could leave the lodge, Hazel Blevins stopped them. "Hi boys, I'm Aunt Hazel. My niece tells me y'all are going to do some sight seeing for elk."

Jesse realized that this must be the establishment's owner. "Well, we'd like to see some of the local wildlife. Are there bears around here too?" he asked, knowing the answer and hoping it would lead to more information.

"Oh sure," Aunt Hazel replied, "there's bears around here. They don't come down out of the mountains much, but some of the surrounding counties are starting to see more and more black bears every year. I guess they come up from Tennessee and such."

"You know," Jesse began, "I've heard that there's also cougars, or mountain lions, seen in these parts occasionally. Is that true or just one of these tall tales you hear about?"

"Honey, there's hills and hollers so dark and dense around here that I wouldn't be surprised if an elephant walked out of one. Sure, people see cougars every now and then. Department of Wildlife folks say they don't exist in the state, but most folks around here've gotten kind of used to them popping up on occasion, whether the state says they're here or not."

"Huh," Jesse commented, trying to steer the discussion in the direction he wanted. "I wonder what else lives around here that's not 'officially' recognized. I bet there's a few animals we'd be surprised to find in these mountains."

"Oh boy, the stories people could tell you about that subject," Aunt Hazel began, but then stopped short.

"What sort of stories?" Jesse asked, hoping not to seem too eager.

"Well, I don't really want to get into," Aunt Hazel said, with an obvious mood change. At that time her niece, Laura, walked into the room.

"Well look who's here, it's my beautiful niece Laura. Isn't she pretty boys?"

Laura interrupted before Jesse or Brad could answer. "Aunt Hazel, knock it off please, that's embarrassing." She had a strange look on her face when she then asked, "What didn't you want to get into? Were you getting ready to tell one of your goblin stories?"

"Goblins?" Brad asked, speaking up for the first time. He was tired of the small talk, not understanding that Jesse had used the same subtle method countless times to get people on the subject of unexplained creatures. "What do you mean by goblins?"

"Jesus, Hazel," Laura scolded, "I can't believe you were going to tell them all that nonsense. Those are the kind of stories that give people around here a bad reputation."

"What kind of stories?" Brad asked excitedly. "Why don't you go ahead and tell us and we'll just decide for ourselves if it sounds crazy or not."

"Oh all right," Aunt Hazel gave in, "but this happened years and years ago and you just have to take it for what it is – a story. Don't go spreading rumors about the crazy woman at the bed and breakfast."

Brad and Jesse swore that they would take the tale simply at face value without passing judgment upon its teller. Laura shook her head and left the room, obviously embarrassed that her Aunt was going to tell the story.

"Well, when I was about five years old," she began as she searched her mind for the right sequence of events, "my family lived in the next county over – Martin County. My daddy was a farmer, and we all helped out around the farm, even during the school year. You know, a lot of the crops are ready to harvest in the fall, after classes have already began. Well, my sister – Laura's mother – and I would help with the corn when it was time to harvest. I guess that would've been about this time of year come to think of it.

"Anyway, one day my sister and I were bored with our farm chores and were playing tag or some other silly game, running through the corn stalks and all over the farm. Well, she caught up to me and we'd both been running and were just plumb tired. So, we plopped right down in the middle of the corn to catch our breath. Then we heard our jackass – a mule you might call it – acting up like he'd gone crazy. Braying and carrying on like the sky was falling. What was that old mule's name? Rufus or Buford or something like that.

"We got up to investigate and made our way through the corn stalks toward the barn where that jackass was tied up. Of course, we couldn't see anything till we stepped out of the corn and were just twenty yards or so from the barn. There he was, kicking and hopping, trying like the devil to snap that rope. Well, then we seen what was agitating him. There, next to the barn was what we first thought was a big old black fella. Now, back then there wasn't many black folks in these parts. And this one was huge, and had a beard that hung down to his knees. At least, that's what it looked like at first. But then he moved from underneath the shadows of the barn's overhang and we could clearly see it was an 'it,' and not a 'him.'

"It was tall as the barn opening, with a chest like a whiskey barrel and

52

arms that hung to its knees. We both stood there looking at it, and it at us. Then it put one giant foot forward with a heavy thud, opened a huge mouth and screamed at us. I swear I saw the planks of the old barn rattle when that thing hollered. Shoot, it was ten times louder than daddy's tractor, for sure. When it screamed, I shook out of my daze and grabbed Sis's arm and took off into the cornfield. We ran and ran, in no particular direction I guess, just screaming and running.

"We could hear it coming after us, shaking the very earth as it ran. I just knew we were going to die. Sis tripped and scraped her knee up pretty fierce. I stopped too and tried to get her up and I could hear it getting closer. Then it stopped, but I could hear – and almost feel – it breathing real heavy. I was looking back at Sis, pleading to her to get up on her feet and she was just whimpering. I saw this big hairy hand reach from way back in the corn. I can still see it clearly – all leathery, with grungy hair and long, thick, yellowish fingernails at the end of long black fingers. It looked like a giant's hand. This was no human hand, or a bear paw or nothing like that. I'm glad Sis didn't see that hand reaching for her ankle. Suddenly, it stopped and withdrew and I couldn't hear the breathing no more.

"I faintly heard Daddy's voice hollering for us. That must've been what that monster heard, because he stopped all that scary breathing and reaching for us. Then it grunted with a deep guttural growl at the end, like it was angry it had to cut its little chase short. As Daddy got closer to us, that thing took off like dynamite blasting through that corn. Daddy finally found us after we yelled back at him. He didn't believe our story at first, but with Sis crying like that, both our faces white as sheets, and that huge path of smashed down corn leading back to the woods, I think he realized we wasn't just making up tales.

"Several years later, when we was grown up some, Daddy told both of us about some of his own run-ins with what he called a 'skunk ape'. In a way, that made me glad that he truly did believe our story from years back and that he'd seen the same thing. But in the same way, it scared the dickens out of me, because what Daddy said meant that such a creature did in fact exist, and that it wasn't just the product of silly childish imaginations. I'm not sure what's worse – thinking you saw one and nobody believing you, or finding out that there really are monsters out there."

Aunt Hazel finished her story on this cautionary note and took a sip of tea. Brad and Jesse had been following her every word – Brad with his mouth hanging open, Jesse thinking how this tale sounded like many stories he had heard before. He did not doubt Aunt Hazel's credibility or veracity, as he figured she had been ridiculed for her story in her younger years and had probably never enjoyed telling it, except maybe by having a good scary story to tell at Halloween.

Hazel quickly stopped as Laura rounded the corner from an adjoining room. "Hazel, are you still filling these guys full of those ridiculous stories?"

"Oh no," Aunt Hazel said with a smile, "we stopped talking about that a long time ago. I just gave them the abbreviated version of my story. No, we've just been talking about some of the local sightseeing opportunities and things they might want to take pictures of. These fellers weren't interested in any of my childhood yarns anyway."

"That's true," Jesse chimed in. "We're really not here to track down anything mysterious. A few shots of the local wildlife and we'll have our mission accomplished. Pretty mundane really."

Brad concurred and they both thanked Hazel for pointing them in the right direction for some good wildlife-viewing opportunities. As soon as Hazel left the room, Laura asked Jesse to forget about the story and hoped that he did not think her aunt was too crazy. Jesse assured her that, in his many years of wildlife photography and outdoors experiences, he had heard similar stories before and some much more bizarre. He tried to play it off as if he did not personally believe Hazel's childhood recollections. Laura quickly reminded him that story-telling had simply been a way of life for generations and generations in this area, and that almost everybody liked to tell a good tall tale every now and then. Jesse promised her that he would chalk up Hazel's account as just that.

Laura had to get to work, as lunchtime was fast approaching. She and Jesse spoke a few words outside of Brad's hearing and then she headed toward the restaurant portion of the building. Jesse and Brad headed out into the daylight to buy some supplies for their expedition and to do some more investigation and story-gathering.

*   *   *

As Jesse and Brad had walked through town, Jesse had been in deep thought about Laura. He did not realize that they had already made it to a small sporting goods store. While Jesse walked absentmindedly through the store, Brad picked through some of the shelves. Although they had brought a lot of camping equipment that Brad had purchased in Michigan, they still looked around for some extra items. Brad had made sure to get the newest, most high-tech equipment he could find. Jesse, however, knew that it would help to make a few in-town contacts by purchasing as much as they could locally. Brad looked at a few high-power flashlights. He was told by the store merchant that they would, "light up the woods for miles."

Jesse considered his good fortune when he discovered a section of local maps. Though they had downloaded several topographic maps from the Internet, and purchased a state map already, the selections in the sporting goods store showed more detail than the others. Jesse could see on the inside flap that the maps had been printed in a nearby town, and he decided that they must have been made by someone with local knowledge. He went to find the store manager to ask about the maps and the mapmaker.

"Oh sure," the manager told Jesse, "those were made just a few years ago by a local by the name of Elijah Hopkins. He used to walk every hill and holler, pine ridge and hardwood creek bottom in this area. Wasn't much demand for the maps outside of the region, so he had them published on his own dime. We've sold quite a few over the years."

Jesse was excited by this news from the shopkeeper. "Does Mr. Hopkins still live in town?" he asked, hoping to get even more intimate details about the surrounding area.

"Well," the store manager began slowly, "that's a good question. We're not really sure if Elijah still lives in town."

Jesse was puzzled. "Did he move or something?"

"No, nothing like that," the shopkeeper answered slowly again. "He's still got his house and everything. But, well, he hasn't been around for a few weeks now. I guess he's still up in the woods, nobody's heard from him."

"Well, do they consider him missing, or lost or something?" Jesse asked, still trying to get the shopkeeper to open up.

"He was just walking the foothills like he always did. Making his maps. No, the last person to get lost would be Elijah Hopkins. I reckon he ran into some trouble up there. Folks told him to wait till the spring or at least later on in the winter. But making them maps was his passion." The shopkeeper shook his head. "It's a shame, but it's not like it hasn't happened before."

Now Jesse was concerned. If bad fortune had befallen the expert mapmaker in the local foothills he knew well, how would Brad's expedition fare? "How long have they been searching for him?"

The shopkeeper was now growing tired of Jesse's questions. "They? Look kid, this ain't the ski slopes of Colorado. We don't have the resources to send a whole team of rescuers into the hills looking for stragglers."

Before Jesse could ask a follow-up question, the shopkeeper cut him off.

"Look, you can go ask Elijah's brother, Vernon, about all this stuff. If you boys want to buy that camping gear, that's fine, but I can't ignore my other customers just to stand here all day answering questions."

Jesse knew that he and Brad were the only customers in the shop, and realized that the store manager simply did not want to be pushed any further on the subject. Brad paid for a few small items and Jesse got Vernon Hopkins' address. The two went outside and got in the Brad's SUV.

"What was up with that dude?" Brad asked, annoyed that Jesse was asking so many questions and mad that the store owner had just brushed them off.

"I don't know, but I was just trying to get some information. Just because I've done this a few times doesn't mean I know all the answers. I mean, you can chime in with your own concerns at times."

After a minute or two of silence, Brad turned to Jesse. "OK, so you think there's something up with this Hopkins guy. Why are you so interested in it?"

"Well Brad, I think we should at least go find out why this expert mapmaker with intimate knowledge of the area has been 'lost' in the woods for a couple of weeks and why no one's out there looking for him. Doesn't that strike you as odd? Like maybe something happened to him that nobody wants to talk about?"

"All right, should we go get the rest of the group?"

Jesse thought about it a minute. He was annoyed enough just having spent the day with Brad. It was more human contact than he was used to recently. He surely wanted to limit his exposure to the rest of the peanut gallery. "No," he answered, then trying to be diplomatic about his reason, "we need to be sneaky about finding out information around here. If this Hopkins guy has lost his brother, he may not even want to talk to the two of us, let alone a whole big group of strangers. So let's go see him on our own and then we'll get with the rest of the gang."

Brad admitted that this made sense. He pulled out onto the street and the two headed towards the Hopkins residence, trying their best to follow the sketchy directions provided at the sporting goods store. After making one wrong turn, they found themselves on Hilltop Lane. The appropriately-named road wound up a steep wooded hill, passing only a few houses.

375 Hilltop Lane would have been hard to miss, even if Jesse and Brad were not specifically looking for it. A 1984 Chevy Monte Carlo sat in the front yard, with its tires replaced by cinderblocks for support. The light blue paint job had yielded in several areas to large swatches of rust. The front bumper was attached on the driver's side, but hung to the ground on the passenger side. Jesse was amused at the "For Sale" sign in the rear window. A similarly-rusted washing machine and dryer combo sat on the front porch. An old dishwasher rested in the side yard, surrounded by tall weeds. Bicycles and other toys littered the rest of the landscape.

Brad was uncomfortable about pulling into the driveway. He suggested foregoing the meeting with Vernon Hopkins. Jesse urged him to relax, while also trying to assure himself that the old adage about books and their covers should hopefully apply in this situation. As they got out of the SUV and walked to the front porch, the pile of empty beer cans did little to comfort either of the two. Jesse pushed the doorbell several times, but could not hear any chimes inside. They could hear, though, a loud television blaring. Jesse knocked on the door and still got no response. Brad decided to give it a try. His caution about the situation had given way to frustration and annoyance. He kicked the bottom of the door hard enough to make it rattle. The television inside suddenly became quiet. Jesse shot Brad an angry look and hoped to himself that Vernon Hopkins would not open the door equipped with some sort of gun.

Vernon did not have a firearm when he opened the door. Instead, he was loosely grasping a plastic bottle of cheap whiskey. He stared wildly at Jesse and Brad and tried to concentrate hard enough to look straight at them, though his head was teetering back and forth. "What y'all mean kicking on my walls?" He asked and took a swig from the bottle. "And what in tarnation do you want? You better not be trying to sell me nothing." He broke his stare and turned back inside. "Where's my gun?" he muttered as he headed back into the house.

Brad and Jesse looked at each other. They were still standing in the doorway, unsure if they should flee or follow the drunk man inside. Before they could make a decision, Vernon came back to the door. It was clear that he did not recognize them from just a few moments earlier. "Can I help you fellers?" he asked cordially. He then appeared a little worried. "This ain't about the other night out in front of the courthouse is it? I can explain that, I was just a little drump. I mean drank." He took an imbalanced step backwards. "I mean dronk." Vernon fell back and tumbled over a footstool and into a recliner.

Jesse decided to see if the man was all right, so he went inside to take a look at him. Brad followed, cautiously looking around the room as if searching for booby traps. Vernon lay on the recliner with closed eyes and a half grin on his face. He was already snoring. "Maybe we should get him some coffee or something," Jesse suggested.

"Maybe we should get outta here," Brad responded, still sizing up his surroundings. "Who's this guy going to think we are the next time he wakes up?"

"Hey, look – we're here already. The least we ought to do is find out the story about Elijah Hopkins. It could be important to the expedition we're going to be on in a few days."

"It could be important to get out of here while we still can," Brad countered cynically. "Jesse, you may have us on some wild goose chase here. What's to guarantee this guy can help us out at all. Maybe he's just a lousy drunk."

"Maybe there's a reason he's drunk, Brad. It's not going to hurt our timetable or anything to stick around for a few minutes and ask him some questions. There's no harm in trying, right?"

"Whatever, man?" Brad said, getting annoyed again. "I hired you to help me hunt down a mysterious creature, not to serve as an interpreter for drunk-ass hillbillies. But if you think this is so goddamned important, we'll just see." Brad plopped down on a sofa covered in newspapers and a few old T.V. dinner trays.

"Like I said," Jesse continued, trying to be patient and a little worried with Brad's surliness, "a few minutes in the grand scheme of things won't cost us that much and it may actually help us a good deal." Jesse headed for the kitchen. "I'm going to see if there's any coffee around here. Keep an eye on your buddy there and make sure he doesn't fall out of his chair or something."

"Oh yeah, that'd be horrible," Brad replied sarcastically. He folded his arms across his chest and fixed a mad gaze on the passed-out homeowner

* * *

"What the ... hey who are you?" Vernon Hopkins asked confusedly as he finally came out of his drunken stupor. He groggily stared at Jesse and Brad and tried to get his bearings. When he realized he was in his own house, he was even more surprised. "What y'all doing in my house? Now look here..."

Jesse interrupted him, "Mr. Hopkins, my name's Jesse McCoy and this is Brad Brown. You invited us in when we came to your door a few minutes ago. Just as you were showing us in, you took a nasty little trip there and must've been out for a little." Jesse looked over at Brad, who cocked an eyebrow up in amusement at Jesse's slight stretch of the truth.

"All right then," Vernon groaned as he sat up in his recliner. Jesse handed him a cup of coffee. "Well, what'd I let you in for? Y'all trying to sell me something or what?"

Brad answered before Jesse could, "We were sent here from the guy down at the sporting goods store. We were asking about your brother and he sent us this way to find you."

"My brother?" Vernon growled in response. "What the hell kind of business you got with Elijah? And what were you talking about him for at the sports store?"

Jesse was annoyed that Brad had been so blunt. He did not want Vernon to know what they were really interested in, and he could tell it was a sore subject. "What my friend means, Mr. Hopkins, is we were asking about the maps your brother makes. We are going to do some hiking and nature photography in the area and were told he was the most knowledgeable person around on the region and its terrain. We were asking about getting some maps from him when the store manager suggested we come see you about it."

Again, Brad was not sure why Jesse did not just tell the truth and say what they were really after. Brad's patience with Jesse's roundabout way of talking to people was growing thin. However, shifting the discussion to the subject of maps and tourism did seem to diffuse a little of Vernon's defensiveness.

"Well shit fire boys, I've got maps out the kazoo around here. Elijah used to come over here all the time with some new place all mapped out. That man must've walked a thousand or more miles in those mountains. It's what he loved," Vernon concluded with a far-off stare passing over his face. Jesse watched as his demeanor turned from recalling fond memories to gloominess.

"I guess you fellers know that ol' Eli's been missing for a while?"

"That's what they told us," Brad offered. He wanted to go ahead and launch into some questions, since that was what they were there for in the first place. "What happened to him?"

Vernon rocked forward and stood up. He swayed a bit as he was still trying to clear the cobwebs out of his head. He went to the corner of the room and grabbed a large chest. He dragged it back to where Jesse and Brad were sitting. "You boys can have your pick of those maps there, I've no use for them no more. If that's what you're really interested in, you can take a few and leave. If you're here on account of something else, you better go on and git now." Vernon grabbed a wooden baseball bat from behind a dilapidated china hutch. Though he was presently using it as a walking stick for support, it seemed dangerous in his hands. Jesse did not want to press him any more, especially since he appeared to still be drunk, agitated, and now wielding a bat.

"We appreciate the maps, Mr. Hopkins," Jesse said in a sincere tone. "Maybe while we're out exploring and hiking, we might run into your brother, or find some clues as to his whereabouts."

"Exploring and hiking? Boys this ain't the time of year to be doing that around here. Elijah knew it, and knew it good. I told him he was a darned fool for going out in them hills by his self. Wouldn't listen to me, and I 'spect you boys won't either." Vernon sat back down into his chair with a resigned sigh. "Y'all know why they hasn't been nobody looking for my brother?" He paused to look at Jesse and Brad, whose silence prompted Vernon to continue. "'Cause everyone in these parts knows it's just asking for trouble to go walking unawares through the mountains around here this time of year. There's things out there a man can't explain. Most of it sounds like fairytale and I'm sure y'all wouldn't believe me, but sure as you and I is sitting here, there's monsters out there. Ghosts, goblins, witches – you call it what you want – but they's out there and they's just as real as you or me."

Brad spoke up, "Whatever you're talking about – if it is real, can surely be hunted down and shot. Why, I've never run across anything, no matter how scary, that couldn't be dealt with a well-placed bullet." Brad's statement was full of false bravado and he knew he was trying to convince himself that he would be able to deal with his fears once their expedition began in earnest.

Now it was Vernon's turn to smirk. A weird smile crept over his face and he raised an eyebrow and squinted the other eye. "You've got some real gumption there sport. I reckon that cocky attitude would turn tail and run faster than a colored feller leavin' a Klan rally if you ever came across what I'm talking about. Tell you what boys, if adventure is what you're after, why don't you head over to the old bridge at Monkey Creek. You just hang out there for a while. It's a good road, not wilderness by any far stretch. Doesn't even require any hiking or 'exploring' as you called it. Nope, just walk down old state road 866 till you get to the bridge. You could even take along a picnic basket if you want. Yes, real civilized. Nothing to worry about."

Vernon leaned back in the chair and stretched his hands back behind his head. He chuckled softly. "Yeah, before you go off hiking in the woods, y'all oughtta test your mettle a little first."

"How do we get to this Monkey Creek bridge?" Brad asked excitedly.

"Oh, it's on one of those maps you got there. But if you go into town and ask for directions, don't tell 'em why you're going and don't tell 'em I sent you. Somebody might try to stop you, to talk some sense into you – and you wouldn't want that," Vernon snorted at the end of his sentence.

Jesse and Brad gathered a handful of maps and thanked Vernon Hopkins for his time, and for the tip about Monkey Creek. They also assured him that they would keep an eye out for any sign of his brother, Elijah, when they began their real wilderness expedition.

"Boys, one more thing," Vernon called out to them as they were leaving. "Elijah was a well-respected member of this community. Solid citizen, nice guy, made real nice maps that everybody liked. The group they rounded up in town to go look for him spent a total of two or three days searching for him after he come up lost, and that was a couple of weeks ago. Don't expect folks around here to come looking for you at all. Not this time of year anyhow. You go off into those mountains against every last shred of God-given sense, and you're on your own."

"I think we can handle it sir," Brad responded. "We've planned for all contingencies."

"Heh," Vernon scoffed, "seems like I've heard that before." He leaned forward in his recliner, extended the baseball bat from his outstretched arm and used it to slam the front door shut. Jesse and Brad could hear the television turn back on through the thin walls of the house. They stepped off the porch and headed to the truck.

"Stupid drunk," Brad said, "acting like we were kids going off on our first camping trip. I'd be willing to bet the Hopkins brothers are probably running a moonshine still or something up in those mountains. Probably use scary stories and dire warnings just to keep people from stumbling upon their little operation. Stupid hillbilly moonshiners."

Jesse refrained himself and replied, "Come on, Brad, you know there's more to it than that. Think about it. Maybe Vernon Hopkins *is* a drunk, but that doesn't explain why the whole town would be weary of spending much time in the mountains looking for Elijah. Why didn't they contact some neighboring counties, or even federal search and rescue to mount a massive search?"

Brad shrugged his shoulders in response.

Jesse was forced to answer his own question. "Well, I'm guessing that nobody from around here wanted to be out in those woods any longer than they had to – and not because of any 'shine still. I'm guessing it's because our hairy friends tend to show up this time of year and nobody wanted to arrive at the same fate as Elijah Hopkins."

This statement finally evoked a good response from Brad. "If that's the case then we should be launching our expedition out into the forests surrounding this town as soon as possible. Let's quit wasting time interviewing these local yokels and get down to business."

"Slow down, Brad. Why don't we start with scoping out this Monkey Creek he was talking about. It may not be all that exciting, but it'd be a good way to spend the rest of today anyway. It'd be a good test of the whole group. We can work out any bugs in our equipment and see how well we all work together on a short day trip before we set off into the woods for a week. What do you think?"

"Yeah, I guess so," Brad said as he started up the SUV. "I guess we are just wasting time till we figure out a place to start the expedition. The rest of the gang's probably tired of being cooped up in that old log cabin lodge.

Yeah, let's go get 'em. We'll see if ol' Vernon Hopkins knows his shit or if the drunk bastard was just messing around with us."

* * *

When Jesse and Brad got back to the lodge, they encountered Mark in the lobby, sleeping in an oversized wingback chair. Brad kicked his foot and Mark snapped out of his slumber. Mark explained that Kelly had come by his room earlier in the morning to visit with Roy and their constant chatter was bothering Mark's headache so much that he came to the lobby. Jesse stayed in the lobby with Mark and Brad hurried up the stairs.

When he got to the hallway, Brad saw Kelly coming out of Roy's room, laughing. When she turned around to see Brad, her face registered a look of surprise and fright. She forced a smile, laughed, and ran up to Brad to hug him. Brad did not return the hug, but instead questioned her.

"What were you doing in there with Roy?" he asked.

As innocently as she could, Kelly responded, "Oh come on Brad – what else am I supposed to do? You and Jesse take off and leave us at this god-forsaken place to sit around and be bored. Roy and I were just watching some T.V. Was I supposed to have been hanging out with Mark, getting to know him? Or just sitting around twiddling my thumbs?"

"Well, next time I'll remember to bring you along whenever we go somewhere."

"That's fine," Kelly replied, hoping she had smoothed things over. "That way I won't be so bored I'm forced to spend my time with Roy." She laughed. "He can be just as much of a bore as sitting around by myself."

Brad stared at her a while, not saying anything. He felt a mixture of emotions, not sure whether to trust his girlfriend or to continue being suspicious. Kelly could read his facial expression and offered, "Look, if it makes you feel any better, just keep closer tabs on me – as in don't leave me here while you go off having adventures. That way I won't get bored to death and you won't have to worry about me. You can keep me safely right by your side." Kelly snuggled next to Brad and hugged him again. After a moment or two, she could feel Brad's tense muscles relax and then he grabbed her in his arms.

"Well, if you want to stay by my side," Brad finally said, "then get your gear ready because we're heading out."

Jesse and Brad studied a map for a while as the rest of the group got ready. They gathered up the gear and all piled into the SUV. They bought sandwiches at the local grocery and drove a few minutes before another pit stop. This time, Kelly needed to use the bathroom and Mark and Roy wanted candy bars and soft drinks. They were all relieved to leave their rooms and be out and about. Jesse, on the other hand, was getting slightly annoyed at the stops and worried about their time frame. He kept an eye on the dashboard clock. Regardless of whether they might encounter anything unexpected or not at their destination, he did not want to be out in unfamiliar territory at night. They did not have the right equipment with them, and Jesse did not think they were quite ready to be stumbling around in the dark.

At the gas station stop, while the others were inside buying supplies, Jesse stepped out and asked the station attendant for some directions. Clayton Mahoney, as his shirt name attested to, described to Jesse the winding road that led to state road 866. By the time they all climbed back into Brad's vehicle, the dashboard clock flashed two o'clock. Jesse sat in the back with Mark and Roy, who began a forced conversation about people and events from Michigan. Listening to their discussion, Jesse decided that they had not known each very well prior to this trip. He wondered how his fellow passengers ended up on this expedition.

Jesse had to speak over them to give Brad directions. In the front passenger seat, Kelly kept her nose buried in a magazine and her ears occupied with a personal CD player turned up loud enough for them all to hear.

Forty-five minutes later, after a wrong turn onto state road 86, the group barreled down a dilapidated asphalt two-lane road where the occasional 866 sign provided welcome encouragement that they were on the right track. That track soon turned to gravel, though. Then, following a sign pointing to Monkey Creek, Brad took a hard right turn down a narrow one-lane gravel road that became a dirt road, then ended. In front of them was an ancient hickory tree lying right across the road. Jesse hopped out of the back and checked the tree to see if there was anyway around it.

"Well, I would've thought the county would maintain these roads better, but it looks like this tree's been sitting here a while," he said to Brad through the rolled-down driver's side window.

"Maybe there's not a whole lot of traffic going down this stretch," Brad replied, "or a whole lot of people wanting to get where we're going."

"Regardless," Jesse said, "I suppose we're on foot from here," This comment elicited some moans from the back seat. It was already a little past three o'clock, so Jesse suggested that they either get going soon or call it quits. Brad refused to simply turn around and head back into town. "This whole day's already almost gotten away from us. I'm not about to let it end that way without at least a little field work," he said. Brad turned to his fellow passengers, "We've got plenty of daylight left and the bridge's probably only a short walk from here. You guys can either come with us or sit in the car." He then turned to look directly at Kelly.

Kelly unbuckled her seat belt. "Well, let's go then," she said unenthusiastically.

"What about you guys?" Brad asked, looking at Mark and Roy. Then, more directly to Roy, he said, "I'd hate for either of you two to look like a pussy having to stay here at the car."

"What, are you the boss now?" Roy asked. "I didn't sign on for you to be ordering us around the whole time. You on some kind of power trip or something?"

"Whoa, turn it down a notch," Brad laughed. "Don't be so sensitive buddy." He slapped Roy on the back with slightly more force than Roy expected.

Roy teetered forward but caught himself. Without looking at Brad he grabbed a backpack from within the car and turned around. Brad did not pursue the conversation any further, but instead turned to Mark, who was already getting his gear ready for the hike.

Jesse looked across the hood from the outside of the car and saw a strained expression on Kelly's face after the display between Roy and Brad. Jesse was getting ready to go over to her and say something, but stopped short when she shot him an icy stare. He decided he would do his best not to get involved in the complex and – as he thought to himself – weird relationship between his four fellow travelers.

In nicer tones, Brad asked them all to grab a video camera, a digital still camera and flashlights. Jesse also saw him go the back of the truck and pull out a handgun from a bag in the cargo area. Jesse shook his head and wondered and worried about what kind of affair he had gotten himself into. He pulled on a lightweight jacket and zipped it up as he glanced at the others while they prepared for the day's activities.

As they got started, Brad confidently led the way, though none of them really knew where they were going. He crashed through some thick honeysuckle and thorns to get around the hickory tree blocking the road. Kelly then picked her way gingerly through the thicket, followed by Roy, who was even daintier in passing through the thorns. Mark tried to fit through the temporary gap in the thorns, but it closed as Roy passed through it, slightly scratching Mark. Jesse took a few steps to the right of the thicket and merely stepped under a low dogwood branch to get through. He was not about to start blindly playing follow the leader this early in the game.

* * *

Warm early fall sunlight draped the trees and gravel road with a sense of cheeriness. Jesse looked around the woods as they walked toward the bridge. In the mid-afternoon sunlight, the hike to the bridge turned out to be pleasant and scenic. Jesse's earlier worries faded somewhat. The group was making good time down the dirt and gravel road, nobody was arguing or getting on his nerves, and they still had a couple of hours of daylight left to get to the bridge, look around, and get home.

Mark kept up with Brad's quick pace, giving him a chance to ask the occasional question and show his interest. Roy and Kelly lagged behind, talking and joking around with each other. Roy carried a video camera to document their outing, and occasionally he took some footage as they hiked along the rough road. After almost two miles, though, there was less joking and even some grumbling. Kelly needed to stop because her feet were hurting. Mark and Roy agreed with the decision to stop. Jesse reluctantly acquiesced. He and Brad were determined to make good time to the spot in order to have a longer time cushion to get back before dark.

The group got going after a short five-minute breather. Another mile and a half down the road they finally came to the dilapidated bridge spanning Monkey Creek. The hike had taken them nearly forty-five minutes, so they now only had an hour or two of good daylight left. Jesse glanced at his watch and decided that they were not too far behind schedule. The other four were in better spirits now that they had finally arrived at their destination.

However, after a quick glance around, Mark was the first to point out what the rest were thinking. "This is it?" he asked with disappointment.

In fact, the bridge was only about thirty-five feet long and the creek below was not much more than a wide, shallow ditch. Jesse looked down at the creek, which was about fifteen feet below. There was a gentle current to it as it funneled into the narrow gap underneath the bridge. A deep, sluggish pool lay upstream of the bridge. Above that, a set of riffles broke up the glassy surface of the water. Past that they could not see the creek as it came from around a sharp, steep bend in the hillside. Jesse was not impressed with the creek either, though the fisherman in him quickly catalogued the likely places to locate hiding fish and wondered what species might be found in this small habitat.

"Oh yeah, this is awesome," Roy declared sarcastically. "Our fearless leader has brought us to a bridge at drainage ditch. Exciting."

"Well, we're here," Brad said in a frustrated voice, "let's film some of the surroundings. We can at least test out our equipment and stuff. Hey Jesse, remember what that guy said was such a big deal about this place?"

"You mean Vernon Hopkins?" Jesse asked, confused.

"No, I'm thinking about one of those guys said this used to be a big make-out spot or something."

Jesse did not remember hearing that, though Brad could have gotten the information from talking to any number of people at the lodge or around town during their many stops en route. It could have been true, though. This was an out-of-the-way spot, and considering how little there was to do in the town, it did not seem unlikely that restless teenagers would find their way here to get into trouble. Jesse looked out over the downstream side of the bridge at a wide portion of the creek. In the afternoon sunlight filtering through the treetops, Jesse could picture people coming out here to enjoy the scenery and solitude.

Roy began setting up the video equipment on a tripod. Mark walked around taking a few still pictures with a digital camera. Brad stood in front of the video camera and discussed their expedition and this current stage of information-gathering. He tried to be as meticulous as possible in his descriptions, but soon wanted some commentary from Jesse. Brad waved over at Jesse, who felt silly coming to his side to do an interview in front of the camera. Jesse talked about the terrain and surrounding environment in regards to possible bigfoot habitat. He noted the lush vegetation, plentiful timber and shelter, and the flowing water supply just below the bridge. He then pointed out that not only would the creek provide water and possibly fish, but also would likely function as a travel corridor as well. Jesse was just hitting his stride in discussing the topography of the land when Mark yelled at them to come see what he had found.

Mark kicked some leaves up from the ground as the others made their way over to his position at the foot of the bridge. Underneath the leaves rested a rusted car door. This in itself did not seem too unusual to anyone, until Mark made an astute observation. "I mean, where's the rest of the car? I know old junk parts probably aren't that strange, but why would this car door be here without the rest of the car? Either somebody hauled a single car door all the way out here to dump, or somebody left a car door here and drove off with the rest of the car."

Jesse digested Mark's musings and walked around the car door. He almost twisted his ankle on something underneath the leaves. He kicked around the leaves and found a decayed, faded woman's high heel shoe. As they scanned the area further, they all started noticing out of place objects. Besides ancient beer bottles and other random trash, Kelly also discovered a pile of spent shotgun shells and a torn mesh baseball cap.

Mark wondered about the possibility that in times of flooding, the creek could have easily risen out of its banks and deposited trash from upstream onto this spot of ground next to the bridge. Jesse contemplated a more ominous explanation for the presence of shotgun shells and a car door that looked torn off its hinges. Kelly expressed a feeling that she was "getting the creeps" from hanging out in this area.

Brad would hear none of that. "Oh come on Kelly – you've got to be braver than that on this trip. We're on a man-made road in broad daylight, and you're letting some odds and ends bits of redneck junk get to you. You're just psyching yourselves out. We've got a whole lot of ..."

Brad's voice trailed off as he recognized that all the hairs on the back of his neck were involuntarily standing on end. Mark, now standing next to Brad, had just noticed the same thing on his own neck. Brad wheeled around and scanned the area quickly, looking for anything out of the ordinary. His senses were suddenly on high alert. He was the first to notice something that Jesse then addressed.

"There's no birds anymore," Jesse said quietly. "No insects either. The whole area's gone silent." He crouched down close to the ground and reached into his backpack. He picked up a listening device that would amplify the forest sounds.

"What's going on guys?" Kelly asked worriedly. "Why are you all being all quiet and fishy all of a sudden?"

"It's just Brad trying to make this all seem more exciting than it is," Roy answered.

Brad shushed them with a finger over his mouth and motioned to everyone to be still. Kelly did not have to wait too long to find out what they had already begun to pick up on. Just imperceptibly at first, but then in a sudden wave, they all smelled a horrible stench that resembled a mixture of pungent body odor, rotten garbage, wet dog, and a musky sweetness that was overpowering. Kelly sniffed in the air at first, then upon catching a powerful whiff of the smell, began to gag uncontrollably. She then bent over and threw up on the ground. Next to her, Roy tried to cover his eyes to keep them from watering. The stench stung his eyes and burned his throat.

Jesse, Brad, and Mark also began to cough and gag. Jesse pulled a bandana out of his backpack and tied it over his nose and mouth. This helped with the stench somewhat, but his eyes were still moistened with uncontrollable tears. He wiped these away, then grabbed Brad on the shoulder. Brad wheeled around just in time to see what Jesse had pointed to. They both caught a quick glimpse of a large blur move from one side of the road to another, about fifty yards away in the direction that they had originally hiked in from.

Mark had also seen something dart across the road, though from a slightly different vantage point. He called out to Jesse in Brad in a hoarse whisper, "Did you guys see that? Did you guys see that?" He scrambled over to them. Brad asked him if he had gotten it on film, but Mark had forgotten that he was toting around the camera. In the onslaught of odors that had just hit them, Mark had been more concerned with his own instinctual response to the smell rather than in somehow documenting his surroundings.

Brad cussed him under his breath and then ordered him to start filming anything and everything that happened. Meanwhile, Roy had pulled Kelly close to him and they slowly moved toward the rest of the group until all five of them stood nearly shoulder to shoulder. The stench slowly dissipated and each person recognized that they could breathe normally again. Jesse removed his improvised facemask and stuffed the bandana in his pocket. He took a big swig of water and splashed some on his face. He passed the canteen to the others, who followed his lead. It was as if they were trying to wash the smell off of them, though it had been so strong and concentrated at first that it seemed it was impregnated in their clothes.

"I feel like I've been sprayed by a skunk," Kelly complained. "Isn't there some folk remedy like bathing in oatmeal or washing your clothes in vinegar that'll help get the smell out?" She looked at Jesse for an answer, but he had none.

"Hell, I don't know Kelly," he finally answered. Jesse did not say anything else for a while, but then walked close to Brad. "I've smelled that before," he said under his breath so that only Brad could hear. "It's unmistakable. My gut reaction was unmistakable too."

"Which was what?" Brad whispered.

"The desire to get out of here as fast as I can." He paused for a while and then continued, "I guess I didn't really get a good look at it," Jesse admitted. "But that smell..." He continued mumbling something that Brad could not hear.

Besides the hushed conversation between Brad and Jesse, the group was quiet for a while as they listened to the normal forest sounds gradually returning. Brad wanted to take a few more pictures of the surrounding terrain, so Jesse sat down on the ground to get more comfortable while he waited. Mark had resigned himself that he was not going to be heading home just yet, so he started fishing through his backpack for a snack. As Brad walked along the trail taking pictures, Roy turned to Kelly. He rolled his eyes and whispered with sarcasm, "Oh yeah, this is real exciting."

Suddenly, a loud rustling noise sounded out from the creek bed behind the group. Jesse wheeled around to look in the direction of the creek. He could not see anything, though he felt like the noises had come from right behind a sharp bend in the creek. Whatever had made the noise was most likely located just out of sight around the bend in the steep creek bank.

Jesse had pulled out his own binoculars and studied the stream bank where the noise had originated. He then grabbed a notebook from his backpack and feverishly scribbled some notes and flipped the pages, looking for a particular entry. Brad yelled something from his position on the trail and Jesse looked toward him to see what he wanted.

While Jesse's attention was focused ahead, something heavy splashed in the creek behind them again. Jesse quickly turned back, hoping to catch the culprit crossing the creek. Instead, he saw nothing. What he did see, though, was a cloud of mud coursing downstream. Something had obviously stepped in the creek and disturbed its muddy bottom.

Brad finally stopped filming. He returned to the rest of the group who were all now staring at the ripples and muddy swirls gently flowing down the creek. "What's going on?" he asked.

"Something just splashed in the creek," Jesse answered.

"Beaver?" Brad offered.

"I don't know. Whatever it was has been making some racket in the bushes on the stream bank, though."

Then, catching everyone off guard, Kelly let fly a shrill scream of terror as she hopped up and broke into a full-fledged sprint. Without waiting for an explanation, Roy took off after her. By instinct, Jesse, Brad, and Mark grabbed their gear and followed.

After a few minutes of all-out sprinting, the group slowed down to a trot, then a complete stop. Roy collapsed on the road. Kelly stood over him, bent over with her hands resting on her knees. Brad breathed heavily as he struggled to keep his composure. Jesse leaned against a tree next to Brad. "OK, Kelly, what were we just running from? Did you see something?" Jesse stammered as he tried to catch his breath.

"Yeah I saw something," she quickly replied. "When I was leaning against that bridge back there I felt something on my neck going down into my shirt. I reached back to grab it and it was this huge gross spider."

"A spider?" Brad asked incredulously. He quickly turned to Roy. "And what were you running from Roy?"

"Well, I don't know," he answered defensively. "We had that smell and then something splashing in the creek and then Kelly starts screaming. I guess I just reacted to her scream. Thought she saw something." His voice trailed off into a mumble.

Jesse could not contain his laughter, though he was still short of breath from running. "Oh man," he chuckled, "this is some fantastic expeditionary force we've got here. Skunks, beavers, and spiders, and now we're all running for our lives."

Brad did not respond to Jesse. Instead, he simply slung his pack over his shoulder and barked at the others. "All right, let's get going. We might as well head back to the car before it gets any later in the day."

Mark, Roy, and Kelly agreed. The hiking and exertion so far had been enough for them. Jesse initially felt like they should return to the bridge and investigate the source of the pungent odors they had smelled and find out what had been splashing in the creek. However, as he looked at his companions he decided that it probably would be best to head back. Also, he knew that the commotion they had just created would mean that any animals in the area had probably long cleared out.

As they walked, Brad filmed and took occasional pictures and Jesse listened to the woods with his parabolic microphone and headphones. Jesse could hear the normal sounds of the forest clear and amplified through the device. Suddenly, he halted and threw his arms out to stop Roy and Kelly, who were walking next to him. At the same time, the others heard louder versions of what Jesse had picked up on the microphone – a series of loud cracks and groans. Then, from a few dozen yards ahead, a huge shadow lurched forward in the tree-lined edge of the woods. Branches swayed, leaves quivered, and an electric-like feeling pulsed through the area all in a split second as a towering, dead oak tree swayed violently forward, then with a final snap, crashed to the ground with a thunderous boom. The loud thud sent bark and twigs flying.

The tree had fallen exactly between the group's position and that of Brad's SUV, parked just around the corner. Not a sound was made for a few seconds after the tree crashed to the ground. Slowly, though, the surrounding woods came back to life. Jesse spoke first, using quiet, calm tones, "Now look, before anyone freaks out we should just take a deep breath and settle down. I mean, we are in the woods, and sometimes trees do fall."

"Are you crazy?" Kelly lashed out. "There's not even a hint of a breeze out here. Trees don't just fall on their own – especially not crashing down almost on top of us."

Roy looked at her, with an unsure expression, "What are you saying – that something *made* this tree fall? Don't tell me you think one of Brad's monsters is lurking around in the woods out there. Come on, Kelly."

Mark spoke up tentatively, "What about the fact that there's already one tree down across the road up by where the car's parked. Maybe somebody or something really doesn't want us around here."

Jesse, who had walked over to the tree, called to them, "Look, this thing's rotten to the core. I bet it's been standing here, dead and rotten for years.

It was just its time to fall. We were just in the wrong place at the wrong time – doesn't mean anything more than that." Though he was personally unsettled by the series of events they had all encountered throughout the day, he did not want everyone working into a frenzy the way Kelly had done earlier. Jesse knew that gross overreactions and keyed-up nerves were not a good recipe for the group's success later on in the expedition.

Brad, who had videotaped the entire incident, was still filming each person as they spoke. "Well, I'm going to agree. We never really *saw* anything that should've made us all worked up like we've been. But, this tree did just about fall on us, and my car. I'd like to get back to the lodge and go over all my footage. I think we might've gotten some good stuff on tape."

Roy did not say anything, but was already scaling the prone tree trunk and hustling on toward the truck. Brad tried to interview Kelly on camera about the day's events, though she was not cooperative. Mark pulled Jesse to the side as they rounded the corner and neared the car. "Be honest with me, Jesse. What's going on here? I can understand a random tree falling, maybe – but two in the almost the same place? And what about that awful stench earlier? You sure seemed to react to it in a certain way. Do you think we're seeing some signs of this creature Brad's fixated on?"

"Look Mark, I don't know what Brad's told you about his plans for this upcoming week." Jesse took a drink from his water bottle and wiped his lip. "If we do eventually come across one of these animals, it'll be a life changing event for you – for all of us. Seeing one in the flesh is a whole different experience then hearing some noises and seeing some trees rustle. Save your energy and enthusiasm for the day – if it happens – we actually see one of these hairy critters." Jesse capped the water bottle and put it back in his backpack. "You'll need it then, for sure."

* * *

Back at the Elk Mountain Lodge, they all met in Brad and Kelly's room. After looking at the film footage, they realized that no one had recorded anything of value. The audio was equally inconclusive. Brad was upset, but tried to use the outing as a practice run, to see what they had done wrong. Jesse mentioned that they would all have to try much harder to maintain composure once the expedition really began. Similar to what he told Mark earlier, he noted that the random events they experienced at Monkey Creek would pale in comparison to seeing a seven- to eight- foot tall apelike creature in the mountains of Eastern Kentucky.

Jesse revealed that the smell they had experienced distinctly reminded him of his own encounter years earlier. However, despite Brad's inquiry into the matter, Jesse insisted that the area at Monkey Creek bridge would not make a suitable spot for their exploration. The fact that it was on public property and had obviously seen a high degree of visitation from the locals in the past was enough to rule it out in Jesse's opinion. "We don't need to go to all of the effort and expense of setting up for a week of hunting an elusive animal only to have the county road crew show up to do tree removal so people can begin driving right up to our spot for picnics or beer drinking."

"But you said yourself that that horrible smell might've come from one," Brad replied, unwilling to let the subject go. "I'd just hate to give up such a promising spot and go deep in the woods somewhere and never run into one again."

"Look Brad, the odds of us duplicating the encounter we *might* have had today are slim. But we can start focusing our search on nearby areas that Monkey Creek or its tributaries flow through. It's the perfect-sized little stream for them to use as a travel corridor. It was small, shaded, and tree-lined for security, but with a fairly level stream bed for easy movement."

Jesse and Brad kept going back and forth on the subject of site selection. Kelly did not participate much in the conversation as she was busy checking her cell phone messages and making calls from the bathroom. Roy tried to put a comic twist on everything they discussed in an effort to assuage his own fears and concerns. Jesse and Brad both attempted to impress on him the need to take the upcoming expedition seriously, but it was clear that Roy was going to stick with his defensive mechanism of mocking everything he could.

Mark left the room while Brad and Roy were arguing. He had never seen them at odds before, and was uncomfortable being in the small room with them. He went back to the room he shared with Roy and plopped down on the bed. He was glad to be alone and done with a long day – a day that had been equally frustrating and exciting. He picked up the phone and made a collect call to his fiancée. Though she was happy to hear from him, Vanessa wanted to know when he would be back.

Mark wondered if her urgency to have him return was because she missed him or she feared he would somehow miss an opportunity at his job. Mark knew that she was just trying to help, but the nagging comments quickly got on his nerves. He used a pleasant voice and feigned interest in her chit chat – anything to avoid getting asked about what he was doing on this expedition. The subject came up anyway. Vanessa again wanted to know when he would be returning from his camping trip and hoped he had not done anything stupid yet. She was having a tough time back at home explaining to her family where Mark was and what he was doing without mentioning the crazy idea of hunting down make-believe monsters.

Mark endured the conversation as long as he could. Then, he pressed a few buttons on the phone. He told Vanessa that their lodging lacked several amenities and that the phones were old and probably did not operate quite right. This only provoked a lecture about how many times Vanessa had insisted that Mark carry his cell phone like everyone else. "You never listen to me, do you?" she asked. In response, Mark grabbed his electric razor out of his suitcase and held it close to the phone. The buzzing drowned out Vanessa's voice for a few seconds. "Sorry honey," Mark said in his sweetest voice, "like I said, these phones are no good. I'm going to have to call you back tomorrow."

"Mark Dunston," Vanessa replied. Before she could continue, Mark turned on his razor again and yelled over the buzzing. "Vanessa… Vanessa … I can't hear you anymore. I'll call you tomorrow." Then he hung up.

* * *

Brad brushed his teeth and rinsed with some mouthwash. He checked his hair in the mirror, then noticed a small pimple on the side of his nose. Cursing, he pinched it till the puss popped out. He wiped the area with some toilet paper. Finally satisfied with his appearance, he walked back into the room where Kelly was reading a popular magazine in a corner chair.

"What's going on in the world of celebrities?" he mockingly asked.

Kelly ignored him, still reading. Brad walked over to her and yanked the magazine out of her hands. "How can you read this crap?" he asked, looking at the magazine's cover.

Kelly, trying to control her temper, responded, "Maybe I read it as an escape from this miserable situation you've dragged me into. Maybe it's more interesting than this desperate quest you're on. Maybe *I'm* desperate for anything that reminds me of normalcy."

Brad got red in the face and his body tensed. He rolled up the magazine and thrust it at her, pointing. "You don't look so desperate when you're hanging out with Roy. You two carry on like we were on a middle school field trip. It's hard to imagine you're that desperate when you're laughing and seem to be having a good time."

"Because he's not out to track down some make-believe monster. Brad, *you're* making me desperate." Kelly paused. "It's bad enough that almost seven years into our relationship we're still just boyfriend-girlfriend," Kelly continued hesitantly, "but add to that this crazy situation…" she gestured to their surroundings and trailed off.

Brad did not respond, so Kelly picked back up with her train of thought. "I've always been there for you. I've gone on plenty of your little escapades, and never once complained. I think I was hoping that this would be the last of those. Maybe I wanted to be along when you finally got over what's been troubling you all these years. Maybe I thought then we could get on with *our* lives."

Brad sensed something in her tone. "Is there an alternative or ultimatum you wanted to add to those statements? Like, that this needs to be the last of my 'little escapades,' or else?" he asked.

Though Brad had just voiced what Kelly had been thinking and feeling for a long time, she realized that she was not prepared to confront that scenario just yet. She was not ready to make her decision.

"Look," she said, switching to a sweeter tone, "we've both had a long day. My feet hurt a little from the hike and I guess it's making me a little cranky. Maybe we could just go to bed and call it a night." She stood up from the chair and put her arms around Brad's waist. She nuzzled her face into his chest and then looked up at him.

Brad's tenseness eased. "It was pretty awesome out there, wasn't it? Just getting out into the field gets me going." He paused for a minute and then his tone eased up. "You can go on to bed, I'm going to look at this video and listen to Jesse's tapes again."

Seeing that the conversation had shifted to Brad's favorite subject, Kelly felt relieved. "Do you want me to stay up with you?" she asked.

"Nah, go ahead and get some sleep. Hopefully tomorrow will be even more action-packed than today."

"That was pretty exciting at the bridge, even if I did get a little carried away," Kelly offered, hoping to get their earlier conversation completely out of Brad's mind.

"You haven't seen anything yet," Brad said as he turned to smile at her.

Kelly smiled back, though for a different reason. She rested her head on the pillow. As Brad's attention focused on his digital camcorder screen, Kelly pulled out her magazine and picked right up where she had left off just minutes ago.

* * *

Jesse entered the small bar area next to the lodge's restaurant. Just as he had hoped, Laura Calhoun was working at the bar, serving drinks to a few locals. Jesse ambled up to the bar and situated himself on one of the bar stools.

"What'll you have stranger?" Laura asked with a smile.

"I'll settle for a beer right now," Jesse answered. He then rolled his shoulders and reached back to massage the base of his neck.

"Rough day?" Laura asked, as she filled a frosty mug with a draft beer.

Jesse reached for the beer and took a healthy swig. "You have no idea," he finally answered, after wiping his mouth. "Man that hits the spot."

As Laura tended to another customer, she asked over to Jesse, "Did you get any pictures today?"

Jesse looked confused, and slightly panicked. He did not know how to respond. Laura finished with the other customer and walked back over to where Jesse sat. "Of elk – did you get any pictures of elk?"

Jesse relaxed. "No, we thought we might've heard some, but they were just out of sight."

Laura rinsed off a glass and wiped it dry with a towel. "It's amazing how such big animals can be so elusive in the forests. As big as they are, you'd think we'd see them all the time."

Jesse grinned. "You don't know the half of it." Laura raised an eyebrow at this comment and, remembering Aunt Hazel's story-telling, Jesse quickly followed up, "I mean, you're right. A huge animal weighing a half a ton or so, it's impressive how well they can stay hidden."

"And we probably make enough noise to scare 'em off from miles away," Laura laughed. Jesse hoisted his glass in agreement and took another long drink. He thought to himself that everything they had just said was equally applicable to certain other large forest creatures, ones that were even better at staying hidden and avoiding human encounters. He wondered how they would ever be able to track those creatures down. Perhaps, as he thought, the encounters usually happen much more on their terms than ours.

"That beer must be pretty good," Laura kidded. "You've been lost in thought since you finished your drink. Maybe it's time for another?"

"You drive a hard bargain," Jesse said, as he pushed his empty glass toward Laura. "Maybe one more for the night."

Jesse sat in the bar for another hour and a half, actually having a few more beers. He talked with Laura off and on when she had the time in between her chores.

Midway through one of the beers, Jesse got a chance to ask Laura about her own background.

"Well, I'm surprised my aunt didn't tell you every embarrassing story and family secret there is about me," Laura laughed. "It's been an interesting journey," she continued after a pause. "After my daddy died I swore I'd never set foot in this town again. People here always seemed so foolish and backward. After my travels up north, though, I guess I realized that those same kind of people live everywhere."

"I can second that," Jesse offered.

"But what you can't find everywhere is the support structure that exists in a small town like this. It can be annoying 'cause everybody wants to know your business all the time. On the flip side, it's nice to have those folks caring what happens to you, especially during the tough times. You know what I mean?"

Jesse did not answer first, but swallowed the remainder of his beer. "I guess I don't really. It's been a long time since I had a 'support structure,' as you call it. And hell, I've been living in a town not much bigger than this for several years now. But besides a few acquaintances, I haven't found a whole lot of folks caring about *my* goings and comings."

"Well, maybe you haven't been looking hard enough, or in the right place," Laura responded with a smile. "And you have to offer people something in return too. But I'm sure you knew that."

Jesse shook his head. "I knew that at one point," he admitted. "It's been a while, though."

Laura poured him another beer and then tended to some of the few other customers at the bar and in the surrounding restaurant. When she came back, she pressed him about what he meant by his last statement. Jesse was reluctant to reveal too much about his own background, because so much of his recent life had been tied to the very subject that had brought him to Laura's town.

"I guess I've been sidetracked for a while," he answered in response to a question from Laura about his history.

"Are you on the right track now?"

Jesse pursed his lips and furrowed his brow as if in deep thought. "You know, I just may be."

"On this trip with your buddies?" Laura continued.

"No, I think I can see now that this trip may be part of my sidetrack. I can't get off that path right now, though. It's something I've got to do. But I think if I do it, I just may be able to step off that track and get back on the right one – one I haven't been on in a long, long time."

Laura looked confused. "Well, I'm not sure I understand which track you're staying on and getting off, but take it from me – it's never too late to make that switch. I left the bright lights and vibrant culture of the big city to come back to a town where coal mining and farming are the two biggest occupations."

Laura smiled again, "And where people like my Aunt don't have anything better to do than tell ghost stories to strangers. I've got to warn you, though, that you might get a lot of that around this crazy town."

Jesse questioned her about the local legends and folklore, though being careful not to give away his reasons for doing so. He also did not want to push too hard considering Laura's upbringing and her aversion to the more colorful stories from the region.

Jesse then shifted the conversation to a neutral topic to avoid revealing too much to Laura. They talked about sports for a few minutes until they both realized that neither had much interest in team sports like basketball or football.

"Well, with all the great outdoor opportunities around here, do you like that kind of stuff?" Jesse asked. "Like fishing maybe? That's always been my favorite pastime."

"I didn't figure you for an angler, McCoy," Laura responded. "You better not be just trying to get on my good side – I can wade a creek and cast a lure with the best of 'em. I'll call your bluff if you're just making talk."

"I'd be glad to spend a day on the water with you," Jesse offered. "I could try to prove my own abilities while learning from a true master all at the same time."

"Now I didn't say I was a 'master.' No need for the sarcasm."

Laura did enjoy recalling several old stories about fishing on her grandfather's farm on its many ponds and in a creek that ran along the back of the property. She also related an incident that occurred while on a fishing trip to Canada with her boyfriend.

"Boyfriend?" Jesse asked, without being able to mask the anxious tone in his voice.

Laura told him that the relationship had at one time been very close, though had turned to an on-again, off-again sort of affair over the past year or two. She admitted that since she had moved back home to help with the family business, she and her boyfriend had done little more than call each other a few times a month.

"I guess the only reason I still call him my boyfriend," she said, "is that we've been together for so long – almost four years. It's gone downhill recently, but I suppose I'm still holding on to it as a matter of habit maybe. I mean, you can't be so close to somebody for that long and just quit cold turkey."

Jesse agreed to a certain extent, but he added that, beyond a certain point, it becomes time to "just move on." He tried to remember the last time he was in a serious relationship and realized that he could not. After he left college his life had been pretty messy and he had just not had the time or energy for a relationship any more involved than the kind that lasted for a matter of weeks. Jesse then decided that he did not need to be giving relationship advice to Laura, though he found himself desperately wanting to prolong the intimate conversation.

He recalled the only long-term girlfriend he had ever had and remembered how the relationship had started with such passion and then fizzled out. "I was pretty head over heels," he confessed, "and I'd like to think she was too. But that's not really enough to base a long-term relationship on."

Laura took his empty glass and washed it out. She straightened a few things behind the bar as she was getting ready to close for the night. "You're right on that one, Mr. McCoy. It's better to start out as friends and then find infatuation, rather than vice versa. At least that's my experience." She showed Jesse to the door while she turned off the lights in the room.

With a few beers to his credit, Jesse blurted out, "Well, I hope we can be friends." The awkwardness was apparent before he had even finished the sentence. "Shit," he said, "that came out kind of stupid."

"I understood your point," Laura said, feeling embarrassed in the situation. "Look, you're just a guy who's staying here for a few days and then you leave. This is where I live and where I'll still be long after you're gone. So don't let those beers give you any ideas. Friends is fine, but that's where it's gonna stay."

"Well, that's a start," Jesse said with a brave smile, his inhibitions still relaxed from the alcohol. "Like a wise person once said, it's good to start out friends and then go from there."

Laura broke a smile at this and swatted at him with her bar apron. "You need to go on up to bed, mister, before that mouth of yours gets you into any more trouble."

"Well if it's you I'm going to get in trouble with," Jesse said as he reached the stairs that led to the sleeping rooms above, "that may not be such a bad thing."

Laura tossed her apron at him this time and he bolted up the stairs to avoid it. Before he reached the top of the steps, he bent over and peered at her through the railing. "Good night Ms. Calhoun," he said in a sing-song tone.

"Good night yourself, Mr. McCoy. Now get on upstairs before I throw something else at you."

Jesse saluted her in military fashion and jogged down the hall to his room.

"Damn," he said to himself as he finally got into his room and closed the door. He caught his breath and realized he was well on his way to being drunk. He turned off the light in the room, flopped down on his bed and quickly fell asleep with a smile on his face.

* * *

Jesse was not smiling the next morning. A day of hiking, running, and overall exertion coupled with some heavy beer drinking before bed left him with a dull headache and sore limbs when he woke up. After a warm shower and some aspirin, he felt better. Jesse headed downstairs to the restaurant, but was disappointed to find that Laura was not scheduled to work that morning. Jesse checked his watch several times as he made his way through a plate full of scrambled eggs, cheese grits, and fresh biscuits.

Finally rising from the table, Jesse looked at his watch again in concern that the morning was quickly passing by. He decided to go wake up the others, but met Brad halfway up the steps. Brad had already checked on Roy and Mark, who declined breakfast, and Kelly had declined all activity until a "suitable" time of day.

Jesse sat down with Brad while he had a quick breakfast of toast and coffee. The plan for the current day, as Jesse and Brad decided over the breakfast table, would include collecting more information from the local townsfolk and finding a base for their operations. This latter component to the plan would potentially be the most important. They needed to find a place with either a history of activity, or some very recent activity. They would also need a landowner willing to cooperate with them.

The two young men went out on the streets after leaving the lodge. They first stopped at the local hardware store. Jesse picked up some rope and a small waterproof tarp that could be useful during rainy weather.

"Goin' campin'?" the hardware clerk asked as he rose from a lawn chair behind the counter. The man appeared ancient, with wispy grayish-white hair, wrinkles so deep they cast their own shadows, and a long, gaunt face punctuated with a pointy, crooked chin. The clerk smiled, displaying several missing teeth. "Sure looks like it," he commented, whistling through his missing teeth as he spoke.

"Yes sir," Jesse answered as he plunked the heavy rope down on the counter. "We're going to hit the trails for a couple of days."

"Lordy," the man said, grinning and shaking his head at the same time. "You fellers sure picked the wrong time of year for that." A pregnant pause followed, but the elder gentleman did not continue with dire warnings or scary cautionary statements. "It's too dang hot!" he offered. "No spring flowers, no fall colors. Only a derned fool would take a trip like that this time of year – too muggy. You'll sweat your britches off I tell ya."

Jesse watched as the old man lifted a heavy book to the counter and flipped the pages. Following the page with his gnarled index finger, the man found what he had been looking for. "Rope'll cost you fifteen and the tarp there is five dollars."

At this point, Brad had walked up to the counter to pay for the gear. The manager looked at him up and down and tilted back on his heels. Peering through his newly-adorned eyeglasses, he said, "You don't look like the usual camping type."

"Well this isn't the usual camping type of trip," Brad said shortly as he took some bills out of his wallet.

"Oh, OK," the man said with a twinkle in his eye, "I guess if you're heading up to the mountains with your gals to drink the beer and such – well you probably wouldn't a cared about spring flowers or fall's leaves anyhow."

"Actually sir," Jesse spoke up, "we have been hearing some interesting stories about the area. Different legends or folk tales I guess you could call them."

"If you heard them from one of the locals, they wasn't no folk tale, I can assure you." The manager stopped and looked at Jesse and Brad. He eased into his chair behind the counter and lit a pipe that had been tucked away under the counter. He exhaled in Jesse and Brad's direction. Jesse tried to nonchalantly wave the smoke away. Brad was not as discreet.

"Well I do recall one story in particular, though there were several events that I could probably tell you about. Most folks in town are pretty tight-lipped about this sort of thing, so don't go around expecting everyone you come across to open up to you. As you can see, I've gotten along in years and don't really give a hoot what the rest think. As long as people like yourself come in here to buy my goods, I'll just keep right on tellin' my tales."

After another long draw from his pipe, the old man continued, "The first, and most memorable happened when I was about eight, I reckon. I lived on a farm with my parents and three brothers at the time. Most everybody in this county was farming back in those days. I was playing with Johnny Littlehorse on this particular day. Johnny's dad, Big John, was a Cherokee Indian. They didn't live around here, but just about every year around harvest time Big John and his squaw would come into town with their little ones in tow. He'd work at the grain mill for a couple months till the harvest season had ended.

"Anyhow, me and Johnny got to know each other because his dad would come to our farm with a big truck to haul corn back to the mill. Once I was done with my chores, I would track down Johnny and we'd have all kinds of grand adventures in the mowed down corn – building forts, playing hide and seek or kick the can, that sort of thing. We'd sometimes take to the hills surrounding the farm to escape the heat of muggy August or September day.

"Me and Johnny, well, we were Daniel Boone and Davy Crockett in the making. We'd explore every nook and cranny, creek bottom and hill top we could find. On one such occasion, it was a real hot autumn day, so hot that it's almost hard to breathe. You know the kind – so hot and humid that you break out in a sweat just standing around. So Johnny suggests we go to the mountains to explore a sink hole we'd seen on an earlier adventure. It weren't more than ten minutes of a hike from the farm, but we loaded up canteens, and wrapped a couple sandwiches in wax paper to take with us.

"There's caves and sinks all around those hills, which you may discover if you go camping out there. Some of them are formed by little creeks that find their way underground. Well that was how this big ol' sinkhole was made. So there stood me and Johnny, peering down into this depression. Thinking back on it now, it wasn't really that deep, maybe five feet below the rest of the ground level – but straight down, no gentle slope. Of course we wanted to explore it, so we came up with the brilliant idea that Johnny would lower me in. There was some fallen logs and dead tree trunks down in it we were going to push together to get back out.

"So Johnny stands at the edge, kind of with his feet in the creek to lower me down. Where the creek entered was probably the shortest distance to the bottom. Unfortunately, though, Johnny was standing on a old, moss covered slickery rock – slicker'n coon shit on a pump handle as the saying goes. When I started to lower down in the sink, my weight threw Johnny off balance and he slipped on the rock and flew backwards, letting me go in the process. I fell like a ton of bricks right onto a gnarled tree trunk, with all my weight landing on one leg. I screamed, but I heard Johnny scream above.

"Seems he landed pretty hard too, he hit his head on a rock when he fell backwards. So there I am, pretty much crippled and Johnny's woozy from a crack in the back of his head. There was no way I could scale out of that sinkhole, whose top was well above my head. And Johnny was in no shape to come down and help me out either. So he says, 'hang on, I'll go git your pa.' He wasn't gone more than three or four minutes when an awful peal of thunder broke out overhead.

"Like I said, this was one of them days when it's so hot and muggy, you just know that it's gonna storm at some point. Well, storm it did. Rained so hard it hurt and the sky got all dark. Didn't take too long and that little creek was flowing pretty good. I will admit that, considering the circumstances, I started bawling. Next thing I knew, there was a face peering at me from above the crater. It wasn't Johnny or my pa. It was a real hairy, dirty face, like a hobo. Then this hobo stood up and I seen that the hair wasn't just on its face, but the whole danged body. And it was a giant body too.

"At that point, my crying turned to hysterical screaming. This thing steps down into the sinkhole. Notice I said 'stepped' down. The rim of the hole only went up to this creature's breasts, making it probably about eight feet tall. Now, notice I said 'breasts.' By then, I had my little boy's body crammed as far as it would go under that tree trunk. Well then she – and I say it was a her because of the breasts – just reached under the tree and plucked me out like a rag doll. She tucked me into the crook of her arm, even though I was screaming and hollering and kicking something fierce. She puts her free arm on the rim of the sinkhole and just hoists up to the ground like you or I would do to hop over a short fence.

"I don't know if I blacked out or what, but next thing I know I'm hurtling through the forest at break-neck speed. We were cutting through honeysuckle and thick messes of rhododendron like a hot knife through butter – going in seconds through brush so thick it would've taken me half an hour with a machete. Then we reached a clearing and I recognized that we were on the outskirts of my farm. At this point, I could hear voices in the distance and then a gunshot. Well the creature dropped me on the soft, rain-soaked ground and just disappeared back into the woods.

"My pa ran up to me and there was Johnny with a nice white bandage on his head. Pa threw a rain jacket around me and hustled me back to the house. Of course I wanted to tell Johnny all about what had happened, but a stern look from my old man told me not to say a word. I think he'd seen the creature, but I don't guess Johnny had. I was later told not to tell anyone about the incident, though I sure wanted to share that story with all the kids at school.

"Several nights later, my folks had some of the other farmers over for dinner. I heard my pa bring up the incident in a laughing manner, until one of the other farmers said something like, 'I guess them ol' monkeys are back in town for the harvest.' One of the others complained about huge patches of his crops that'd been eaten or just trampled on by the creatures. Our next door neighbor was furious that some of his livestock had been missing, and even one of his prized hunting dogs had just up and disappeared never to be seen again.

"A fella from way down the road mentioned that he'd been walking in his fields and came upon a pile of dead deer. But they were weird dead – not shot or nothing – but some were completely broken in half. Others had their legs twisted off and such. After being asked if it was scavengers, like coyotes, the man said that he'd visited the pile a couple of times and the carcasses had not even been touched by a single buzzard. They was just sitting there, laid across each other.

"Anyhow, there was other stuff, but I'm about out of breath and need something to wet my whistle." The old man abruptly stopped talking and reached under the counter for a small flask of whisky. He was about to take a sip when the hardware store door opened and the county sheriff walked in. He quickly put the flask back and sat up in his chair. "Morning sheriff," he said.

"Morning Asa," the sheriff replied. "You don't need to go through that song and dance with your whisky flask every time I come in. As long as I can't smell it halfway across the store, you're fine to do as you please."

"I appreciate that, Harmon. I was just telling these young men some stories and needed a little refreshment break." The storekeeper then took a quick sip of whiskey while the sheriff looked at some items on a nearby shelf.

"Asa, you and your stories," the sheriff replied, laughing gently. "Did he tell you fellas the one about the witch cradling him in her arms and saving the day?"

"Weren't no witch," the storekeeper corrected. "Was one of them big monkeys 'at live in the hills."

"Oh, that one never gets old, does it? I grew up hearing that story, although my parents used it as a warning to keep me from straying too far in the woods. They'd say 'don't get too far from home or Big Momma'll snatch you up and carry you away to feed to the rest of 'em'." The sheriff laughed. "Hell, Asa, how old are you? A hundred and fifty? I doubt Big Momma is still out there carrying lost kids to safety."

The storekeeper puffed on his pipe and deliberately blew some smoke in the sheriff's direction. "Well, she may not be, but I reckon she had young'uns over the years. I bet they's the ones visit Steve Akers' farm from time to time."

The sheriff shook his head. "Asa, you know that was probably some runaway cows that ate his crops last year. And he never came up with one lick of proof about them missing goats. You old folks chalk every mysterious incident up to the monsters in the mountains. But not once has anybody shown any proof that they was the culprits, or that they even exist anymore."

"Anymore?" Jesse asked, inserting himself into the conversation.

"Don't tell me you boys believe that load of nonsense," the sheriff said, still in a lighthearted tone.

"Actually, that's what we're here for," Brad blurted out.

The sheriff's demeanor quickly changed. He walked over to Jesse and Brad and loomed in front of them. Jesse could see his own reflection in the sheriff's shiny silver badge. "Ah, you would be the group staying over at the Elk Mountain Lodge, huh? Well let me make it very clear. This county does support tourism and outdoor activities as they've helped our economy out in some tough times. What we don't promote, however, is a bunch of kids wandering through the woods, getting lost and who knows what else, trying to take pictures of a monster.

"We've had it before," he continued. "Folks getting lost up there and never being seen again. Do you have any idea how many miles and miles of forest surround this county? How every unmarked trail, creek, and ravine pose a threat to unwary travelers? This county's cash-strapped as it is. We don't have the manpower to send rescue teams looking for wayward youths every time someone gets lost in the mountains. Are you hearing me boys? Am I coming in loud and clear?"

"Loud and clear, sir," Jesse answered.

"Give me a break," Brad said as he turned away.

"Hold on there, boy," the sheriff shot back. "Now, I can't stop you from going off looking for monsters or goblins, if that's what you're here for. But the moment you step into the woods, you've got bears, boars, rocky trails, steep cliffs, and a serious potential for getting lost to contend with. And Asa's Big Momma ain't gonna be around to help you out in the clutch. You won't find any friendly faces peering from behind a tree to rescue you."

"Oh, you might still have faces peering at you, but I wouldn't count on 'em being friendly," the storekeeper added.

"Knock it off, Asa, you're only encouraging them. You boys have seen too many monster films. If excitement and danger are what you're after, your safest bet would be to visit the town's movie theater."

"Or you might head over to Steve Akers farm – he's usually got some monkey business going on this time of year, if you know what I mean."

"Asa!" the sheriff shouted. "Quit it. You've been sipping too much of that whiskey. I'm trying to set these boys straight here and you keep interfering. I'll have you shut up now and put away your flask. Got it?"

"Yes sir, sheriff. I don't know what got into me. I'm sorry boys, I just get a little excited at times. Pay no mind to what I've been blabberin' on about. Old folks like me just get to talking sometimes."

Both Jesse and Brad had been overwhelmed by the series of events unfolding in front of them over the past few minutes. They had gone from store patrons to outlaws in just moments. Jesse tried to appear agreeable and compliant to the sheriff's message. Brad glared ahead, purposefully avoiding eye contact with the law man.

Brad finally spoke up in the direction of the sheriff. "We got it already. You can save the lectures for somebody else." Brad unfolded his wallet and plunked down a handful of cash. He grabbed as much of the goods as he could carry and nodded at Jesse to pick up the rest. Silently, Jesse walked out of the door, but not before Brad could mutter a few curse words under his breath.

The sheriff slowly moved to the door and stood behind it as it eased shut. He glared through the screen as Jesse and Brad got in their vehicle. They could see him take out a pen and notebook as they drove away.

* * *

Jesse skipped dinner that night, staying in his room. Using detailed maps of the area and frequent phone calls to the information directory, Jesse had spent the afternoon and was spending the evening searching for the perfect place to launch the expedition. In particular, he remembered the hardware store owner mentioning the name of Steve Akers. He also kept in mind the incidents from Monkey Creek, hoping to find an area at least in the same general vicinity. The conversation with the Sheriff at the hardware store had helped Jesse finally rule out the Monkey Creek bridge site for good. Before, he had worried about picnickers and partiers coming by. After the lecture by the lawman, Jesse certainly was not going to take any chances setting up a base camp that might be too easy for the town Sheriff to locate.

Jesse looked up the Akers address in the phone book and then found roughly the area where the Akers farm should be located, according to his brief detective work. The location on the map, if accurately pinpointed, was almost too good to be true. Jesse looked at the topography surrounding the Akers farm. Immediately behind the farm, the ground level rose constantly and an unending wave of foothills led from there. Though the farm did not directly border the Monkey Creek area that Jesse and his companions had visited earlier, Jesse traced Monkey Creek from the bridge going west. It did not seem to run straight through the Akers land, but tied into several smaller streams that appeared just east of the Akers property. Jesse figured that the stream off-shoots could be just as likely animal travel routes as the main creek itself.

Jesse dug out his atlas and compared the small local map to a regional picture. It seemed to him that, besides a few isolated state and forest service roads, the wooded land behind the Akers farm went on for miles, even possibly to the Kentucky state line. Jesse checked the phone book again and jotted down Steve Akers' phone number and address. He would call first thing in the morning.

* * *

"What's up stranger?" Mark asked Jesse as they crossed paths in the hallway the next morning. "Didn't see much of you last night."

Jesse was still rubbing the sleep out of his eyes. He had forgotten to set his watch alarm and had gotten his best and longest night of sleep since he had left Ohio. "Morning, Mark. Is everybody already up?"

"Yeah, we're having breakfast downstairs in the restaurant. Go ahead and take your time getting ready if you need it. I'll make up something to tell Brad."

"Thanks man," Jesse responded. Though he was not happy that Mark and Roy were tagging along, he was at least finding Mark to be more tolerable than he had initially predicted. "I'll be down in a few minutes."

When Jesse finally did make it down to join his company, Brad was immediately on his case. "What's the deal, Jesse? This isn't some sort of luxury spa vacation where you can sleep all day."

"Take it easy Brad," Jesse said as he sat down at the table. "I haven't just been wasting time. I've figured out where we're going to start this expedition." That statement got everybody's attention. "If you recall from yesterday, the hardware store guy mentioned a farm that has seen a pattern of activity. I found that place on the maps and called the farmer – Steve Akers."

"And?" Brad impatiently interrupted.

"And, it just so happens that Mr. Akers has recently purchased some expensive farm machinery and would be willing to let us use his land for a contribution to help pay off his loans."

"How much of a contribution are we talking?" Brad asked.

"Well, I'll let you settle that with him. I've arranged a meeting with him today at his farm."

"That sounds awesome and all," Roy interjected, "but I might have to sit this one out. Stomping around on some guy's farm just doesn't do it for me." Roy turned to Kelly, "What about you?"

Before Kelly could answer, Brad spoke up. "We are *all* going. You guys didn't come on this trip to hang out in some dumpy lodge all day long, did you? The sooner we get some of this groundwork done, the quicker we can get going with the real expedition."

Kelly looked down at the ground, Jesse turned his gaze to something off in the distance, and Mark pushed his breakfast napkin around on the table. It was obvious that Brad's comments were meant directly for Roy and Kelly. After a few moments of uncomfortable silence, Jesse stood up. "Well, we need to get some gear ready – cameras, video equipment and other stuff to do a proper study on this proposed site. It might be our launching point, so we want as much info on it to review as possible."

"You heard the man," Brad added, "let's get going."

The group broke up and they all went to their rooms to load a backpack with necessities for the day's outing. They reconvened in the lodge lobby for an early lunch before heading on their trip. After loading into the SUV, it took them half an hour to find their way to the Akers farm. They missed the turn to the main house and ended up turning down one of the farm's service roads. They bumped up and down the dirt and gravel path as it curved from the main road toward the farmhouse. This led them eventually to the back side of the house instead of its front.

"All I see is corn," Kelly complained. "What are we doing, camping in this guy's backyard?"

"This is going to be our staging point, honey," Brad explained. "The camping's going to be done up there." Brad pointed out the front windshield to the tree line just visible over the top of hundreds of acres of cornstalks. "According to Jesse, those trees go on for miles and miles."

"Not only that," Jesse added, "but this flat land gets steep pretty rapidly behind this farm."

Kelly hopped out first and stretched. The others soon followed. Roy jumped out and yelled "Woo hoo, let's do some farming, boys" in his best country accent. Then he slammed the car door loudly. A few quick seconds later, two enormous German Shepherds came barreling through the corn. They were running so fast at the group that when Kelly first saw them she reflexively jumped up on the SUV's hood seeking a safe position.

The dogs stopped abruptly just a few feet in front of Roy, who was standing ahead of the rest. They stood silently, not growling or snarling, just standing firm and attentive – poised, like coiled-up energy ready to unleash. Roy took a step to the side, and one of the dogs stepped sideways too. The other stood his ground and monitored the rest of the group.

"What do I do, Brad?" Roy asked as he stood closest to Brad.

"Just don't move any closer to me, that's one thing," Brad said frankly. "In fact, don't do anything quickly. We can all slowly get back in the car for the moment."

Jesse stepped backwards to get closer to the car door. The dog not monitoring Roy shifted his stare to Jesse's movement and took a step forward to maintain his original distance. "Shit," Jesse said.

Then, they heard a voice call, "That's enough boys." Both dogs backed up a few paces and sat down. Their tense muscles eased a bit, but their eyes and ears were still very much focused on every movement from the group.

A gruff old man came around the corner of the house. He wore dirt-stained overalls and a white T-shirt underneath. He had a yellowed handkerchief hanging out of his front overall pocket. He pulled it out and mopped his brow as he walked up to the dogs from behind. "Leave it," he commanded sternly and both dogs got up from their guarding positions and paced around. They settled back down at the farmer's feet and lay down.

"I guess you've met Butch and Duke," the farmer said. "They're really sweet boys once you get to know 'em. Just a tad on the serious side though."

"Yeah, we noticed that," Brad responded.

Steve Akers finally introduced himself and shook hands with each person. He stepped back and patted both dogs. "Yessir, Butch here is the older one. He's the big boss of the two. Once he sent a prowler to the hospital for two months. Duke's never been faced with that type of situation, yet, but I think his brother's demeanor has rubbed off on him pretty good."

Mr. Akers then talked about the dogs' bloodlines and reminisced about some of the farm dogs he'd had in the past. He rambled for several minutes on topics of dog breeding and personality types common to the different breeds he had had around the farm over the years.

Jesse's mind had wandered during Mr. Akers' discussion about canine attributes. Jesse immediately returned his attention when he heard Mr. Akers comment, "…course all that courage and breeding goes right out the window when those damn monkeys come to town." Jesse glanced over at Brad, who had just raised his eyebrows. Jesse grabbed his notebook and prepared to write anything useful Mr. Akers had to say.

Mr. Akers continued, "Heck, I've seen these two chase bears and boars, and even treed a cougar several years ago – absolutely fearless. But when them apes show up, Butch and Duke might as well be newborn pups for as scared as they get. I remember one day, bout two years ago – around this time of year – I went to visit my granddaughter in town. Y'all might've met her, she works over at the lodge with her aunt."

Brad glanced over at Jesse, who visibly blushed, realizing that Mr. Akers was referring to Laura Calhoun.

Mr. Akers picked back up with his train of thought. "Anyway, I had dinner with her and so forth and didn't get back here till later. First thing I saw as I drove onto the property – I was coming down this back road like y'all just done – I saw the split rail fence separating my property from the woods had been demolished in one section, simply knocked over. There was a trail of flattened out crops. My corn crib had been raided and so had my freezer chest on the back porch – about sixty pounds of frozen venison and store-bought meat all gone. Some of the boards on the back porch were a little catty-wampus too – all bowed and cracked and some even popped loose. Something big had been walking around, that's for sure.

"Then, the worst of it was what I could hear from under the porch – whimpering. It took two hours to get these boys to come out from under the house. They was both covered in their own crap and still looked scared to death. Took forever to clean them up. They still react the same way sometimes when we hear the howls and screams out in the forest. They get this long far-off stare to their eyes like they're remembering something. I don't know if it's that night from two years ago or if it's some deeper animal instinct-type memory. They'll bark and carry on, then usually I'll find them later, cowered somewhere in the barn or tool shed."

Jesse looked at the two enormous, fierce-looking dogs as they now stood at attention next to their master's side. He wondered how anything could faze such powerful-looking beasts.

"Yeah, we got lucky last year," Mr. Akers kept going. "Them damn monkeys were hanging out on the other side of the holler, on up towards the Hapley's place. But, lots of farms round here are looking at bumper crops of corn this year with all the good weather we've had. There's a saying around here that you want your corn to be 'knee-high by the Fourth of July.' Well it was waist high if not taller at the beginning of July. Like I said, we had pretty good weather this summer.

"Wouldn't be surprised if we start getting our yearly visitors soon. Those things can eat the hell out of some corn, not to mention raise Cain with the few livestock animals I keep from time to time. I got a good lock now on my meat freezer, but there's nothing a farmer can do about acres of exposed crops. They ain't designed a scarecrow yet that could keep those pests out of my fields."

"Well," Brad interjected, "perhaps we can help with that situation. Now let's get down to business." Brad and farmer Akers discussed matters of compensation for letting the group use the farmland as a staging point. Mr. Akers was very frank in expressing that he thought they were all "a bunch of damn fools," and if he had not had so many bills to pay he would not have even considered letting them use the property. He added, "I feel guilty in a way 'cause by letting you set up on this property I'm basically going to be responsible for what happens to you when you get up in them hills."

Brad responded that they could easily find another local farmer who needed the cash more.

"No, no – I'll take your money all right," Mr. Akers answered. "Still, I feel bad. That, and I'd like you to pay me before you go into the woods. Also, after you park and unload your vehicle, it'll probably be best to leave me the keys. The sheriff'll want to move your truck off my property when y'all don't come back."

The old farmer's frankness in this last statement caught Jesse off guard. He had said it with as much sincerity and at the same time nonchalance as if he had been relaying to them the weather report for the night – not a prediction of their demise. Brad guffawed and blew off the remark and then requested that they be allowed to go ahead and check out the area.

Steve Akers hauled them around on his tractor, pulling a large wagon. He showed them the crop fields with pride and eventually took them to the edge of the cleared farmland. "Beyond this fence," he shouted over the noise of the tractor, "I have several hundred acres more of property. Been in the family for generation upon generation. Yep, my land goes almost up to what folks call the Devil's Ridge." He turned off the tractor so they could talk without yelling.

"It's a steep rocky ridge that rises up over the top of a lot of the surrounding hills. Not sure how it got its name originally, but some folks say ol' Scratch himself used to live there." Mr. Akers paused to wipe his brow with his handkerchief. "Even the Indians avoided that place, or at least that's what folks always said. And in more recent times, back during the Depression you had squatters who'd set up shacks in some of these foothills. But wouldn't a soul put up a cabin anywhere near the Devil's Ridge."

Jesse thought Mr. Akers was done with his story, so he was about to ask a question. But Akers started right back up, "Nobody but old Wendell McClain. Story goes that Wendell wasn't from around here and didn't put any stock in the local sayings or legends. Apparently he stumbled onto a valley rich with ginseng that he could sell back in town. I'm sure y'all didn't know it, but this is the largest wild ginseng-producing state in the nation. Heck, last time I looked it was selling for near three hundred dollars a pound. Even back then a fella could make a pretty penny after a day's gathering in the woods. So old Wendell threw himself up a shack right on the edge of the ridge, despite everyone tellin' him time and again not to. One day he came to town with a basket full of fat knobs of ginseng, then he was gone. Nobody ever saw him again."

"What happened to him?" Kelly asked, absorbed in the story.

"Well, some folks say he went crazy from being out there all alone – that the loneliness drove him to distraction. Some say ol' Scratch showed up and took Wendell away. Whatever or whoever the culprit, Wendell McClain's just another in a long line of weird tales surrounding that piece of property.

Personally, I believe about half of 'em can be chalked up to pure malarkey, and the other half's probably got something to do with those creatures I've told you about.

"Anyhow, the point is that, if the scary stories around the property wasn't enough, it's simply too steep and rocky to farm or graze, so it's pretty much un-sellable. Like I said, we've been stuck with it for generations."

Steve Akers pulled out a weathered canteen of water and took a drink. He continued with his description of the surrounding land. "Up past my property and beyond the ridge is a thin stretch of private timber stands, like a finger extending south from the timber company's main property. Bordering that is some reclaimed mining lands – ponds, sinkholes, caves, and such. Past that and you've got a few parts of the elk refuge you've probably heard about. They tend to enjoy some of the cleared parts of that reclaimed mining land. Beyond all that are miles and miles of forest land that I'm not sure who owns, if anybody. Keep going east and you're in the hills and hollers of West Virginia, and I'm sure it's the same story on that side of the state line. So basically, if you start walking east from my fence line, you'll be in the woods till somewhere in the Mountain State."

The old farmer started the tractor back up and drove them along the fence line for several minutes as they surveyed the property. They stopped at one point when Brad noticed something along the wood line. He jumped down from the tractor wagon and scouted the ground. He had found an animal trail - a deer run. There were tell-tale hoof tracks here and there and also some rubs on nearby saplings. He explained that the rubs resulted from bucks rubbing their antlers on the trees to serve as scent and territorial markers during the mating season rut and at other times to help rub off antler velvet. He had seen similar signs when he first got into hunting a few years earlier. He had learned from an experienced Michigan guide to watch for trails crisscrossing through the woods, rubs on small trees and saplings, and the territorial ground scrapes that deer of both sexes used as calling cards.

Brad also spied another trail running parallel to the deer run. It was an older trail, not used for some time. Brad said it did not have the characteristics of any deer trail he had ever seen, but that it appeared to have been created by a large animal. Jesse was impressed with Brad's keen eyes and analytical tracking abilities. It was a side of Brad he had not seen yet. Jesse hoped that the serious hunter and woodsman side of Brad would replace the huffy, bossy side.

After touring the rest of the grounds, Mr. Akers drove them back to the house. Butch and Duke ran out to greet them, but were still on guard with the strangers present. As the group packed their gear back into the SUV and made last-minute plans with Mr. Akers, he spoke up, "Now, don't tell my granddaughter about this if you see her at the lodge. Just talking about this kind of stuff gets Laura all testy and worked up. She'll tolerate it from Hazel but won't allow me to say word one about some of the strange stuff that happens out here."

Akers continued, "Course, and she'll figure this out one of these days. People up in these hills has been seeing boogers and haints, critters and goblins for as long as people have lived here, including the Indians. Hell, when I was growing up, we had a neighbor family that was Indian. I don't think they lived here all the time, but their people was from this area. They used to tell all kinds of stories about the 'wildman of the woods' – oh they had all sorts of names for them things.

"I just think it's interesting that folks around here have known about this sort of thing for generations and accept it as a fact – not a mystery at all. Hell, we even get used to their hollering and screaming just about every fall. Sometimes you can hear them caterwaulin' and carrying on just as plain as day. Doesn't spook me as much as it used to. You know, those creatures are kinda like the coal in some of these hills – been here a long, long time and most folks has got used to them for a while now."

Jesse's mind had wandered again during Mr. Akers' lecture. He kept thinking about Laura Calhoun back at the lodge. He knew that he would much rather be there, spending the day chatting away with her and enjoying her company, than here with a crew of people he hardly knew, preparing for an event that made him more and more uneasy the closer it got.

* * *

By the time they arrived back at the bed and breakfast, Jesse, Brad, Kelly, Mark, and Roy were ready for an early dinner. First, though, Jesse accompanied Brad to Brad's room in order to go over an equipment check. Jesse wanted to make sure that the group would be properly equipped for a wilderness experience lasting up to a full week. Brad first showed him the audio and video equipment and the array of electronic sensors and other gadgets that would be used around the campsite. Jesse was impressed with the technology, but was curious as to how Brad planned to provide the electricity or power to run his myriad of electronic items. They certainly would not be hauling a generator or giant batteries into the rugged Appalachian foothills. Brad revealed two flexible panels of photovoltaic cells to capture sunlight and power the equipment. Jessed still wanted to focus on the basics.

After they checked items such as sleeping bags, tents, cooking materials, lanterns, flashlights, clothing, rain suits, and other miscellaneous gear necessary on the trail, Jesse decided to ask Brad about firearms. He wanted to see what kind of an arsenal Brad had gathered.

"All right Brad," Jesse said as he sat down in a nearby chair, "we've gone over the essentials and it looks like we're pretty much set for the week. Now let's have a look see at your other gear – what you plan to use along with all those fancy sensors and gadgets."

"Spare me the hints McCoy. You want to see the weapons, right?"

"You got it. I need to know what kind of firepower we're going to be toting around."

Brad pulled out a large duffel bag from under his bed. He brought it over to Jesse and put it at his feet. Unzipping it, he pulled the bag open to show Jesse the wide variety of arms inside. Jesse bent over in his chair and reached into the duffel bag. He pulled out several hunting knives and inspected each one.

Brad removed a piece of liner and started pulling out several firearms. Brad laid each gun on the bed for Jesse to see. First, there were three high-powered hunting rifles, each chambered in .30-06. Jesse also observed that one of the models was an older Remington 700 with a weathered wooden stock. "I'm sure this one's got a good story behind it," he chuckled.

Brad glared at Jesse and quickly grabbed his father's rifle out of Jesse's grasp. He carefully laid it down and covered it up. After a second or two of silence, Brad picked right up on the conversation as though he had not paused at all. "Obviously the rifles will be good for long-range shots," Brad said, "but I've also got these for close-up action." Brad pulled out two semi-automatic shotguns. "They're both twelve gauges and I've got different kind of shells for them – three inch magnum shells loaded with shot and also some deer slugs."

Jesse rubbed his stubbled chin. He hadn't understood Brad's strange actions from a moment ago, but was glad that the focus of the discussion had returned to practical matters. "Those'll be good if we're talking about really close-up encounters."

"Hey, we don't know what we're going to get into out there. Might as well be prepared for anything."

"That's fine," Jesse said, "as long as you're willing to carry it all."

"Well, that's not all," Brad replied. "This is my ace in the hole." He reached into the duffel bag again and pulled out one more weapon - a Romanian SAR-1, semi-automatic assault rifle mirroring the venerable AK-47 platform. The gun had a folding stock that made it fairly compact, and a thirty round magazine that made it deadly.

"Shit fire," Jesse exclaimed as he whistled. He picked up the assault rifle and unfolded the stock. He checked it over, impressed with the weapon. He put it back down on the bed and turned to Brad. "But can we even legally carry something like this?"

"Relax," Brad said, "I've already checked it out. The gun itself is perfectly legal, just not the high-capacity magazines. We'll carry a limited 5-10 round mag with us on the hike in and so forth, but if things get crazy, we'll have two thirty-round high-capacity mags handy."

"All right," Jesse replied reluctantly. "But we can't hunt from jail, so you better know what you're talking about."

"Like I said," Brad offered again, "relax."

Jesse continued, "And you're talking about some pretty serious added weight to be toting around too."

They discussed it for a while longer and then decided to break for dinner. After Jesse left, Brad zipped up his personal pack and then arranged the other guns to be distributed to the rest of the party for carrying on the trail. He laid out a few boxes of ammunition and a hunting knife to go along with each gun. Deciding that was as much as he could do at the time, Brad left the room to join the rest of the group downstairs for dinner.

* * *

While Jesse and Brad had been going over the equipment checklist, Kelly had left the room so as not to get in the way. She wound up in Mark and Roy's room, passing the time until dinner. Mark felt like the odd man out in the trio. Roy and Kelly had a long history that provided for inside jokes, discussion topics, and conversational subtleties that Mark simply did not get. After a while, he announced that he was heading down to the bar until dinner time.

As soon as Mark left, Kelly and Roy were alone for one of the few times so far on the trip. "So," Roy said in a long, drawn-out manner, "how's it going?" He scooted closer to her on the small motel-room-sized sofa.

Kelly playfully responded, "You're getting awfully close there mister. I guess that's all right as long as we're just talking."

"Just talking," Roy echoed as he slid even closer. "I've been wanting to just talk to you for quite a while – ever since that New Year's party."

"Roy," Kelly complained playfully. "This is not the time or place to bring that up."

"Oh but it is," Roy answered seriously. He moved even closer until their knees were touching. "Think about it. Why are we even on this stupid trip?" He paused, then resumed his monologue, "I know the only reason I'm here is because you're here. I thought this might be a situation where Brad's so focused on something else, I might be able to steal a little time with you. So you see, this *is* the perfect time and place to bring up old memories."

"You're only here because I'm on this trip?" Kelly asked in amusement. "Roy, that is the most ridiculous thing I've ever heard." Kelly placed her hand on Roy's knee and then continued, "It's also the sweetest."

Roy leaned toward Kelly and gave her a gentle kiss on the lips. Kelly closed her eyes and returned the favor, kissing Roy. She could feel the heat from his face radiating out and reflecting off her own. She opened her eyes and sat back up. Roy reached his arm around her waist and pulled her even closer. Kelly held up her hand to stop him from leaning in for another kiss.

"Roy, what are we going to do about Brad? I mean, he and I are still going out. I shouldn't even be doing this."

"What are we going to do about Brad?" Roy asked in reply, then repeated, "What are we going to do about ..."

"Brad," Kelly said in a gasp as the room's door flung open and Brad stepped inside. Roy instantly scooted to the opposite end of the small couch and leaned far away from Kelly.

"What's going on, you two?" Brad asked.

Kelly's heart raced and Roy feverishly searched his mind for an answer.

"Are you coming down to dinner or what? For Christ's sake the rest of us are starving." Brad then gestured with his hands, "Come on, come on, we're all waiting on you two."

Roy finally had worked up a response after a moment of awkward silence. "What have you guys been doing, getting drunk at the bar? You should've come up here earlier. I could go for a drink."

"No, we haven't, but that's not a bad idea after dinner," Brad answered. He then turned to Kelly. "Jesus, Honey, you need to get some food in your stomach, you look white as a ghost."

"It's just been a long day," she replied meekly.

As soon as Brad had ushered Kelly through the door and closed it behind him, Roy let fly a volley of quiet cursing. His adrenaline was still flowing from the close call, but the jealousy he had always felt about Brad dating Kelly gave rise to anger. He knew he would always be worried about more close calls as long as Brad kept such a tight rein on Kelly. Aggravated, Roy mused to himself, "What are we going to do about Brad?" repeating Kelly's earlier question.

* * *

Jesse could not concentrate on the discussion at the dinner table. Sitting in the small restaurant portion of the lodge, Jesse had seen Laura Calhoun working in the bar section and back in the kitchen. He kept trying to make eye contact with her, but she was busy. Occasionally Brad would lean across the table and ask, "McCoy, are you getting any of this?" Jesse would nod automatically and the conversation would continue. They were all talking about gear and packing up to get an early start the next morning. Jesse cared more about getting another chance to spend some time with Laura before the whole group was out wandering the wilderness.

After dinner, the party broke up and most headed upstairs. Jesse lingered in the restaurant. Finally, he caught Laura's attention. She gestured to him to wait a minute while she finished with a customer. Then, she walked over to him with a curious look on her face. "I thought you'd forgotten about me already," she said.

"Honestly," Jesse responded, "you're the only good thought I've had in days. Unfortunately, we're leaving tomorrow on our little expedition. I've got to pack my gear tonight."

"Well, maybe I can stop by and help you pack. You could probably use a woman's touch. But if you're going to bed real early or something …"

"No, I'll be up for quite a while," Jesse hurriedly interrupted. "I've got a lot to sort through tonight, and I'm not just talking about the packing."

Laura smiled. "There you go again with your cryptic statements. If that's a ploy to get me intrigued, it's working."

"Just come by later," Jesse said, staring into her eyes.

*   *   *

That night, Jesse was busy stowing his own personal items and clothes, plus his share of the group's gear into his pack. He had agreed to take one of the rifles, and he strapped this to the side of his pack. Cinching it tightly, Jesse checked to make sure the gun was well-secured. He wanted to check the weight of the hefty pack, so he shouldered it and strapped himself in with the waist and chest belts.

The pack's weight was considerable. Jesse questioned whether he would be able to carry it throughout a week's worth of hiking and rough trails. Though he figured that he could probably make do, he really wondered about some of his traveling companions. As he looked at himself in the full-view mirror, someone knocked on the door.

Jesse hoped it would be Laura, and he did not want her waiting out in the hallway. So he lumbered over to the door, peeked through the peephole, and then let Laura into his room. She took one look at him and laughed. "Do you always carry that thing around inside?" she joked.

Jesse realized he still had his pack on, so he quickly shed the cumbersome bag and set it down on the floor, trying to hide the scoped rifle clinging to the side of the pack.

Laura still had on her apron from bartending and waitressing, and her hair was a little mussed. She saw her own reflection in the mirror and exclaimed, "Oh Lord, I'm a royal mess. Maybe I should go change real quick."

Jesse grabbed her before should could even move. "Don't go anywhere," he pleaded. "I think you look cute," he then said with a devilish grin.

Laura rolled her eyes. "You men and your fascination with uniforms. Next thing you know, you'll be asking me if I have a cheerleader outfit."

Jesse rubbed his chin and said, "Now that you mention it …"

Before Jesse could continue, Laura cut him off. "What in the world is all this gear? Is that a rifle strapped to your bag?"

Jesse tried to deflect the questions. "Oh, don't pay any attention to all that stuff. You've met my friend Brad – he's overly cautious about this trip. You know, bears and stuff."

Laura shot him a look showing that she did not accept that explanation. "But what about all this other gear? Do you really need that much equipment just for camping and wildlife viewing?"

"Well, maybe for *some* wildlife viewing," Jesse said guardedly.

"What's that supposed to mean?" Laura asked as her mood began changing from playful to serious. "There you go again with the mysterious answers." She turned to him and squinted her eyes like she was trying to figure something out. "You've got something up your sleeve Mr. McCoy, and one of these days I'm going to catch you with your defenses down."

"Oh I wish you would," Jesse playfully replied, hoping to lighten Laura's serious tones. She continued to stare intensely at him and the backpack with a scowl. Finally, she sighed, and said, "Jesse, you are just too much." She laughed, then jabbed him in the side with her elbow before sitting down on the corner of his bed. She picked up the television remote and turned on the evening movie. "Butch Cassidy and the Sundance Kid," she announced as she turned up the volume. "I saw in the paper that it was going to be on tonight."

"Hey, this is one of my favorite movies," Jesse said as he sat down to watch.

"Mine too," Laura said excitedly. "Newman and Redford were so young back then. Talk about hunks."

"Well, I don't know about all that, but it is a great flick." Jesse looked up in the air and thought for a moment. "I've probably seen this a dozen times."

"Let's make it a baker's dozen, then – or would you rather watch something else?" Laura asked.

"I guess I can tolerate seeing it again," Jesse replied "with some company."

"You've got it, unless you were talking about somebody else."

Jesse paused for a second, then said, "I can't think of anyone else I'd rather sit here with than you," and he meant it. Though he was happy to be in Laura's company, Jesse realized that the good feelings he was experiencing also highlighted how miserable he had been for the past few years. He had allowed his work life, home life, and relationships to all come unraveled because of his harrowing experience in the woods of the Shawnee Forest. He had not spent as much quality time with another person in years as he had with Laura in just a few days.

Laura looked into his eyes and then suddenly remembered something. She reached into her apron and pulled out a small bottle of whiskey. "You looked so frazzled earlier, I thought you could use a little pick-me-up. In fact, you've kind of got a strange look right now."

"It's just been a long time since I've been in the presence of such an attractive, interesting person," Jesse said as he got up.

Laura blushed, "Well now you're just trying to butter me up."

Jesse smiled in response. He went to the nightstand and got two cups supplied by the lodge. He pulled the plastic wrap off the cups and filled each with some ice from an ice bucket. Splitting the whiskey between the two, they then raised their cups in a toasting fashion and settled in to watch the movie.

Both Jesse and Laura pointed out their favorite scenes as the movie progressed, while often reciting certain lines before the actors could say them. As Paul Newman and Robert Redford took their bank robbing to South America, Jesse and Laura had long ago finished their drinks. Laura had leaned back on her elbows to watch the movie. Her head nodded from time to time. By the time Butch and Sundance were battling it out in their last stand, Laura was fast asleep.

Jesse pulled the covers from the sides of the bed and folded them over her when the movie ended. He turned off the lights in the room and lay down next to her. He was soon asleep too, as the exhaustion from a long day finally took its toll. At one point in the night, Jesse woke up needing to use the bathroom. He opened his eyes and noticed that Laura had rolled onto her side and had draped an arm over him. Jesse did not know if she had done it on purpose or not, but he did not want to ruin the moment by getting up. So he lay there smiling, despite the full bladder, staring up at the ceiling and counting the minutes until dawn.

PART IV

DAY ONE

Jesse woke up the next morning with his bed to himself. Somehow Laura had gotten up earlier and left without waking him. He immediately hopped up from bed, still clothed from the night before, and pulled on his shoes. He wanted to rush downstairs and try to find Laura. As he whisked open his door he stood face to face with Brad. Brad looked him over and shook his head. "I don't know what you got into last night, but it ends now. You've got to shift into expedition mode because we're leaving as soon as we can get all the gear together. So get your ass moving."

Brad turned around and walked off before Jesse could say anything. The previous night's encounter with Laura had been such a pleasant and welcome change from being around Brad and the rest of the gang. Unfortunately, now Jesse had to face the fact that they were actually going to go through with this scheme. His mood darkened quickly as he thought about the week ahead and what he was leaving behind.

Jesse grabbed his heavy pack, slung it over his back, and then draped a rain jacket over the rifle strapped to the side. He navigated the stairs cautiously under the heavy load. Jesse then saw the rest of the crew already in the lobby. Mark and Roy joked with each other nervously and Kelly flipped through a magazine. Brad entered the room just as Jesse stepped off the last stair. He ushered everybody into an adjoining private room so they could check their gear. Jesse set his pack down on a sofa next to Brad's, and once everyone else was in the room, they did an inventory check of the items needed for the trip.

Brad was upset about several pieces of equipment that they were going to have to leave behind. He had originally planned to have the group use ATVs as a means of transportation, allowing them to take along larger items of equipment. At first, he had wanted to bring a portable gasoline generator to supply electricity to the campsite.

However, once the plan had matured and he had discussed it with Jesse, Brad realized they would primarily be hiking and carrying everything on their backs. The ATVs would be too loud and would likely ruin their chances of getting anywhere close to the elusive forest animals they sought.

Brad had found a solution to small-scale electrical supply for the electronic detection materials by using the portable solar panels.

But today, Brad learned that some other gear would have to be left behind. Brad had several massive spotlights that were simply too big to lug around. Instead, they opted to carry a single six-million-candlepower spotlight that Brad had bought locally as a backup. Also, a large stove and heater were replaced by propane-powered alternatives. These replacements would be less powerful, but more portable.

Brad complained to Jesse as more and more items were vetoed or switched out. "I'm worried that the solar panels will barely provide enough juice for the perimeter alarm systems. With some of the other things we're leaving behind, this is turning into more of a primitive endeavor – not the high-tech, well-equipped expedition I had envisioned."

"Relax Brad," Jesse said as he tried to ease some of the tension. "We can make do without some of that stuff. Plus, we've got replacements for the others."

"Well, they're half-assed replacements," Brad replied in a surly tone.

"No – more portable replacements," Jesse quickly countered. "Besides, it's the replacements we've found, or no replacements at all."

Brad muttered under his breath, "Maybe we should replace you."

"What?" Jesse asked sharply as he spun around to face Brad.

"Nothing. I'm just on edge, ready to get this thing going. Let's at least go over the few items we *can* take."

The group was definitely taking more than just a few items. As they looked over the checklists and confirmed them by looking in their bags, each team member read out a lengthy variety of gear. Night-vision devices and infrared digital video cameras for catching movement in the dark, two three-man backpacking tents, bed rolls, sleeping bags, flashlights, fire tools, water bottles, and clothes were some of the items they would be hauling on their backs.

To save space, most of the meals they would eat were of the freeze-dried, self-heating variety. These packed easily and did not require any cooking utensils to prepare. They would be using small backpacker's propane stoves and lanterns. Each team member would be responsible for carrying two fuel canisters. Brad and Jesse both had water purifiers in their packs to resupply the group with potable drinking water. Roy's pack contained a small camp axe and saw, while Mark's had a well-appointed first aid kit inside.

Additionally, each person would be loaded down with ammunition and one or two firearms, depending on what they could physically handle. The weight of the weapons, plus that of various digital cameras, GPS units, recording equipment, and walkie-talkies gave the packs incredible heft.

The inventory check took quite a while, and the delay made Jesse jittery. He wanted to be either on the road headed to the site, in the woods already on the trail, or back in his room conversing with Laura. The standing around drove him crazy.

Finally, they were ready to load the SUV. Brad checked them all out of their rooms and settled the tab. While he did this, Jesse took the opportunity to scour the lodge for Laura. He checked upstairs, downstairs in the lobby, in the restaurant, even around the outside of the building. He was anxious to at least talk to her for a minute or two before they departed. He thought that the previous night had meant something – like a beginning. Jesse swore at himself for feeling like a school kid with a crush, but at the same time hoped that last night's experience with Laura was a sign that she might feel the same way. He would never know, however, if he could not get a chance to talk to her.

Jesse did not get his chance. Brad told everyone to make one more quick check of their rooms and to meet out front at the SUV. So, the five explorers made last minute sweeps of their rooms to make sure they had not forgotten anything. As Jesse checked his room, he took the opportunity to write a quick note to Laura. He grabbed the complimentary stationery pad from atop the dresser.

"Dear Laura," he wrote, struggling with each word that followed. "I have to leave this morning and have been looking all over for you to tell you goodbye. It was nice to spend time with someone like you. I know I'm just a guy passing through town and you probably get this a lot, but I really mean it. I have feelings when I'm around you that remind me of how good life can be. That's something I haven't been able to think much about in a long time. Thanks, Jesse"

Jesse stood back after the laborious act of trying to put his thoughts and feelings onto paper. He studied the note and was instantly disgusted with it. Jesse grabbed the paper, crushed it into a tight ball and threw it into the wastebasket. He stood over the bin a minute staring at the crumpled paper within.

It dawned on Jesse that he really did not know what he was getting himself into with Brad's expedition and that the only thing he could be absolutely, positively sure about was that he liked Laura very, very much. Jesse smiled with the insight and smiled even broader as he decided to just put this concise thought on a new piece of paper and it would express everything he had wanted to say. As he was leaving the lodge with his fellow crew members a few minutes later, he took a quick moment to approach the front desk and ask to have the short note delivered to Laura.

*   *   *

The ride from town out to Steve Akers' land was eerily silent. Brad concentrated on directions, making sure to get out there as directly as possible. Jesse sat next to him in the passenger seat with a map, though they did not talk unless Jesse mentioned turning down one road or another. Jesse stared out the window, thinking about Laura. With her, he had felt alive and invigorated about something other than the subject of hairy hominids for the first time in many years. He hoped she had felt at least a small amount of that excitement. Jesse tried not to think about what lay in store for him and the others over the next several days.

Kelly kept to her magazine. She seemed to be reading it intently at times, though she would often just stare at the page or straight ahead at the back of the passenger seat. Mark and Roy were quiet too. Once Jesse turned around to see what they were up to in the backseat. Roy was asleep, with his head nodding rhythmically. Mark was reading a book about wilderness survival, though Jesse figured that it was too little too late. He thought it probably would not make up for Mark's inexperience in the woods, but was impressed that he was at least trying.

*   *   *

Steve Akers stood next to his tractor on the outskirts of the cornfield, holding both of his dogs by their collars. The German Shepherds tensed up as Brad's SUV pulled onto the property. Mr. Akers whispered a few calming words to them and they obediently sat back down.

"I guess you brought the whole dang crew," he called out to them as the group filed out of the SUV. "Looks like you really are fool enough to try a hare-brained scheme like this." He sauntered toward them, still holding the dogs. "I don't suppose you'll take any advice from an old feller like me, but I'd call it quits right now and save yourself the trouble – if I was you, that is."

Brad spoke up first as he walked up to the farmer. "We're here and we're ready to get started. I've got your money here if you're ready to seal the deal. So, are you going to cooperate or just nag us the whole time?"

Steve Akers stepped back, looked at Brad, and shook his head. "You young folks – all piss and vinegar, but not an ounce of sense." He paused as he surveyed the group. "Oh, I'll cooperate. If y'all are in a hurry to get in trouble, just be my guests."

Mr. Akers helped them load their gear and packs onto the wagon behind the farm tractor. Once they were all piled in, he drove them to the spot they had seen earlier with game trails and a fairly easy entrance into the thick woods.

"If I didn't know any better," Akers said as they hopped off the wagon and shouldered their packs, "I'd say it looks like you folks are aimed right at the Devil's Ridge." He shook his head with genuine worry. "I'm offering you one last chance to turn back now and end this foolishness."

Brad tossed him the keys to the SUV. "Don't go joyriding in my truck old man," he said with a half smile. "I'm gonna want her in good shape when I get back."

There was no smile on Steve Akers' face. He spit a stream of tobacco juice that sailed through the air and splattered on the dusty ground. "I ain't holding my breath," he muttered lowly as he turned the ignition key and the engine throttled to life.

The noisy tractor slowly drove away, kicking up a dust trail as it moved through the fields. A moment of silence then passed over the group. They were on the threshold of the unknown. Their preparations and activities up to this point had been adventurous and exciting, but also safe and escapable.

"The point of no return," Brad announced loudly with a grand gesture. "There's no turning back now. It's do or die."

A response occurred to Jesse. "I just hope it's not do *and* die," he thought.

* * *

Brad took the first step. "All right guys. We won't get anywhere just standing here looking at the cornfield. Let's follow this trail here and see where it leads." He then turned to Jesse and smiled. "You keep your eyes peeled for any monster sign." Brad looked at the others next. "The rest of you just try not to trip over your own feet. Look around, look for animals, look for things out of place. As we go, I'll point out the normal sights of the forest – animal tracks, broken limbs, deer browse – that sort of thing. This should be nice and educational for everybody."

Jesse did not appreciate Brad's condescending attitude, but felt somewhat assured that Brad had at least a decent background of hunting and tracking to guide them through the forest. They took their first steps away from civilization and weeks of planning and into the woods to begin the actual hunt. They did not plan to hike very far on this first day because they were uncertain of how much headway they would be able to make relying on game trails and rough maps of the area. As they soon found out, the terrain dictated their pace. Just a few hundred yards into the forest and away from Mr. Akers' fence line, the ground rose up sharply.

After a half hour of hiking, Kelly asked if they could take a break. She complained that her feet were hurting and that her pack was digging into her shoulders. Jesse admitted to himself that his pack felt pretty heavy at this point too. It was only noon, so they still had several hours of sunlight left to hike. As Brad was still leading the group at this time, the decision came down to him. He looked at Mark and Roy, who were sweating in the mid-day September heat and agreed that they could take a quick rest.

After un-shouldering his pack, Jesse sat down on a fallen tree trunk. He pulled a water bottle out of his pack and took a deep drink. Roy sat down next to him and clumsily unfastened his pack. It fell backwards off his back and onto the ground behind the log. Brad cautioned him, "Take it easy with that pack, Roy. It's got a lot of gear we're going to be needing on this trip. We don't want your lazy ass breaking everything on the first day."

"Why don't you take it easy, Brad," Roy replied. "Jesus, this isn't the damn trail of tears death march or something." Roy then leaned over to pick his pack up from the ground. As he reached behind the log to pick it up, he suddenly jumped up and several feet away from the tree trunk. "Look out!" he yelled.

Jesse had instinctively jumped up too, and was looking for the cause of Roy's concern. As they both looked over the log, a five-foot-long black snake quickly slithered across the ground and hid in the forest litter a few yards away. Jesse announced, "It's only a rat snake everybody. No need for concern from that little guy. Y'all are gonna have to get used to normal forest animals around here if we expect this trip to keep going smoothly." Then he turned to Brad, "Especially if we're looking to run across a big old hairy ape out here."

Roy announced, "It didn't really scare me or anything, just startled. You know what I'm saying? Just startled."

Kelly had found the whole incident amusing, and enjoyed the moment of entertainment at Roy's expense. It also provided her with a second or two of distraction from her foot pain and aching back. "Well gang," she said, "I guess I'm about ready to hit the trail again." She looked at Roy and then said, "Unless Crocodile Dundee there needs to wrangle some more snakes before we can get going."

Roy deflected this embarrassment into anger, and blamed it on Brad. "If the king of the jungle had any clue where we were going, maybe we wouldn't just be blindly stomping around these woods. Your feet wouldn't be tired and I wouldn't be running into snakes all over the place." Roy turned away and went to grab his pack. This time, he checked the area before reaching down to shoulder his bag.

"Hey, settle down there good buddy," Brad said, trying to diffuse the situation. "We're on the right track here. You and Kelly just need to learn to get along better or you two are going to make us all miserable."

Roy enjoyed Brad's suggestion that he and Kelly should get along better. He wondered if Brad had any clue that there was a budding relationship going on right under his nose. "Well, I'll try," Roy finally said as he suppressed a smile.

After they had all taken another drink of water and hoisted their packs, the group set off again into the woods. They kept up a mild level of chatter during most of their hike, except when the exertion got too strenuous. The early afternoon sun peeked through the dense canopy of trees and gave the woods a cheery feel. Though the heat took its toll, Jesse preferred the security of the muggy daytime hiking to what he imagined was an unsure, anxious night ahead.

As Brad led them through the woods, he often checked the GPS unit to locate their position. When they took their third break of the day, Brad announced that they had almost gone two miles. Roy could not believe what he had heard. "Two miles?" he asked incredulously. He could not resist the temptation to add a jab in at Brad. "We've been hiking all day following your lead. What, are we going in circles or something?"

Brad dismissed the question and pointed out that most of their trip had been either straight up or straight down a series of ridges, which translated into very slow going. He unfolded a topographic map of the region and compared it to the coordinates from the GPS unit. He estimated where they were, and showed the group on the map. Their location was a dishearteningly short distance on the map from the farm fields they had left that morning.

Jesse said, "Look guys, we're not out to set any distance records here. I mean, really we're right where we want to be. If these animals are moving from the woods to the crop fields to feed, they're not going to stray too far from this general area."

"That's right," Brad chimed in, "besides most game animals will stay in the general vicinity of a ready food supply. If they're working those corn fields, then we might just be smack dab in their staging area already."

Kelly perked up hearing this. "I like the sound of 'already.' No need to keep on hiking just for the sake of hiking – especially if it takes us farther than we need to be."

Brad raised an eyebrow. "I didn't know you were so keen on getting to the bottom of this mission right off the bat."

"Hell," Roy said, "she just wants to quit walking – like the rest of us."

Brad looked around them and surveyed the surroundings. He then studied the topographical map one more time and suggested that they change direction a little and head north to the top of the next ridge. It appeared to him, from the map, that that area would be more suitable for the first night's campsite. So, the group trudged on. They had to descend into a hollow first before they could head uphill to the ridge. At the bottom of the small valley, a stream carved a path through the ridges.

The creek had a lazy flow to it and the bottom was muddy with silt. It did not have a steep gradient like some of the smaller streams that cascaded down the hillsides throughout the area. "Does this remind you of anything?" Jesse asked Brad.

"Well, it sure looks like that Monkey Creek we went to, but I don't think it is from looking at the map."

"Yeah, I don't think it is either, but it's got the same type of water flow, mud bottom, and stream bank like Monkey Creek." Jesse studied it some more. "I'd be willing to bet it's in the same drainage system – if not a direct feeder or tributary."

Brad agreed and marked the stream on his map as a promising spot for future reference. Jesse took one of the water purifiers and refilled his water bottle and topped off everyone else's. Brad pointed out some deer tracks in the soft mud along the stream banks. He also saw a different set of tracks – wild boar. Brad mentioned that they would have to be on the lookout for the hogs, which could be dangerous if confronted. As they gathered their strength to hike up the last hundred yards to the top of the steep ridge, Brad took out some binoculars to spy the terrain ahead. He noticed that the ridge looked clear at the top. Upon hearing of this, Jesse said it was most likely a rocky ridge top where only small plants and grasses could grow – commonly called a bald. He and Brad decided that such a spot would in fact be a good place for the night's campsite because it would be open and relatively safe. It would also be easier to set up a camp in a cleared area.

Jesse took the first step up towards the bald, and groaned under the weight of his backpack. Roy followed closely behind, breathing deeply as they climbed the steep ridge. Halfway up the ridge, Roy stepped on a loose rock, which gave way under him. He fell forward first and grabbed at Jesse's pack. The grab threw Jesse off balance too, and he teetered backwards. Jesse managed to snag a tree and right himself, but Roy slid down the steep incline, crashing into Kelly, who had been behind him.

The collision knocked Kelly off her feet, and she fell to the side, landing on her backpack. Roy's fall scraped his hands and knees as he had tried to arrest his momentum on the way down by reaching for anything. Brad had been bringing up the rear and saw the whole event unfold up above him on the narrow path. He rushed up to check on Kelly.

"Are you OK, baby?" Brad asked as he knelt down over Kelly. Before she could answer, though, Brad was unzipping her backpack and checking the contents.

"What are you doing?" she asked furiously.

"Well," he began, "you're carrying some important stuff in this pack. You've got the thermal imager and two of our walkie-talkies. We need that stuff."

Kelly shoved him away. "Well, *I* don't need your help," she said. "*I'm* fine thank you, and so's your precious equipment."

"Hey, I'm all right too, in case anybody was concerned," Roy said, struggling to his feet.

Jesse came over to study Roy's scrapes and bruises. He poured some water over Roy's hands to wash away the dirt. Roy then wiped the rest of the blood and dirt on his own shirt, making quite a mess. Because the scratches were all just superficial, no other medical attention was required and they all started back up the ridge. Roy paid close attention to where he stepped until they got to the top.

Besides Jesse, none of them had seen a bald before. He told them that no one knew for sure what created these rocky, barren habitats, but that one theory suggested that native large mammals, such as bison and elk, were responsible for creating and maintaining these balds and that early settlers grazed the same sites with domesticated livestock.

"You mean, there used to be buffalo around here?" Mark asked, speaking up for the first time in a while. "I thought they all lived on the plains and stuff."

Jesse explained, "Well, from what I've read, it seems that back in frontier times you had all kinds of huge animals living in areas that are now cities and asphalt. Bison used to roam all over Kentucky and the surrounding states. In fact, that's how the early settlers used to make their way through the thick forests – following buffalo trails." Jesse then squatted down and picked up a handful of rocky soil. He gazed off into the distance, studying the surrounding landscape of ridges and valleys, easily seen from the height of the cleared, grassy bald.

Brad had appreciated the history lesson. He also thought it had a valuable application to their purpose on this expedition. He too looked out over the scenic vista and tried to imagine what other creatures lived and moved about under the thick forest canopy that spread out for miles and miles around them.

Mark interrupted Brad's thoughts. "Hey Brad, not trying to sound pushy or anything, but shouldn't we set up camp now before it starts getting dark? I mean, if this is the place we're going to stay at tonight."

They pulled out the two tents. It only took a few minutes to snap together the aluminum poles, thread them through the tent fabric, and pop the tiny structures into shape. Brad and Kelly would share one of the larger tents and Mark, Roy, and Jesse would lodge in the other.

After setting up the tents, Brad directed Roy to deploy the video cameras and other monitoring equipment around the camp. The setup was such that they could record or photograph in any direction around the campsite. The electronic sensors had just enough charge to last through the night before they would need recharging by the solar panels. The group had an excellent field of vision because of the unobstructed, grassy nature of the bald. As Brad and Kelly got the freeze-dried meals ready, Jesse and Mark went to the tree line to collect some firewood for the night.

Jesse bent over to grab a few dry sticks off the ground. He cradled them in his arms and turned to Mark. "Hey Mark, can I ask you something?"

"Sure, what is it?" Mark replied as he pulled a long dead branch from a thicket of rhododendron.

"A few minutes ago, you had a strange look in your eye – like you were really thinking about something."

"What of it? I think I was just looking around and stuff, like everyone else," Mark answered.

Jesse searched for the words. "Well, I guess it was just a look that caught my attention – like you were deep in thought."

Mark set down his load of firewood and faced Jesse. "Well, this is probably nothing, and I'm only saying it so you'll get off my back. I don't really know much about this kind of thing. I don't want to make a big deal out of what could be nothing and then have everyone mad at me."

Jesse gestured with his hand to get Mark to keep revealing his story.

"OK, back at the creek down at the bottom of this ridge – where we saw the deer and hog tracks. Well, there was something else too. I didn't show anyone because I wasn't sure what I was looking at, but I think I also saw some bear prints. At least, that's what they looked like according to the book I've been reading."

"So you're not really sure they were bear prints?" Jesse asked.

"Well, hell, of course not. I'm just going on what I've read in my book. I thought they were, but they were kind of all smudged up. I don't know if they were sliding around on the mud or what, but what should be a circular kind of print was longer, more like elongated. Actually, just forget it – I don't really know what I'm talking about – it just seemed curious to me."

Jesse shook his head. "I wish you'd showed that to me earlier, when we were down there. I would've taken a picture or two."

Mark responded, "I didn't see these till you guys had started up the ridge. And you guys were all were having a hard enough time making it up the hill – I didn't want everyone coming back down just to see some tracks. Like I said, I'm a rookie when it comes to wilderness adventures. I guess I didn't want to be the 'boy who cried wolf'."

Jesse bent over to grab his bundle of wood. When he straightened up he said, "Mark, we're pretty much looking for anything out of the ordinary – so strange footprints are just as good a start as any. Got it?"

"OK, sure. I got it. Do you think Brad'll want to look at them tomorrow?"

"Well, *I* want to look at them and that's what matters right now," Jesse replied. "My responsibility here is to make sure we're on the right track. Brad wants to hunt some monsters, but we've got to find them before we can hunt them."

"We shall go a-hunting then," Mark stated in an official-sounding voice. He loaded his arms with the wood he had gathered and the two headed back to the campsite.

* * *

Jesse finished off his re-hydrated beef stroganoff and tossed the plastic container into the campfire. He took a long drink of water and opened a granola bar. The autumn heat had dwindled and the cool evening air felt pleasant. The usual night chorus of crickets and other insects buzzed all around them. There were even a few dog-day cicadas left over from the end of summer creating their loud rhythmic droning songs in the treetops. With a belly full of food, Jesse relaxed on his fold-out stool with a sense that this trip might just turn out all right. They had a clear evening sky and a few stars were already twinkling overhead. In fact, there was a harvest moon out that night – a moon that glowed with an orange hue and seemed much larger and closer to earth than usual.

Jesse was not the only one in a better mood. Though Brad and Kelly sat silently, they sat close together and seemed to be on friendly terms. Mark was doing his best at whittling a long walking stick. Occasionally used it to poke and stir up the fire. Roy had smuggled in a bottle of rum from which he took an occasional sip.

Brad, Kelly, and Roy quietly reminisced about a few memories from college. For his part, Jesse did not mind listening to their recollections. He thought it was a good idea that everyone be in an easy-going mood for this first night. It would take their minds off what possibly lay ahead. Eventually Roy's bottle of rum got passed around to everybody. Jesse declined as he preferred his own stash of bourbon, though he was not drinking any tonight. Kelly had a few too many sips and Jesse saw her sleepily lean her head on Roy's shoulder. Brad turned to see this too. He stood up from his chair and pulled her away from Roy. "You two have been getting awfully close the last couple of days," he said. He turned to Kelly and continued. "I don't know what's going on, but you better just remember whose tent you're sleeping in tonight."

Kelly stood up with a stoic look on her face. She turned around without saying anything to Brad, and walked away from the campfire. Brad sat back down and stared into the fire. Mark focused on his whittling, while Roy took a long hit from the rum. After an awkward moment of silence, Jesse got up from his stool and walked back behind the tents to find Kelly. She sobbed quietly in the darkness several yards away from the fire, the tents, and her boyfriend. Jesse approached her, feeling that she probably needed some consoling, or at least to talk to someone.

"Are you OK?" he asked, trying to muster some tenderness. "I hope everything's all right."

Kelly shot back, "This isn't your problem, Jesse."

"Well, I just thought …" Jesse began.

"Thought what?" Kelly said, cutting him off. "You don't know anything about me. You don't know anything about Roy. You don't know anything about Brad either. You're his little errand boy for this stupid trip and then after that, he won't ever see you again. But he'll see me." She stopped to wipe her face.

"You see this watch?" she asked Jesse, showing him her wrist. "Eight hundred bucks for this little watch. Brad got it for me for my last birthday. And my hiking boots? Two hundred dollars. They're brand new and I probably won't ever wear them again as soon as this stupid trip's over. I mean, who gets to do that?"

Jesse shrugged, not sure of the point she was trying to make.

"I get to do that," she continued. "Brad takes care of me. What do I care if he says stuff about me and Roy? We're just friends and that's all there is. I mean, for now anyway. I wish Brad would just get over all of this. He and I could move on and take that next step in our relationship. We've been together for so long, but …"

Kelly turned away from Jesse at this point and faced the dark woods beyond them. Jesse could tell she had begun to lightly cry again. "Don't stand there feeling sorry for me, Jesse. Feel sorry for yourself. My decision will be made in the next few days and I'll return back to a normal life with one of those two rich, successful men sitting by that fire. What kind of life will you be returning to? To think that you believe in all this hocus pocus – that's the real pitiful thing around here."

Jesse stood in silence. He retreated a few steps and turned to go back to the campfire area. Obviously Kelly did not need consoling, or at least pretended she did not need it. Jesse wondered how much of her strong statements were real – whether she really was that devoted to Brad and the hope of a developing relationship with him, or whether she was trying to mask something going on between her and Roy, or perhaps both. Jesse thought to himself that the mystery of Kelly would certainly not be the last thing about this trip that would defy easy explanation.

* * *

Back at the campfire, Jesse joined the others. Kelly soon sat back down and the conversations started again. Jesse pulled out his plastic bottle of bourbon from his pack. He had hoped to save it for later in the trip, but after his confrontation with Kelly, decided he needed it sooner. The bourbon tasted good and had an immediate effect. Jesse stared into the campfire and tuned out the talking around him. Mark was back at his whittling and Roy sat quietly, nursing his own bottle of liquor. Brad and Kelly appeared to have gotten over their tiff and resumed their subdued whisperings.

Jesse's eyes glazed over as he looked deeply into the hypnotic dance of the fire's flames. The flickering mesmerized him and he zoned out for several minutes, enjoying his own personal reverie. However, Jesse was soon jolted out of his trance when Roy yelled, "Did you see that?" Jesse swung around and started scanning the nearby tree line, trying to get his night eyes working again after staring into the fire for so long. Brad grabbed his rifle and stood up, ready for action.

"What was it Roy, what did you see?" Brad asked, springing into readiness.

Roy was not looking at the forest. Instead he gazed upwards. "I just saw a shooting star," he finally said. "Man, it was a big one – went from one end of the sky to the other. I've never seen one like that before. It's so clear out here that you can see stuff in the sky really well ..." Roy trailed off as he realized that his companions had taken his startled exclamation to mean something quite different. Brad took off his hat and swatted it at Roy. They all sat back down and eased up a bit.

Jesse did not want someone to start firing shots or do anything rash by being startled by something harmless, like the starry night sky. "Look, everyone's on edge and also probably beat from today's hiking," he said. "Before we see any more shooting stars and get all riled up again, maybe we should turn in for the night. Besides, Mark and I were talking earlier and decided we want to go back and visit some trails we passed by. We need to get an early start tomorrow."

After his short speech, Jesse looked up and saw part of what had so excited Roy. On top of the bald and miles away from any city lights, the immense expanse of sky above them was so clear and seemed so close to earth that the scene was awe-inspiring. It had been years since Jesse had seen so many stars so brilliantly twinkling over head, and even they could not compete with the light from the harvest moon which had moved further up into the sky.

Brad kicked the campfire apart and poured a few sprinkles of water on it to douse the main body of flames. The embers continued to glow, but no more flames licked upwards from the remaining logs. Jesse walked a few yards away from the tents to relieve himself. He had his headlamp switched to a red light to preserve his night vision. Jesse then walked to the tent he shared with Mark and Roy, unzipped the D-shaped door and climbed in. Fortunately, he had the sleeping position right in front of the door. This would make for an easy exit if he had to get up in the night for any reason. However, he worried about being in between two potential snorers. The night was already getting cool and Jesse had been on enough camping trips to know that cool night air and sleeping in the outdoors was a perfect combination for head congestion and loud snoring.

The day's exhaustion did not let Jesse worry long. He fell asleep quickly and before either of his tent mates. Jesse's sleep was not a deep one, though, because he had to struggle to get comfortable in his mummy sleeping bag. The light sleep led to various dreams, including a very vivid imagination of the campsite and its inhabitants. In his dream, Jesse saw Brad standing behind Kelly, who sat in front of the campfire. Brad stroked Kelly's hair as she poked a stick in the fire. Her feet were resting close to the fire, and the rubber sole of one of her hiking boots smoldered a bit.

Kelly turned to Jesse and spoke directly to him, saying, "Brad will just get me new ones you know." Brad laughed behind her, then gave Jesse a wink. Then, suddenly, Brad spun around and pulled two cowboy six-shooters from his waist and began firing indiscriminate shots into the woods surrounding the campsite. After emptying the guns, Brad turned to Jesse. With smoke curling up from the barrels, Brad holstered the guns and mumbled that he thought he had heard something in the trees.

At this moment, Mark and Roy roared up to the campsite in Brad's SUV with the windows down and loud music blaring out from within. They skidded to a halt in front of the fire, sending clumps of rocks and dirt flying through the air. They stumbled out of the vehicle, reeling in drunkenness. Mark balanced precariously on his whittled walking stick. Roy opened one of the back doors and stammered, "Look what we found back in town – it's the bartender from the lodge."

Laura jumped out of the truck and ran up to Jesse. He grabbed her in his arms, wanting to protect her from his crazy companions. He was so excited to see her, and the embrace was sweeter than any he had had in ages. However, their happiness at seeing each other was interrupted by a snarling growl from the woods surrounding the camp. The snorting continued in a rhythmic manner – growling loudly, then sputtering and fading. It got so loud that Jesse felt the sound was almost in his ear, ringing and pulsing every few seconds.

Suddenly, a gargantuan creature burst through the trees and rushed the camp. Jesse only saw the blur for a second before it was right before him. The huge animal ran right into Jesse, knocking him down to the ground. Jesse lay there for a moment, then Mark leaned over him and grabbed his shoulder. "Jesse, are you all right? Jesse?"

"Jesse, are you OK?" Mark asked again. Jesse opened his eyes to see Mark looking at him in the darkness of the tent. Jesse realized that he was in the tent, still wrapped up in his sleeping bag. Mark had a hold of his shoulder, gently nudging him. Jesse shook his head, trying to clear the cobwebs. He then heard the growling and snorting again, and turned in his sleeping bag to see Roy next to him, snoring violently.

"I'm all right, Mark," Jesse whispered. "Just having a bad dream, part of which was thanks to Roy's ridiculous snoring."

Mark settled back down into his sleeping bag. It was only 2:00 AM and they still had a lot of night to get through. "Just relax," Jesse said. "Morning will be here sooner than you know." Jesse did not really find comfort in his own attempts at valor. He stared up at the nylon ceiling of the tent. With the rain fly covering the whole structure, the moisture from their breath collected on the inside walls in tiny droplets of dew. A small insect fluttered about and crawled along the inside top of the tent.

Mark broke the silence. "I keep hearing all kinds of animal sounds out there, like hoot owls or something."

Jesse whispered, "Well, I'd say that's pretty normal out here. I imagine it's just squirrels and birds and stuff. Let's try to get back to sleep."

"Try's the right word there," Mark whispered back. "Especially with Old Man River over there sawing logs. I haven't been out camping since I was a kid in my own backyard. Takes a little while to get used to I guess."

Jesse closed his eyes again and turned to his side to block out Roy's snoring. Mark kept rambling for a while before finally drifting back off to sleep. Jesse stayed awake for a few minutes, trying to hear the owls that Mark had been mumbling about. He heard nothing other than a few small animals rustling around in the leaves, though, and soon fell asleep for the rest of the night.

DAY TWO

A faint light filtered through the blue nylon of Jesse's tent. He pulled his arm out of his sleeping bag and checked the time. It was already morning, but Jesse had no urgent desire to leave the warm cocoon of his sleeping bag to brave the chilly autumn morning air. So he turned on his side and tried to burrow even farther into his bag. He pulled the flaps up over his head and left a small opening for his mouth and nose to breathe.

After lying still for almost an hour, Jesse decided to emerge from his sleeping bag and get the day started. He unzipped the side and hurriedly threw on a hat and jacket and then pulled on his pants. He shook his boots out, put them on, and stepped outside of the tent. Jesse laced up his boots and straightened up in an early morning stretch. He felt sore all over, almost as much from the night's sleep as from the previous day's hike. As Jesse sifted through his pack to find some gear, his commotion slowly woke up the rest of the party.

Brad was the next to get up, rising slowly out of the tent he shared with Kelly. He walked over to Jesse and fired up one of the small camp stoves to heat up a tiny pot of coffee. The two stood silently, recognizing the awesome spectacle unfolding before them. Atop the bald, they could see the hills, ridges, and valleys outstretched in front of them, enveloped in fog and mist.

"Sure were a lot of owls out last night," Brad said as he sipped his scalding hot cup of coffee.

Jesse raised an eyebrow. "Yeah, that's what Mark was telling me in the middle of the night. What kind of owls were they?" Jesse asked.

"Not really sure," Brad answered. "A couple of times I could've sworn they were screech owls, but every now and then you'd hear a call with a lot more bass to it. I guess I'm a little ashamed to say I just couldn't put my finger on which species would make a call like that. I don't have that much experience in an eastern Appalachian forest like this."

"Well, maybe we'll hear them again tonight," Jesse said while opening a granola bar. "You ready for breakfast?" he asked, changing the subject.

Brad snapped out of the deep thought he was in and agreed that they should get the others up and get breakfast ready. He pulled out a tube of powdered drink mix and instantly created lemonade in one of the water jugs. They would not be cooking breakfast this morning other than the coffee they'd already made, so granola bars would be the table fare for this second day of the expedition. Brad thought this was the best idea to keep it simple and fast until they had settled into a permanent campsite and gotten more used to the camp life.

After eating, they all worked on striking camp and packing up. Jesse took this opportunity to remind them that he and Mark had talked about back-tracking to revisit some of the strange footprints and tracks Mark had seen down in the valley below. This news upset Brad as he wanted to push forward and deeper into the forest first, and then maybe double back. His best hunting adventures had always had more success the further from civilization they were.

Jesse tried to remind him of what they had talked about just yesterday – the possible tie-in with Monkey Creek, and that these animals were likely hugging close to civilization because they could take such advantage of crops and other ready food sources. They could also potentially be hunting the abundant deer that frequented the local agricultural fields. Thus, it might make just as much sense to concentrate on the areas closer to cropland than far out into the deep forest. Brad continued to complain for a while, despite recalling that the idea seemed reasonable to him the first time he heard it. Jesse and Mark shared a look as Brad cussed his way through the whole process of taking down his tent.

After a tent stake refused to pry free from the ground, Brad exploded in frustration. He vented by interrogating Jesse concerning the reason for the new plan. Jesse answered, "Calm down Brad. Look, it's hard to say what the best way is going to be to track and find an unknown animal. But a good way would probably be to look out for unusual signs and follow up on them. Mark says he saw some pretty strange track arrangements down at that creek bottom yesterday. That's just as good a starting point as any." Jesse studied Brad's still-angry face. "Hey Brad, what we're doing now hasn't been done much before, if ever. This is how we're going to have to play the game until we figure out all the rules."

Brad was still not satisfied. He bent over and wrestled again with the tent stake. Finally, it popped free from the rocky ground and sent Brad tumbling backwards. "Goddammit," he yelled as he got to his feet and brushed himself off. "We're out in the middle of nowhere and now you're telling me we don't even know what we're looking for. That's just fucking brilliant." Brad looked down at his elbow, which was now bleeding from his encounter with the tent stake. "And now my fucking elbow is fucking bleeding," he continued cursing.

Fortunately, Kelly came over to Brad and tended to his slight wound. She also managed to calm him down a little. She pulled a small box from her pack and then lit cigarettes for Brad and herself. Jesse suddenly realized that he had not seen either of the two smoke in the last several days. At least, they had not done so in his presence so far. Though he felt that the nicotine cravings might have contributed to Brad's edginess, he was not sure he liked the idea of having two smokers in a hunting party trying to track down a very elusive and aware animal. He felt that the constant smell of smoke that would follow them would alert everything in the forest to their presence.

Jesse then thought for a minute and mused to himself, "On the other hand, we're hunting just about the only animal that might turn around and hunt us. I'd say we'd be a pretty easy bunch to locate in the woods. If the smoking brings them to us, it might save us a lot of fruitless walking."

* * *

After Kelly had seen to Brad's injury, she got up to get her meager breakfast. While Brad and Jesse continued to argue a little bit more about the day's course of action, Roy took the opportunity to pull Kelly aside.

"What's with Brad this morning? Could he possibly be more of a dick about things?"

"I guess he's just anxious to have everything go right on this trip," Kelly offered. "Or, at least go his way."

"Well, I just don't want him to take his frustrations out on you, like he did last night," Roy continued. "That stuff pisses me off."

"He's usually pretty mild-mannered," Kelly responded. "Like I said, I guess it's just that he's got so much riding on this expedition."

The two stood quietly for a few moments then Roy revived the conversation. "Look, you and I both know we're not going to find any kind of magical giant ape running around out here in the boondocks. Why don't we cut our losses? You and I can head back early and just wait for everybody else back in town. We'd have a little time to ourselves too."

Kelly studied Roy's grin. "I don't know Roy. I can't leave Brad out here. I'm not at that point – yet. He's still my boyfriend and I've got to stick with him for the time being to help him work through this." She looked down at her feet and kicked around a bit of loose dirt. "Maybe this trip will really help him in the long term."

Roy didn't miss a beat in responding, "What about the short term, Kelly? Are you still going to let him treat you like he does? What if we don't find Brad's make-belief monster out here? Aren't you fed up with getting dragged all over the world in his 'pursuit for inner peace,' or whatever it is he's trying to get at?"

"Roy, stop," Kelly answered. "You know how difficult this is on me. But I just can't make that break from him right now," Kelly said as she gestured to the thick woods surrounding them, "especially not out here. I've got to give him the benefit of the doubt for the time being."

Roy rubbed his chin as his brow creased. "What if he wasn't in the picture – just for hypothetical's sake? What if he wasn't around and we weren't out in the middle of nowhere on a stupid camping trip?"

"Roy, what are you getting at?" Kelly asked, somewhat alarmed.

"Oh, nothing … nothing. Just forget about it. I'm talking to myself. Look, we better get back with the others. It looks like Jesse and Brad are getting geared up to go."

Kelly and Roy walked separate directions and joined back up at the campsite where Mark, Brad, and Jesse were taking down the last of the equipment and packing it up. After a few more minutes, they were all ready to hit the trail again.

* * *

Jesse shouldered his pack and followed Brad back down the ridge as they made their way from the bald to the valley below. As he and the others hiked cautiously down the ridge, they were presented with a wide variety of environments. The midmorning sun brought a rising temperature and the moisture emanating from the surrounding forest created a tropical feel, despite the elevation and autumn date. In some places, though, the sun barely filtered through the dense canopy of mature hardwoods and evergreens. The forest floor underneath these sun- and rain-grabbing giants was fairly clear and open. In other areas, the tangle of rhododendrons and creeping vines made travel almost impossible.

Brad and Jesse managed to locate the creek that they had stopped at the day before, but they had to travel a while to find the mysterious tracks Mark had seen earlier. They passed by deep sinkholes where the ground simply opened up and swallowed the forest floor. Tiny streams dropped into some of these depressions, creating microclimates of moisture and shade. One tributary they had followed ended in an immense bog created by a beaver dam. Shallow water and deep mud covered the trunks of numerous trees in an area of several acres. The group retreated to higher ground to avoid getting stuck in the boggy area.

After making it back to the main branch of the creek, they only had to travel a short distance before they found the tracks Mark had discovered on the previous day. They took a break, glad to finally be back on the right track. Jesse unpacked his water purifier and refilled the group's water supply. The water from the stream ran cold and clear, and having a cool drink on this muggy morning was a welcome relief for the weary hikers. Jesse sipped from his water bottle and sat down on a large, flat boulder. He was joined by Mark and Roy. Kelly walked with Brad to look at the tracks, still evident in the soft riverbank soil.

The two came back a few minutes later. "Everybody up," Brad barked. "We've finally got something to look at."

Just twenty yards away from the mysterious tracks, Brad had discovered a game trail that extended from the creek all the way back into the woods. As Jesse arrived at the scene, he immediately noticed characteristics often associated with bigfoot activity. Framing the entrance to the trail was an arch of two bent-over pine trees. The trunks of the young trees had been broken approximately seven feet above the ground. Jesse stood on his toes to get a closer look and saw that the trees appeared to have been twisted at the break. He pointed this out to Brad who initially argued that the breaks could have been weather-related.

Jesse disagreed. "Look at the breaking point on these trees – they've been twisted, like someone wringing a wet dish towel. That would take some serious wind to do that. Surely that type of storm would've left some other damage around here. But all we have are these two, isolated trees. It would be one awfully selective type of storm to do that." Jesse reached up to feel the twisted, broken trunks with his hands. "This is bigfoot sign," he said quietly and solemnly.

Brad admitted that he could not come up with a better explanation. His face then displayed a strange look as different realizations about this expedition began to swell up in the back of his head. At this point, though, Brad did not want to confront the theoretical struggle getting ready to take place in his psyche. He shook his head as if trying to physically clear the emerging thoughts and get back to the task at hand.

While still inspecting the trail entrance, Brad found a small pile of rocks about four feet farther into the trail from one of the pine trees. Jesse came over to look at the pile. It was not a random deposit of rocks. Instead, several flat stones had been laid on top of each other in a pyramid fashion, reaching to a height of about six inches.

"You got an explanation for that?" Jesse asked Brad as they studied the rock pile. "That sure isn't the result of some strange weather phenomenon. In fact, this could be surer evidence than the arches."

Brad did not respond. A look of puzzlement had spread over his face. He got down on his hands and knees and looked closely at the stones, then stood up and stroked his chin for a while. He was losing the battle to keep his thoughts and concerns at bay. Brad looked back at the pine tree archway, then turned to Jesse. "Supposing an animal did do these things. What are we talking about – something with intelligence enough to make signs and markers?"

Jesse responded, "Brad, this is classic bigfoot stuff and I think it does show that they have decent intelligence. I've read about chimps at zoos that they've trained to do sign language and use tools. I'd say a bigfoot would have at least a similar primate level of brainpower and could make signs like the ones we've seen out here."

Roy had come closer to inspect the latest find and overheard Brad and Jesse talking. "I'm betting that all we're dealing with here is a wicked storm and some crazy squirrels or something," he declared. "All we gotta do is find a pile of acorns next and I'll be at ease again."

"Not trying to be spooky or anything," Jesse said, "but I doubt if any of us will be at ease again for the rest of this expedition."

Mark and Kelly walked up to them to see what was going on. Jesse explained that they had found an awfully large trail, pointed out the arched trees, and also took them to look at the small stone pile. "So what's with all the markers, what are they – bigfoot crossing signs?" Mark jokingly asked.

"Well," Jesse began, "you might not be too far off." He turned to Brad. "Brad," he asked, "before you found this trail, did you notice any other game trails around here, like deer paths?"

"Sure, they crisscross all over this area," Brad replied.

"So, Mark," Jesse continued, "these might just be road signs to any of our large forest dwelling friends. Seems like a good place to hang out and wait for an unwitting deer to come by."

Roy looked at Jesse in disbelief after hearing his explanation to Mark. "Hold on a minute there. You're not suggesting that these things eat deer are you?"

"That's exactly what I'm saying," Jesse responded. "They're probably omnivores, just like a lot of primate species. Think about it – they're likely the top of the food chain around here, except maybe bears. When winter gets harsh and the local agricultural crops are gone and vegetation is scarce, what better source of protein and nutrients than fresh venison? I don't just mean the backstraps and tenderloins either. Livers, kidneys, other internal organs – they're all power packed with everything one would need to get through the lean times."

Roy was still having trouble tackling this concept. "Let me get more to the point. Is this thing a predator, and if so, does that mean it's smart?"

Brad had also been experiencing a rising level of concern as he listened to Jesse and as he had been addressing his own thoughts and emotions over the past minutes. He had come out to this forest in search of a shadowy figure that may or may not have been the cause of fear and nightmares for years. Brad realized that he had never honestly, fully believed that anything like a bigfoot could exist, but that the vague notion of hunting one had been enough to keep him going.

Suddenly, though, he was faced with physical evidence that he could see and touch of a real animal altering its surrounding environment. Brad squatted down and picked up one of the rocks. It was worn and polished – obviously from a river or creek bed. Having not seen any such a waterway nearby, Brad pictured the image of some creature carrying these stones all the way through the forest and deliberately placing them on the ground. The small stone structure worried Brad because of what it represented – a creature that he wanted to confront, but that he had not truly expected to actually be walking through a forest leaving arched trees and intricate piles of river rocks.

As Brad rubbed one of the smooth stones between his fingers, he also grew excited that this trip might actually provide the result he had sought

— the most striking chance yet to outwardly confront the inner demons that had plagued him for so long. Already, this was the most unique hunt he had been on. Now that they were finally coming across signs of the quarry he sought, he could feel a resolution and closure within his grasps.

This new feeling of excitement and eagerness helped Brad overcome the shock of discovery he had been reeling from. Mustering his usual bravado, Brad stood up and turned to Roy, to answer the question posed moments ago. "Come on Roy," he chided. "You've watched enough nature programs to know that the predator's usually a whole lot smarter than the prey."

"Oh Christ man," Roy spouted, with a mixture of disbelief and anger. "Now you're telling me there's a giant fucking smart predator gorilla out here. No, no, no! I thought this was going to be some Jane Goodall business where we're just hanging out and documenting some new tribe of monkeys or something."

"Roy," Brad said sharply. "Calm down. What the hell did you think we're carrying all these guns for? You knew we weren't coming out to take pictures of some new type of cute baby chimp or something. Did you think I'd come out with all this manpower and firepower to hunt a sweet fuzzy little animal? Get a hold of yourself." Brad paced feverishly, kicking up dirt as he tried to calm himself down too.

His bravado and adrenaline were getting carried away as he tried to mask something that had been creeping up from his stomach and threatening to unglue him this whole time. One emotion had accompanied the puzzlement, shock, and excitement he had been going through as he came to grips with the notion that they were actually tracking a real animal. That emotion almost never left him and it was making its presence known despite Brad's best efforts to force it back down. He was feeling what Roy's concerns and questions stemmed from – fear.

At this point, Jesse stepped in between the two. "Let's all just settle down a little bit. Look, we've seen some pretty definitive bigfoot signs here. But Roy, if it makes you feel better, just think of this stuff as weird storm damage, or termites, or woodpeckers – whatever. Keep playing the skeptic. I think that's an important role right now. Besides, there's five of us, we're armed to the teeth, and we're only a couple miles from civilization. When you consider…"

"Shit!" Mark exclaimed from a little further back in the woods where he had been looking around.

"What is it?" Kelly asked. She was a few feet behind him, just aimlessly walking around the arched trees with the rest of the group.

"It's shit," Mark responded.

"What's shit?" Jesse asked, trying to see what had gotten Mark agitated.

"It's crap. I just stepped in a pile of crap," Mark replied, disgusted. As Roy, Brad, and Jesse caught up, they all stood around Mark. Just ten yards from the arched pine trees, Mark had stepped into a mammoth pile of dung hidden in the leaf litter. Although the smell released by Mark's disturbance of the pile was nauseating, the curiosity of the discovery overcame their disgust. After Mark wiped his boot on the ground, Brad moved closer and bent over to look at the feces. "It's not deer, elk, or bear," he announced. "I'm pretty familiar with that stuff - at least, compared to what I've seen out West."

Roy squatted nearby, looking at the pile. "It looks like human shit."

"Yeah," Jesse agreed, "except it looks like it came from Paul Bunyan."

Brad stood up. "A bear the size of a grizzly could've done this, but not one of the local black bears. What's interesting, though, is the contents."

"Oh, this is just too gross," Kelly complained. "I'm not going to stand here and listen to this." She walked past the group and sat down in the opening of the trail's entrance, under the arched pine trees.

"What's so interesting about crap?" Roy asked.

"Well," Brad began, poking at the pile with a stick, "it's got bits of corn in it for one thing – so whatever left this has been visiting the farms a couple miles away. There's some berries and other vegetation mixed in, which isn't too strange. But if you look closely, there's tufts of undigested hair all through this."

Brad squatted back down to look closer. Using his stick, he dug out a chunk of hair and held it up to investigate. "This is deer hair all right, so we're definitely dealing with a scavenger or a predator. Again, that *could* indicate a bear, but I'd say that it's awfully unlikely."

Mark spoke up. "If it is a bear, would it be dangerous?"

Brad answered, "Again, I'm only speaking from experiences from hunting them out West and up in Canada, but I'd say a black bear can sprint pretty fast – somewhere in the thirty mile per hour range. But looking at this dung pile here, we'd be dealing with a lumbering giant who might have been scavenging off a carcass."

"So now you're leaning toward it coming from a bear?" Jesse asked.

"No, I'm not saying that at all," Brad answered while still staring at the pile of feces covering a solid foot in circumference and almost five to six inches in height. "I'm saying a bear would be the likeliest of explanations under *normal* circumstances." He turned to Jesse with a serious expression, "But nothing has been normal to me since we set sight on those arched trees."

Brad then stared out into the forest with a strange look on his face. On one hand, he was glad that they had finally come across some signs that would indicate the real existence of a bigfoot creature. That meant that the whole expedition would not be just one grand wild goose chase. It also meant he might soon be able to address the nightmares that had plagued him for decades. Yet, in thinking about the confrontation needed to accomplish that very goal, Brad was now experiencing something he had not counted on – fear of an animal, not just a memory.

*   *   *

The early afternoon sun shone directly over their heads as the group took a break underneath the arched pine trees. Brad took a bearing with his compass and noted that the trail marked by the arch headed west, back in the direction toward the Akers farm. Though he had been reluctant earlier in the day to head back to their starting point instead of deeper into the woods, the clues they had uncovered convinced him that they might be on the trail of one or more of the creatures they sought.

They hiked on the trail for almost a half hour. The going was easy, as the trail was wide and the ground fairly worn from the footsteps of countless animals – both known and unknown. Brad was still leading the pack and was the first to come to the fork in the trail. At a large, dead oak tree, the main trail split to the right of the tree and a smaller route branched off to the left. Jesse caught up to Brad and studied their choices. Brad pulled out his binoculars and scanned down each trail. Through the trees shading the smaller lane, Brad saw something out of place in the dense forest.

"It looks like there's something down that trail," he said, still squinting into the binoculars. "I can't really make out what it is, but it's something solid, and kind of whitish. It's hard to see through all the trees, but you can make out something large and white in the background."

"What, like a big boulder?" Jesse asked.

"No, it looks flatter than that, like maybe a wall of some type," Brad answered. "Here, hold on a minute," he said as he reached into his pack. "I've got my spotting scope with me. It can pick out the pupil in an elk's eye at three hundred yards. It should help us see what we're looking at."

Brad raised the scope up to his eye and stared down the trail. "Well, I believe I was right," he announced. "Looks like a wall or the side of a building of some kind. We might as well go check it out."

Roy and Kelly voiced that they did not want to do any unnecessary walking, so they protested the side trip. Mark, on the other hand, was curious to see the shed. "Maybe it's an old miner's shed or something. There could be old axes and lanterns and rustic memorabilia in it – Vanessa loves that old antique kind of stuff."

Brad frowned at him. "Mark, grow some balls. We're not here to loot old shacks and hunt for treasure for your fiancée's decorating desires."

"All the same, I'd like to go see it," Mark quickly responded, unfazed by Brad's comment.

"Well, it's settled then," Jesse said. "It's not too far of a walk and it's still early in the day. We can go check it out and then just come back to this tree if the shed turns out to be a dead end."

The skinny trail leading to the shack presented more obstacles than the wide, clear path they had been hiking on. Overhanging branches and exposed tree roots made the going slower, but they eventually found themselves staring at a small shack. The structure consisted of four square walls and a moss-covered roof. The roof was sunken in along the back corner, near a stove pipe. The flimsy walls were warped as well, and the front – and only – door to the small abode was off its hinges and lying on the ground. A grimy window on each side of the shack indicated it had once been inhabited, though now the windows were cracked and so covered with dirt that they were nearly impossible to see through. Almost two miles away from the Akers' farm, it instantly reminded Jesse of the local legends Mr. Akers had told them. "I wonder if this is Wendell McClain's old place?" he asked to no one in particular.

Still standing several feet away from the entrance, Jesse detected a musky, dank smell. He turned to Brad, who was also sniffing the air. Brad's face registered his determination to figure out the odor. He turned to meet Jesse's gaze. "I can't tell if that's wet dog or urine I'm smelling," Brad said.

"I think it smells like wet, moldy leaves," Mark contributed.

"Well it's probably a combination of all those things," Jesse concluded, trying to sound upbeat. "This place's certainly been abandoned for quite a while – decades upon decades if this is the place Mr. Akers was talking about."

"Hey, look at these," Roy called out. He was standing near the steps that led into the shack. As the others gathered around, they could see what Roy had discovered – small bones scattered to the left of the steps. Brad knelt down to study them. He picked up a few and examined them. "This one probably belongs to something small, like a rabbit," he explained holding up a bone for the rest to see, "and you can see what look like a few squirrel skulls here and there. We might've had a fox or even a bobcat denned up in this shack at one point."

Brad stopped as he spied something sticking out from underneath the wooden steps. He reached toward the step and started pulling out a bone from underneath. "Hello," he said quietly. "this is big enough to be a deer's thigh bone." He kept pulling, though the end of the bone was stuck underneath the steps. Brad changed the angle of his pull, and the bone popped free, though with it came a section of the pelvis, still barely attached to the femur.

"Oh that's disgusting," Kelly exclaimed.

"Dude, that's awesome," Roy said as he moved closer to the newest discovery.

"Still think all this is a fox's handiwork?" Jesse asked Brad.

"Well, it wouldn't be uncommon for a fox to nab a piece of carrion to bring back to some pups," Brad answered. "Problem is," he continued, "there's not any little teeth marks on this bone to suggest a couple foxes working on it. That, and it's weird how this pelvis could be shattered in two like it is."

"Oh man," Mark shouted, "I think I just found something even stranger."

Except for Kelly, who had decided she had had enough gruesome discoveries, the others rushed over to Mark. He was standing a few yards from the corner of the shack in some knee-high weeds. With a large stick, he shoved something free from the weeds and it rolled out in front of the group. Jesse stared down at his feet, looking at the obvious skull of a wild boar, with four-inch tusks still intact.

"Well, that pretty much rules out any small predator like a fox or a bobcat," Brad said. "Probably also rules out bigger ones too, like coyotes. Even in a pack it's not too often you see coyotes willing to take on a full grown boar." Brad squatted down and ran his fingers along one of the boar's tusks. "Still sharp as a goddamn razor," he said. Then he placed his open palms over the top of the skull to measure the skull's length. "I've seen guides do this with a bear's skull before," he explained. "I don't know if the same would hold true for a pig, but I'd still say this was probably an adult male – a big one at that, maybe three hundred, four hundred pounds. I suppose that's just a guess but you can clearly see this isn't the skull of some newborn piglet."

"Could this have been done by that bear you were talking about earlier, when we found that pile of crap?" Roy asked.

Brad thought for a minute. "Yeah, it's possible. Coyote and black bear do sometimes prey on wild hogs, but it'd have to be a large pack of coyotes or one bad-ass bear to have taken down this big boy. But you're right – we could be dealing with one very large, very hungry black bear. Or," he paused and the same expression as earlier crept onto his face, "one very bad-ass unknown hominid." He looked over at Jesse.

Then Mark asked, "Yeah, I mean, do bears even live in shacks like this? Is it normal for them to take up residence in an abandoned shack and scatter bones everywhere?"

"Well, I've never heard of anything like that," Brad admitted. "But let's look inside first before we make any conclusions. Maybe we'll find some clues to answer this little mystery."

* * *

The smell hit Jesse first as he stepped through the decaying doorway. Brad followed close behind him, then Mark. Roy squeezed in behind them, while Kelly stayed outside. Roy pulled his shirt over his nose to keep out the stench. The musky smell some of them had noticed earlier was intense inside the small cabin. It seemed to emanate from one corner of the open room, where leaves, sticks, and various odds and ends were piled into what looked like a bedding area. Amongst the bits of leaf debris, moss, and hair, Brad also spied some items not from the natural surroundings. He picked up a mound of shredded foam that must have come from what had once been a pillow or cushion.

Jesse noticed some trinkets spread around the bedding area, including bits of colored glass, two marbles, and a flattened beer can. Brad continued walking around the small room, picking something from cracks and crevices.

"What is it?" Jesse asked.

"Some sort of hair," Brad answered, holding up several strands of long, stringy, grey-colored hair. "It's not fur, that's for sure," Brad continued. "Looks more like coarse human hair than anything." He walked over to Roy, who happened to have the longest hair of the group. Without permission, Brad yanked one of Roy's hairs loose to compare. Brad held Roy's hair strand and the unknown sample side by side.

"Well, they look similar to me," Mark said.

At this point, Kelly had stepped into the shack's entrance. "Oh my God, this place reeks. How can you guys stand in here?"

"You get used to it after a while," Jesse answered.

"Not me, I think I'm going to gag," Kelly responded. "Besides, this place gives me the creeps. I'm going to be waiting back outside. Can you guys hurry it up please, I don't like being here."

"She's right," Roy spoke up. "I've got an eerie feeling just standing in here. I'll go keep Kelly company outside."

Jesse looked out through the grimy windows. The forest canopy surrounding the tiny ramshackle cabin was thick and the late afternoon sunlight barely filtered through. He surmised that the shady nature of the location contributed to the musty, moist smell and feeling the place gave off. He also decided that they would need to get back on the trail soon. He suggested this to the others still inside and they agreed. Mark and Brad took some digital photos and video of the interior while Jesse bagged as many hair strands as he could find into a zip-close sandwich bag.

As they were walking through the door to the outside, Mark leaned over to Jesse and whispered, "Kelly's right. This place is pretty creepy. I don't know what's been living in here, but I've felt more comfortable reviewing revenue documents in front of a bunch of mafia types than standing around here."

Jesse looked surprised at Mark's off-hand comment, so Mark added some clarification. "My accounting firm sometimes represents some less-than-reputable clients in Detroit. I've spent many an hour sifting through receipts, invoices, and tax forms surrounded by pretty shady characters.

But like I said, at least then I knew who I was dealing with. Here, I just can't put my finger on it."

Jesse nodded in agreement to the point Mark had just made. He also realized that Mark might just have a little more backbone that he had first supposed. Jesse made a mental note that that might be important in the ensuing days.

Outside, Kelly was pacing and nervously smoking one of Brad's cigarettes. Though Jesse had seen Brad smoking a few times already, he had not seen Kelly smoke as much and had hoped that she would not.

"We need to be pretty infrequent with the smoking guys, or we'll be sending out scent signals the whole woods can smell a country mile away. That may actually help us, or it could send every animal in the forest scurrying away from us."

Kelly had no use for Jesse's reasoning. "Look man, I'm just a little freaked out right now. I think something's been watching me from out there in the trees."

"Like what? Did you see something?" Brad asked.

"No," Kelly answered, "but I can just feel it. You know what it's like when somebody's staring at you – you can just feel it."

"She's not the only one," Roy said. "I've felt it too, just in the few minutes I've been out here with her. And I could've sworn I heard movement in the woods. Could've been squirrels or something – I don't know. Still, it's kind of unsettling standing out here."

The group stood still for a while, listening for what Roy had described. They did not hear anything, and Kelly admitted that she no longer felt like she was being watched. While they were standing there, Jesse asked Brad, "Supposing this is that guy's shack, wouldn't we be at the edge of the Devil's Ridge?"

"What guy?" Brad asked "You mean that Wendell McClain who disappeared and was never heard from again?"

Jesse nodded and Brad checked the map. "Doesn't say anything about a Devil's Ridge on here, so I'm guessing that was just a local nickname given to it. But you can clearly see on the map that we're not too far from a pretty significant ridge rising up from the forest floor."

Jesse studied the map and saw what Brad was talking about. Before trying to find the ridge, they all agreed to move on and find a suitable place to camp while they still had daylight to work with. Kelly took one last drag from her cigarette, tossed it to the ground at the foot of the cabin's steps and smothered it with her boot.

*   *   *

The group moved from the shack and its small clearing back into the canopied forest. They hiked in a westerly direction again, searching for a suitable campsite. As they walked, Jesse would occasionally point out potential signs of bigfoot activity. Near the small trail could sometimes be seen more bows and arches like they had seen earlier in the day at the entrance of the big trail. Brad stopped them once to look at a curious site just off the trail. He pointed to a medium-sized tree, whose trunk had been damaged several feet off the ground. Brad walked up to the tree trunk to survey the tree's wound. The markings were about a foot above his head. He stood on his toes to get a better look.

"Come here, Jesse," he said, "and bring a flashlight."

Jesse pulled his flashlight from his bag and walked over to Brad. The late afternoon sun was not penetrating deeply into this part of the woods, and Brad needed the extra light to examine the destruction.

"Hold that light so it's shining on this spot here above my head," Brad instructed.

Jesse pointed the flashlight's beam at the damage while Brad peered at it and picked at it with his pocketknife.

"That's a bite wound, folks," Brad declared. "You can even see the teeth depressions in some spots."

Jesse stood back and looked at the deep gouge in the tree. The circumference of the bite was enormous. Considering this, and the height off the ground, Jesse asked Brad, "That's no squirrel looking for acorns, is it?"

"Nah," Brad agreed, "I'd say whatever did this was biting into the rotten tree trunk looking for grubs. I'm not seeing any claw marks, though, so I'm having trouble saying this could be a bear. Again, you're talking grizzly proportions for something that could just stand on its hind legs and take a chunk out of a tree almost seven feet off the ground."

By this time, the others were listening closely to Jesse and Brad's conversation. Mark and Roy were sizing up the tree damage while also videoing the scene for documentation. Mark spoke into the microphone as he filmed. "OK people," he said, "we're looking at evidence of a deep bite mark in this old tree trunk. Whatever left this has a mouth the size of a dinner plate and almost seven feet off the ground."

"All right guys, that's enough footage," Brad said as he pulled his backpack back on. "We don't want to run the camera batteries down before we get the solar panels put up for recharging. Besides, we need to get on the go to find a good campsite before dark."

* * *

After another hour of hiking and several stops for breaks and photographing more suspicious indications of a bigfoot presence in the area, the group arrived at a small clearing along the trail. Two massive oaks had fallen recently, creating an opening in the canopy above and room enough for a few small tents below. With the trail running right past the front of the clearing, there were thick woods to both sides and across the trail. Behind the campsite, a steep rocky outcropping jutted out over twenty feet above the ground and a steep ridge rose in the distance behind them.

Brad consulted the map again while they were checking out the area as a potential campsite. "Now I'm only guessing since this map's not labeled very good, but based on my GPS readings, we're pretty damn close to the bottom of this ridge here, which is significantly taller than any others close by on the map."

"The Devil's Ridge?" Jesse asked.

"I'd be willing to bet on it," Brad replied.

Jesse suggested, and Brad agreed, that this would be a good location to stay put for a while. It seemed like an ideal place from a strategic defensive view and some of Steve Akers' stories had mentioned this general area.

Jesse then instructed that they put their tents facing the curving trail, with their backs to the straight rock wall behind them. With this setup in the D-shaped clearing, they could see and hear anything on the trail, while having a slight sense of security that nothing could sneak in from behind. They placed the tents around a small spot they cleared for the campfire. Brad and Kelly erected their tent while Jesse enlisted Mark to help put up the tent they would be staying in for the next several days.

Roy filmed the coming-together of the campsite. "Here's where we'll be camping for the next couple of days," he said into the camera. "We've got shelter behind us and the trail clearing in front of us. Once we get the cameras and Brad's fancy sensors up, nothing's gonna get by here without us knowing." Roy turned the digital video camera around to film himself. He pointed at the lens, "For you folks back at home, get ready for a couple of days of nonstop nonaction as we sit here bored off our asses. The great white hunter has got us all involved in the grandest wild goose chase I've ever been on. I hope you viewers can appreciate the sheer stupidity of all this."

"Damn it Roy! Stop screwing around and lend us a hand," Brad yelled. "We still need help getting all this gear set up before dark."

Roy set the camera down and assisted Brad and Mark setting up the motion-sensing still and video cameras that would be tied in to the sensors around the perimeter of the campsite. Assuming they all worked and had enough power from the solar photovoltaic cells, the array would provide continuous monitoring of the trail running in front of the camp and out into the woods in every direction. Brad had also brought a thermal-imaging camera that could be viewed remotely. He had Roy set this on the rocky ledge behind the camp, resting a little over seven feet off the ground – as high as Roy could safely place it. It faced the campsite from the rear in order to capture any movement in and around the area. Though it could not see through the massive tree trunks of the forest, the thermal device could pick up body heat clearly through the dense tangled underbrush and detect such a presence when night vision and the naked eye could not.

While they were working on these projects, Jesse started to get dinner ready. The propane lantern cast just enough light for him to see what they were doing. Mark came over to help and heated up water over the campfire while Jesse gathered up enough dehydrated meals for the group. They poured the steaming water into the packages to heat up the prepackaged meals of spaghetti, lasagna, and even meatloaf. Kelly sat in her compact camp chair, watching all the activity. She was exhausted from the day's trekking. Though Jesse resented her unwillingness to help out, he decided that things were probably going just as smoothly without pressing her into service.

After Brad was satisfied with his camera setup and the motion detectors, they all sat down to eat. He talked excitedly as the waning evening light faded. Mark asked Brad and Jesse repeatedly about the strange signs and markers they had seen on the trail. Though neither had sure answers, this did not temper Mark's interest. Unfortunately, it left Roy – who had been listening to the conversation – to supply his own answers. His cynicism about the expedition and the creeping jealousy he felt toward Brad did not block feelings of concern and nervousness from emerging as he took note of the discussion.

The mood around the campfire grew more and more tense as the evening wore on. Kelly lit up another cigarette to calm her nerves. Jesse shot her a disapproving look. "This is only my second of the day," she snapped at him.

"That's two too many," he snapped back. "Your secondhand smoke's gonna get us in trouble – and I'm not talking about lung cancer either."

Brad spoke up. "Give it a rest, Jesse. We haven't seen any monsters lurking in the bushes just yet." Brad kicked the ground at his feet, picked up a rock and threw it angrily into the darkness. "I mean, I'll admit that I've been excited all day looking at these possible clues and stuff, but we need something more concrete than rock piles and twisted trees."

Brad stared at Jesse with an accusatory glare. Jesse knew that Brad expected Jesse to share responsibility for this expedition and its success. However, instead of joining in the fray, he put his head down and finished eating his beef stew.

Not getting a reply from Jesse, Brad stood up. "Come on," he barked at Kelly. "We're hitting the hay. One of you guys figure out who's staying watch tonight. Or, divvy it up how you like, as long as someone's awake."

"Aye, aye captain," Roy said sardonically.

Brad did not acknowledge Roy's comment. He simply ushered Kelly in front of him as they walked to the tent and climbed in. Roy stood up and watched as they zipped up the tent's door and sealed themselves inside. "What a jerk. I'm starting to regret coming on this shindig."

"Look," Jesse interrupted, "It's getting a little tense around here. Maybe we should all go to bed and get some good sleep tonight. Maybe we're all just a little crabby."

"Yeah, crabby – that's it." Roy stood up and grabbed his crotch. "I've got your crabby right here." Without another word, he walked over to the three-person tent and got inside.

"I don't even want to know what's going on there," Jesse said.

"Well, I think it has to do with the girl in Brad's tent," Mark replied with a smile. "I can't remember a golf game yet where she hasn't been discussed in some form or fashion. Of course, that's probably what they say about me and Vanessa."

"Vanessa's your fiancée?"

"Yeah." Mark paused for a while. "She thought I was crazy for coming on this trip. Was sure that I'd always hated camping and had been afraid of the woods. I don't know where she got that idea, but it's clearly not accurate. I mean, I'm out here, right?"

"You got that right," Jesse answered. He reached into his jacket and pulled out the plastic flask of bourbon that had been stashed in his backpack. He and Mark sat around the campfire, talking softly and occasionally taking a sip from the flask. An hour passed quickly, and soon it was almost ten o'clock. Having forgotten Brad's instructions for someone keeping watch, Jesse suggested going to bed soon so they could be fresh in the morning. Mark stood up to stretch and yawn. He stopped in mid-stretch and dropped back into his chair reflexively as a long, mournful howl erupted from deep in the woods. The two men sat in silence for a few seconds. Mark was getting ready to ask Jesse about the noise when an answering call sounded from the east. The howl was more like a scream – a sharp, piercing scream from a frightened woman. However, as the shrill scream trailed off, the voice got deeper and deeper, and the call ended in what could only be described as a growl – a growl loud enough to be heard throughout the forest.

Mark grabbed the flask and took a deep drink. "Please tell me that was a coyote, Jesse."

Jesse shook his head doubtfully and said cynically, "Well to make a sound like that, it could've been a coyote hopped up on crank and hollerin' through a megaphone." Jesse shook his head again and looked down to the ground. He mindlessly traced in the dirt with the stick he had been using to poke the fire.

"Oh come on, what's that supposed to mean?" Mark asked.

Instead of answering, Jesse held up his hand in a gesture motioning to be silent. Next he put his finger to his lip to make sure his meaning was understood. Then he cupped his hand around his ear and pointed out to the forest. Mark caught his meaning and strained to listen to the surrounding woods. The whistle was almost inaudible at first, but then pierced clearly through the dense forest. Mark's eyes shot open. "Is that somebody whistling to us," he asked excitedly.

"Shut up and listen closer," Jesse scolded. "That's not a somebody, it's a something."

The whistle was not a clean sound, but had other tones mixed in. The next time it sounded, they could both make out a series of hoots and grunts that accompanied the loud whistle. Again to the east, an answer called out. The same scream from earlier tore through the night silence. The penetrating shriek sent shivers down Jesse's spine. He turned to Mark, who looked pale and whose jacket cuffs were pulled back enough to reveal wrists covered in goose bumps. "Mark," Jesse whispered, "look at the goose pimples on your arms."

With his eyes still fixed on the forest in front of them, Mark said out of the corner of his mouth, "You should see the hairs on your neck."

In truth, Jesse's neck hair was all standing on end. He ran his hand down the back of his neck to feel his raised hackles.

"Something tells me that's not an owl either," Mark said quietly to Jesse.

"I know what those noises sound like to me," Jesse cautioned. "I've listened to plenty of bigfoot recordings that sound dead-on like what we've just heard."

Jesse realized that his words had made Mark look even more worried. "I'll take the first watch," he offered. "After all that carrying on, I don't think I could sleep a wink right now. You go on and get some rest and I'll get somebody up in a couple hours to relieve me."

Mark readily agreed to the plan. Before he left for the tent, though, he asked Jesse, "You got enough wood to keep this fire going?"

Jesse nodded and reached over to his backpack and unstrapped a shotgun. He laid it across his legs and settled into his chair. "I've also got my thunderstick chief, so don't worry about me."

"You can get me up first if you want," Mark offered. "I don't think I'm going to get much sleep anyway."

* * *

Jesse dutifully sat watch until after midnight. The forest had grown quiet and the period of normalcy lulled him into a relaxed, sleepy state. He nodded occasionally, catching himself and pinching his skin to stay awake. Eventually, though, the day's exertion and excitement caught up to him and his chin fell to his chest. He slept for over an hour in this position, until he suddenly jerked awake. He quickly rubbed his eyes and scanned the trees with his flashlight, trying to find what had roused him from his slumber. He saw nothing and put the flashlight down. He settled back into the chair and zipped his jacket up tight against the cool night air.

Jesse's eyes were drooping again when a loud twig snap forced him to attention. The noise had come from just beyond the tree line on the other side of the game trail in front of the camp. Jesse reached for the high-power spotlight to get a better view of the area. He panned the strong beam across the trees. Despite the intensity of the beam, the light did not penetrate far into the thick forest. Then Jesse thought he saw a quick blur of movement. He stopped his scanning and focused on where he had seen the swift motion. At the same instant, a strange whistling noise came from the woods and high into the sky above Jesse. He took his eyes off the tree line and pointed the spotlight skyward – just in time to see a softball-sized rock hurdling towards him.

Jesse watched in amazement as the stone sailed overhead and landed behind him, right next to one of the camp chairs. The rock thudded heavily into the soft ground with a thump. Jesse then spun around quickly to face the forest in front of him as something large barreled down the game trail in front of the camp. He swung his spotlight to shine on the direction, but was not fast enough to see what had made the commotion. However, both motion-activated cameras flashed as they recorded the event and the perimeter sensors began beeping loudly. Jesse jumped out of his chair and panned the tree line with his spotlight. All he saw were tree trunks and darkness.

"What's all the ruckus?" Brad asked as he unzipped his tent to step outside. "Did you set those sensors off by knocking something over?"

Jesse put a finger to his lips to silence Brad and then motioned to the forest. Brad understood and stopped talking. He walked up to the campfire and whispered to Jesse, "What's going on? Did you see something?"

Jesse turned on a smaller flashlight to illuminate the now-imbedded rock. "Rock came out of the sky, things moving around on the perimeter of the camp. The trail cameras flashed so we might've gotten some pictures."

At this time, Mark exited his tent as well. "What's all the whispering about?" he asked quietly as he walked up to Jesse and Brad.

"Something just threw a rock at Jesse then ran away," Brad answered.

"Let's check it out on the cameras." He went back to his tent, grabbed his pack, and pulled out a small device used to view the trail camera images. He and Jesse cautiously walked to the edge of the clearing to the cameras. Brad reset the motion sensors to stop the beeping and rearm them. He then plugged the viewing device into each camera and downloaded the images. They walked back to the campfire area and sat down so that all three could look at the pictures.

The first photo showed a brown blur of something moving in front of the camera within a foot or two of its position. The picture from the second camera showed an almost identical image.

"Those cameras are attached to trees at a height of five feet off the ground," Brad said. "So whatever passed in front of them was at least five feet tall, and if you look at the picture, you can tell that the top of whatever it was is well above the camera's height."

"That doesn't rule out a deer," Brad continued. "We might be looking at the upper neck of a big buck." Brad thought about his statement for a moment, then added, "Well, maybe a really, really big buck."

Jesse had been studying the time and date encoded on each picture. "Look at this guys," he said, "The blur passed both camera positions roughly within one second of each other on that trail. I'd say that those two positions are probably forty, fifty feet apart maybe. We'll compromise and say forty-five. That means that something was trucking through here and made it past forty-five feet of game trail in one second. Now that includes a lot of estimation, but that's really moving."

"How fast is that?" Brad asked.

"About thirty miles an hour," Mark answered quickly.

Both Brad and Jesse looked at Mark in amazement.

He shrugged. "I work with numbers all day long. It becomes second nature to a nerd like me. I'm just doing it in my head, but I come up with something like thirty miles an hour."

"Again, that doesn't rule out a deer. Even a bear can reach that speed on a short sprint," Brad said. "But whatever it was, it was freaking big and freaking fast. Besides, last time I checked, deer aren't necessarily known for picking up large rocks and tossing them at people."

Mark spoke up, "What about that big, rocky ridge that rises up steeply behind us. Maybe the rock dislodged from that and tumbled down till it hit the ground."

"I thought Jesse said it came from the direction in front of him – from the woods in front of us," Brad questioned.

"Well shit," Jesse replied, getting frustrated. "I was sleepy and it all happened real fast. I'm not sure what I saw anymore."

"Ok, take it easy, Jesse," Brad counseled. "Why don't we try to get some sleep. Let's not tell the others about all this since we're not even sure what happened. Mark, what about having you stay watch for a while, since you're up anyway?"

Mark definitely did not want to stay watch after listening to Jesse and looking at the blurred camera images. Stronger still, though, was his desire to prove himself to his camping partners. He grabbed some warmer clothes from the tent and headed to the campfire area. Jesse handed over the spotlight and the shotgun as Mark settled in to the chair Jesse had been using to keep watch. Brad and Jesse were both so tired, and Mark so seemingly eager, that they were more than happy to have him stay watch. Brad knew Mark was not overly familiar with firearms, but reasoned that the shotgun was at least a fairly user-friendly gun for a novice. After getting a quick safety lesson from Brad, Mark insisted that he was smart enough to figure out how to pull the trigger and which end the shot came out of.

* * *

After Brad returned to his tent, he explained the situation to Kelly, who wondered what he had been doing for so long. Brad crawled back in his sleeping bag and promptly fell back asleep. Though he was exhausted, Brad slept fitfully, tossing and turning in his sleeping bag. His light sleep led to frequent and vivid dreams. Though the dreams began as a mixture of unconnected sights and sounds thrown together in a strange collage, the image sequences racing through Brad's mind soon became more crisp and coherent. As the dream developed, Brad could see the campsite out of his peripheral vision. Ahead he could see the thick forest of tall trees. It was pitch dark – the woods were enveloped by an overcast night with no stars or moon and no campfire or lantern to provide light. It was so dark that Brad could only see blackness in the voids between the barely visible vertical grey of the tree trunks.

Yet, somehow, he detected movement. He could make out three dark shapes moving through the forest. They were almost as black as the surrounding night. Their movements were unnerving as they strode easily through the shadows with a strikingly human-like gait. It scared Brad to see them walking through the darkness so easily when he could barely see them. In fact, for a second he questioned whether he saw them at all.

Then, the three black figures moved again as the dream progressed – one near, one off-center, and one farther back and almost indistinguishable against the dark forest. They were moving at will and Brad had no power to foresee their next step or to prevent it. He had an instant desire to flee away from the beings pacing between the trees. Yet, he could not move. Brad looked down at his own feet – alarmed that he was still standing put despite his fear. He tried to lift a foot up so he could run away, but his feet and legs did not obey his commands. Brad was nearing panic as the black shapes kept walking through the darkness.

When Brad returned his focus to his feet in an effort to will them to move, he saw his father lying on the ground a short distance away. His father appeared motionless and perhaps dead, but a familiar voice filtered through the air anyway.

"Come on Brad," the distant voice urged, "you've got to get moving. Don't you remember what happened before?"

"I'm trying, Dad," Brad pleaded, on the verge of tears. "I'm trying."

He stared intensely at his feet and focused hard on lifting them up but they would not move. Suddenly, he saw his father get up and stand, dusting himself off.

"OK, Brad, you stay put. I'm going to go into those woods and see what these things are." He pointed to the mysterious humanoid shapes that moved stealthily through the forest even as they were being pointed to.

"No, Dad," Brad protested, now fully crying. "Don't go in there by yourself."

Suddenly, Brad was awake. Kelly was lightly shaking him. "Brad," she asked, "are you still asleep?"

He mumbled a reply, still disoriented.

"Were you having that dream again? You were kind of whimpering and you were thrashing your legs back and forth like crazy. Are you all right?"

Brad did not answer immediately as he was still trying to figure out where he was. "Yeah," he finally said. "I'm awake. And yes, it was the same dream – same as I've been having since I was a kid."

Brad was quiet again, still trying to shake the images from his mind. "But, there were a few things different I guess. It didn't take place back on that mountain in Utah. It was here, and now. And I wasn't a little kid anymore – I was the age I am now."

"Could you move around?"

"No. That *was* the same."

"Was your father in it?"

"Yeah, I already told you it was pretty much the same," Brad said in an irritated manner. He was silent for a while. "This time I could see the creatures moving around, though. They were fast, and they kind of walked like people. That freaked me out a little."

"Well, can you get back to sleep?" Kelly asked before falling back asleep herself.

"I'll try," he replied. Brad clutched his sleeping bag tightly and thrust himself further down into its warm interior. He kept his eyes open for as long as he could, staring at the cold, dark ceiling of his tent. After his dream, he did not feel safe closing his eyes, so he forced them open as long as he could. Eventually, though, the toll of the day took over and his heavy lids drew closed.

* * *

Jesse had fallen asleep shortly after hearing Brad's quick firearms instruction lesson to Mark. After some frustrating maneuvering, he finally settled into a comfortable position in his sleeping bag. At 3:30 in the morning, though, Jesse jolted out of his slumber after the deafening blast of a gunshot sliced through the nighttime silence. He looked over at Roy, who was sitting bolt upright in his sleeping bag, with his eyes wide open. They both climbed quickly out of their bags and out of the tent.

Jesse could see Brad and Kelly getting out of their tent when he switched on his flashlight. Jesse then shined the light toward the barely-glowing campfire to see Mark sitting in one of the chairs. He trotted over to Mark, who was still staring straight out at the woods with wide eyes and breathing short, quick pants of breath exhaling vapory clouds in the cool night air. Jesse also noticed smoke rising from the end of the shotgun Mark held.

Without taking his eyes off the woods, Mark spoke to Jesse in low hushed tones, "They're here."

"Ok Mark," Brad said as he approached from behind. "I want you to slowly put the safety back on the gun and cautiously just hand it over to me when you feel like it."

Mark did not move, so Brad reached over and pried the shotgun out of Mark's tight grip. This action finally snapped Mark out of his gaze and he took his eyes off the forest in front of him. He turned to look at the group now assembled around him. "Right out there in front of us," he tried to explain, "the eyes … they were huge." He stopped for a moment as he tried to put his experience into words.

"Come on, Mark, spit it out," Brad ordered impatiently. "What did you see?"

"The eyes," Mark continued, "two sets of them. Right out there." Mark pointed to the empty, dark woods beyond the clearing. "The eyes were huge, like baseball-sized." He then quietly added, "And red."

Roy did not like the sound of that, and the expression on Mark's face was unnerving to view. "Did you say 'red'?" Roy asked. Then he turned to Brad. "What exactly are we talking about here – some kind of demons or something?"

"Now hold on there Roy, just slow down," Jesse interrupted. He leaned over Mark. "Think hard for a minute, Mark," he said, "were the eyes themselves red, or could they have been catching some red or orange light from the campfire and reflecting it back?"

"Yeah, I guess that's possible," Mark answered. "Hell, I don't really know. But they were definitely big, and quite a ways up off the ground. Two sets of eyes, maybe ten, fifteen feet apart – and swaying."

"Swaying?" Roy asked in disbelief.

"Yeah, it seemed strange at first, like maybe I was seeing things. But I rubbed my eyes, looked down at the ground, then back at the woods and they were still there, just kind of moving from side to side. That's when I fired the gun. After that, they were gone." Mark paused for a moment. "I don't think I hit anything. I'm not even sure I was aimed in the right direction. I was pretty worked up at that point."

"Well now you've got us all worked up," Roy complained.

Jesse was personally worried about Mark's descriptions. Jesse had often read reports or heard first-hand accounts of bigfoot creatures exhibiting swaying or rocking back-and-forth in apparent irritation. This activity frequently led to intimidation behavior or some other attempt to get the human intruder out of the creature's territory.

Perhaps more disturbing to Jesse was that Mark had seen two sets of eyes. Had he observed the eyes of a single individual, this would be exciting, if not cause for some concern. The presence of two of these animals, given what little Jesse had heard of their social behavior, could suggest more members of a larger group nearby. They were not simply dealing with a lone wanderer. While this certainly increased their chance for seeing and even hunting one of these creatures, it also certainly increased their chances of getting involved in a very dangerous situation.

With these thoughts in mind, Jesse walked back over to Mark to ask him a few more questions. Mark declined, however, stating that he was so tired that he was no longer sure what he saw, if anything. Brad suggested that somebody else should take watch for the rest of the night so that Mark could try to get some rest.

While Mark was walking back to the tent and Brad was trying to get a volunteer to watch over the camp for the rest of the night, Jesse stopped Mark for one more question.

"I already told you, Jesse – I'm so tired that I don't really know what I saw anymore."

"I know Mark, but it was the expression on your face when I first came over to you after the gunshot. That look in your eyes told me that you at least thought you saw something."

Mark did not respond at first. Then, quietly, he said, "Jesse, I know I didn't see an owl, that's for sure. I also know I've never felt a fear like that before. It was deep, like almost in my stomach. It wasn't like any nervousness before a test, or even the anxiety I felt before asking Vanessa to marry me. It was something else."

Mark trailed off as he was searching for the right word to use.

"Something innate, instinctual?" Jesse offered. "Something that lets you know right away that you're not just looking at an owl?"

Mark breathed out a sigh and did not answer Jesse. He shook his head and then crawled inside the tent.

* * *

Hearing no offers to take watch, Brad reluctantly volunteered to sit up during the night if he could get some help stoking the campfire back to life.

Roy headed back to the tent to join Mark. Jesse and Brad gathered some firewood and tended to the fire.

After tossing on some pine cones and dried pine needles, the fire quickly blazed into a steady, soaring flame. Jesse piled on a couple of thick logs to increase the burn time of the fire. On top of this, Brad tossed an armful of more pine needles and small twigs. The fire smoldered and choked under the new fuel, then burst into a tall, bright, roaring pillar of fire. It even illuminated the surrounding trees during the quick-lived flame-up. After the pine cones and needles burned off and the flame returned to a normal size, Jesse was convinced that the fire was steady and solid enough to last for a few more hours. As he turned to head to his tent, a loud noise halted him in mid-step.

From far into the woods a deep resonating call crescendoed into a deafening, bass-filled roar that lasted for several seconds. A more shrill, high-pitched scream answered from the east. A few seconds of silence passed and then two sets of rapid-succession hammering noises responded to each other from the same general areas as the calls had originated.

Jesse listened in fascination and fear. "Tree knocks," he said aloud. "I've only heard that once before. They say it's a kind of signal or communication between the creatures, knocking heavy branches or logs against the trunks of trees to make the noise. Sometimes the bigfoot will respond to each other from completely different areas of a forest when the conditions are right."

He turned to say something else to Brad, but stopped when he saw the expression on Brad's face. Brad had never heard the tree knocks before, but he instantly recognized the roar and scream that had cut through the night. His face had gone white – drained of blood, and chills shot down his spine. Brad identified the eerie, unnerving call as nearly identical to the one he had heard as a young child shortly before his father's death in the snowy mountains of Utah, and it matched a version of the scream that played routinely in his dreams.

Brad strained to hear any follow up noises, but the forest had gone quiet. After a few moments of silence, his adrenaline levels subsided and he shook himself free of the paralyzing daze he had been in. He finally looked over to Jesse, who appeared to have been waiting for a reply of some sort from Brad.

"You staying up with me?" Brad asked. "If so, let's keep this fire going good the rest of the night."

"Uh, yeah, I guess I'll stay up," Jesse slowly answered, still concerned with the strange manner that had come over Brad. "You OK? You look like you've seen a ghost."

"Or heard one," Brad mumbled quietly.

Jesse did not catch Brad's comment. After a moment or two of silence, he observed, "First time hearing something like that can be quite a shock."

"It wasn't my first time hearing that scream," Brad said, still with a far-off stare.

Jesse decided not to pursue the conversation any further. He reached over and picked up two pine cones from a small pile next to the fire. He tossed them at the base of the blaze and they fueled the flames even higher. The bright light and warmth from the fire put him a little more at ease as far as their safety. It did not, however, relieve any of his apprehension about the sudden change in Brad's demeanor.

* * *

DAY THREE

After a few hours of calm, dawn broke over the camp with a welcoming splash of sunshine darting through the forest canopy and illuminating the clearing the expedition had staked out as its base camp. Jesse and Brad found themselves still sitting in their camp chairs, facing the woods. Jesse stretched as he slowly awakened. He rubbed his eyes and scratched the stubble on his face. "Sure could go for some coffee," he said in a coughing mutter. Then he kicked Brad's chair. "Up and at 'em," he said hoarsely. "We made it through the night."

Brad wheeled around in confusion, then as his memory resurfaced he settled down. "I guess we didn't have any more visitors last night?" he asked.

Jesse shook his head as he stood up, "None that we know of anyway. I'm pretty sure I sacked out about an hour before dawn. I could just make out the faintest bit of blue spreading across the sky before I finally fell asleep. I guess you caught some winks too."

"Well, I tried to fight it, but things got so calm I just drifted off." Brad stood up too and poked the embers and coals of the campfire with a stick. After straightening up, arching his back and stretching his hands over his head, Brad said, "It's so chilly and damp here in the mornings. It takes me at least half the day to get the kinks out of my back." He picked up a small stick and tossed it at the tent holding Mark and Roy. "Time to get up you lazy-asses," he barked. He then turned to Jesse and said, "I'll go get Kelly up, she can be tough to get going in the morning."

Roy struggled out of his tent like an insect emerging from a cocoon. He shivered and pulled a wool toboggan tightly down over his ears. He walked up to the campfire and set a small backpacking stove down on the ground next to Jesse, and put a small pot on top of it. "Want some coffee?" he asked.

"More than just about anything right now," Jesse replied.

Roy gestured toward the direction of Brad's tent. "What's his deal this morning? What's he planning, another big day of traipsing through the woods?"

"I don't know," Jesse said as he leaned over the pot of already-boiling water. "I don't think he's one to stay put, though. He probably considers himself as a man of action and will want us to go along with that."

"Shit man, from last night it sounded like those things know we're here," Roy said.

"So, you're saying now you believe they exist?" Jesse asked with a grin.

"I'm not saying anything till I see one," Roy answered, "but I will admit that there's been a lot of strange stuff going on that I can't quite explain. Hell, that's enough mystery for me. I've had my spooky camping fun already. I don't need anymore. Besides, it's fucking freezing out here in the mornings."

As Roy continued to complain, Brad surfaced through his tent door, with Kelly following sleepily behind him. He picked up the stick he had thrown earlier and whacked the other tent several times to wake Mark up. "What do you two have in store for us today?" he asked as he approached the campfire area.

Jesse was in the middle of pouring a cup of coffee, so he waited till that task had been accomplished before answering. "Well, Roy and I were talking about just taking it easy today. Seems like everybody's sore and tired and based on Mark's possible visualization and the screaming and carrying on last night – well, they know where we're at. I think we've got a much better chance of running into them here rather than trying to find them out in the woods, their home turf."

An image instantly flickered through Brad's mind recalling his father desperately trying to follow a mysterious creature up the steep hills of the Uinta Mountains as he remembered the last time he had been involved in tracking an unknown animal deep into its 'home turf.'

"All right," he finally said. But I don't like the idea of sitting around here doing nothing. That seems like wasted time to me. We should at least search the perimeter of the camp for footprints or other sign."

Jesse was visibly annoyed with Brad's insistence on leaving the campsite. After a long sip of coffee, though, he finally surrendered. "OK, I'm willing to look around the immediate camp area for anything out of the ordinary. We can take pictures, video, whatever you want. But that's where I draw the line."

Brad agreed to limit the search to the area immediately surrounding the campsite. After a quick breakfast and some camp coffee, Brad and Jesse set off to scrutinize the perimeter of the camp while Mark, Roy, and Kelly stayed at the campsite.

Brad first checked on his motion detector alarms. They had not sounded during the night when Mark had had his sighting. Brad quickly realized that the solar charging system was not creating enough juice to run the sensors. The constant shade of the surrounding forest simply did not permit enough light in for efficient solar charging.

"Well, these have already crapped out on us. They're totally useless," he said to Jesse.

"I imagine they won't be the last thing to prove so, either," Jesse replied. "Especially the longer we stay out here."

They extended their search past the immediate perimeter of the camp. Their exploration yielded very little results, partly because they were not exactly sure what to look for. To the east of the campsite, though, they found a small creek. They followed the tiny drainage as it gradually circled around the campsite and ended in a low, boggy area. Brad warned Jesse to stick to the high, rocky areas surrounding the bog because of the potential of getting stuck in the thick, swampy mud. As they edged along the rim of the bog, Brad stopped suddenly and motioned to Jesse to come over to him.

Right at Brad's foot, and almost under it, was a deep depression in the soft earth. Brad gingerly stepped back to avoid disturbing the track as Jesse came closer to examine it. The footprint was almost two inches deep into the soil. By comparison, Brad's print next to it barely even left an impression. Jesse leaned over and studied the track, guessing its length at about eighteen inches. It was a flat, elongated, elliptical shape that ended with what clearly looked like four large toe prints. Jesse took a few pictures, including close-ups with his measuring tape next to the print for comparison.

Jesse stood up to look ahead for the next print. Almost five feet in front of the right foot print that Brad had found was the corresponding left footprint. He and Brad were both amazed at the stride length between the two prints. The left print was not in as good shape, though. Brad said that its muddled appearance was probably due to the foot twisting upon impact, as if pivoting.

"He's changed directions," Brad announced.

"Yeah," Jesse agreed, "right towards our camp."

*   *   *

As soon as Brad and Jesse had left, Mark settled into one of the camp chairs to tend to the fire. Kelly found a fallen log near the edge of the clearing and sat down. She was busy doing something when Roy walked over.

Roy stopped in surprise as he realized why Kelly was positioned in a certain way on the log. "Whoa, hey – a little warning would have helped."

"Give me a break Roy," Kelly answered after getting herself re-situated. "At least I had the courtesy to get to the edge of camp. If I could stand around and pee like you guys, I definitely would. Believe me, it'd be a whole lot easier than having to find a spot like this each time. You boys just have no idea."

After finishing her business, Kelly stood up and walked over to Roy. "Let me borrow some of that waterless soap you have. I know you carry some around in your pocket."

Roy pulled out a small bottle of sanitizing gel for Kelly. As she used the fluid to wash her hands, she noticed that Roy was staring at her intently.

"What?" she asked, annoyed.

"You look hot," he said while breaking into a grin.

Kelly ran a hand through her mussed hair and straightened her wrinkled shirt. "Don't be an ass, Roy."

"I'm not kidding," he protested. "It's a good look for you."

Kelly playfully shoved Roy and he caught her wrist. He pulled her close to his chest. "Come on, let's get out of here. I'm pretty sure I can find our way back to that farm. We could be back in town by this afternoon. Let's get out of this whole horrible situation."

Before Kelly could respond, Mark called out to them from his seat next to the campfire. "Hey you two, did you hear that?"

Roy put his hand to his forehead. "Christ, what now?"

Kelly laughed and whispered to Roy, "He probably scared himself with his own imagination. I'm sure it's nothing."

Regardless, she and Roy walked over to Mark.

"Listen close," he said.

It did not take long before they all heard the noise that Mark had first detected. It was quiet at first, then quite clear – a loud "whoop" or "hoop" called out from the woods opposite from the direction that Brad and Jesse had headed.

"That's not Brad or Jesse," Mark said, "they went into the forest on the other side. I wonder if they're hearing this."

A few moments later, a small shower of pebbles and rocks landed on the campsite, sounding like hail as the stones hit the ground and camping gear. Roy and Kelly ducked behind the chair Mark sat in. Most of the pebbles fell harmlessly to the ground, but a rock struck one of their backpacking lanterns, shattering the glass. Kelly stood up after the rock shower ended and had walked over to the lantern to make sure it still worked, which it did.

Roy was still standing behind Mark when a second volley of rocks flew from the woods to the left of the camp. Simultaneously, a handful of larger stones came flying at a higher speed from the right. One of these rocks hit Mark square in the leg, right below his knee. He yelled in pain and Kelly screamed in reaction.

*   *   *

Brad had found the second set of prints without much trouble. They were not nearly as distinguishable, as they emerged from an area thick with fallen pine needles and other forest litter. Jesse attempted to measure a few of the vague impressions. The measurements would not be as exact as the clearer, larger print, but provided an estimated track size of approximately fifteen to sixteen inches long.

"I don't know if you agree," Brad said, "but it looks like this smaller one joined up with the bigger one here." He pointed to an area next to a sprawling rhododendron. "Then smaller guy falls right in step with the bigger one, but hanging back about a foot or two."

Jesse admitted that he could not really see all of that in the few, faint impressions, but conceded that Brad had a lot more tracking experience than he. Brad said, "Well, why don't we follow these tracks into the woods right in front of us, it leads back toward the camp anyway."

"That's a scary thought," Jesse muttered to himself.

They pushed their way through the thick underbrush and tried to follow the meandering trail tracks. They busted through tangled rhododendrons and ducked occasionally under low-lying tree limbs. At times, Brad wondered how such supposedly tall creatures could navigate through the tight, cluttered understory, noting that it might require getting down on all fours to get through some spots.

Suddenly, they found themselves in a small clearing. Branches had been broken on surrounding bushes and trees, and the groundcover was trampled absolutely flat. The clearing was circular, with a fairly even diameter of about ten feet.

"Well, now," Jesse said, "this looks like a cozy little bedding area doesn't it?"

As they studied the plant debris, looking for hairs or tracks, a yell and simultaneous scream shot through the air.

"Did you hear that?" Brad asked with a mixture of excitement and fear in his voice. Before Jesse could respond, though, Brad had realized something. "That's Kelly," he shouted as they looked in the direction of the scream. He sprang instantly to his feet in order to head toward the camp.

Jesse did not move at first. He was too busy looking at his surroundings. He had discovered that they were only about a hundred yards from the camp, and could actually see the tops of their tents and smoke curling up from the campfire quite well.

"Fascinating," Jesse said to himself. "We could sit here all day with a clear view of the camp without them having the slightest idea we were here."

Brad turned around to grab Jesse. "Save the observations 'til we get there," Brad replied edgily. "Let's get moving."

* * *

It took Brad and Jesse a few minutes to bushwhack their way to the clearing. The mid-morning sun illuminated a disconcerting scene when the two searchers arrived at the campsite. Roy and Kelly were standing over Mark, who lay on the ground next to one of the camp chairs, clutching his leg in agony. As they checked on Mark, Kelly recounted the events of the past few minutes. Jesse explained that he and Brad had followed some footprints that led to an observation site or bedding area or perhaps both.

Brad helped ease Mark back into the camp chair. He then knelt down to feel Mark's leg. The impact zone below his knee was already inflamed and swollen with bruising. He decided that it probably was not broken, though Mark complained of shooting pain when Brad tried to straighten it.

"It's hard to tell with all this swelling," Brad said as he stood up. "I think he'll be fine after a while, but he may not be able to put much weight on it."

"Fine?" Mark asked incredulously.

Brad ignored the comment, "Come on Mark, let's get you situated where you can elevate that leg a little."

As Brad reached down to help Mark up, he noticed something out of the corner of his eye. He looked up to see a fist-sized stone sailing through the air in a high arc, only to come hurtling down toward the campsite. With its weight and speed on the way down, the stone easily tore through the thin mesh at the top of one of the tents and crashed into something inside.

Brad quickly abandoned Mark, grabbed his large backpack and pulled out the Romanian SAR-I, which he had been hoping would not be needed. He unfolded the stock, slapped in a magazine, and began firing indiscriminately into the woods. The heavy sound of the AK-47 derivative filled the woods with noise as the semi-automatic spewed out round upon round of ammunition. Bark and leaves went flying as most of the shots bounced off of, or imbedded into, nearby trees. Brad did not stop firing until the magazine was empty.

Jesse had been yelling at him the whole time. When the echoes of the gunfire finally subsided, Jesse's voice could be heard. "Knock it off," he screamed, "before you get one of us shot. You're not doing a damn thing but wasting bullets."

Brad coolly ejected the spent magazine, folded the rifle stock, and set the weapon down. "Well, I only had twenty in the mag anyways. Besides, that should stop the rock-throwing for a while."

Roy stood still with a shocked look on his face. He finally muttered, "This is fucking nuts. Fucking nuts. We've got who-knows-what out there in the woods, and Rambo here firing off bullets like crazy – and I don't know which one I'm more scared of. Dude, Brad, get control of yourself man."

Brad began to protest Roy's characterization, but Roy cut him off before he could speak.

"We should all be getting out of here," Roy continued. He turned to Kelly, "Kelly?" he asked, "what do you think?"

"Hold on there, Roy," Brad shouted. "You're not the one calling the shots around here. Nobody's going anywhere right now."

Brad had always considered himself as the most integral part of this expedition, and his anger rose as his ego took a bruising listening to Roy's pleadings to Kelly. "Or you know what, asshole," he said to Roy, "go ahead and leave. All you've done so far is criticize everything. What help have you been?"

Roy did not respond at first. He shook his head and muttered to himself as he studied the group of ragged, frightened individuals. "You guys are all crazy to stay out here. We've only been camping about three days and you're already looking worn down and broke. With things getting worse each day, I can't believe you'd want to stay for more."

Roy looked pleadingly at Kelly for some support. She turned her eyes from his gaze and looked at the ground. No one replied to Roy's comments. A long period of silence ensued and finally, with a look of acquiescence, Roy declared, "OK, fine, if no one's sane enough to go with me, then I'm staying put too. I'm not hiking back by myself." Roy turned to face Brad, "But Brad, you better chill out man before you end up getting us all hurt. This whole trip was your goddamn great idea in the first place, so don't screw it up now by shooting one of us."

Roy walked away from the group and crawled in his tent. After a few moments of quiet, Brad set down his rifle. "Let's get this place cleaned up a bit and make sure all our gear is intact and accounted for."

Glad for something to take their minds off the threatening presence in the woods and Brad's erratic behavior, they all focused on looking busy and tidying up the campsite.

* * *

A little after noon, Jesse finally broke the silence by asking if anyone wanted lunch. Nobody had spoken much since Roy had retired to his tent. Mark was still dealing with the pain in his legs and had taken several pain medication pills from the first aid kit. Brad stalked around the camp, checking on the gear and pointing his gun toward the surrounding trees occasionally. After Jesse mentioned lunch, Brad finally spoke up.

"Look guys," he said, "let's all have some lunch and that'll make us feel better. I mean, it's a nice sunny day, we've got plenty of food and water, a pretty good supply of ammo, and most of our equipment still works. Yes, Mark's got a little bruise on his knee. But that shouldn't be enough to unravel this whole group. No need to be so glum everybody." Brad's pep talk did little to raise the spirits of Jesse or Mark, who were sitting closest to the barely-smoking campfire.

Roy had emerged from the tent upon hearing talk about eating lunch. Brad then turned to Kelly, "How 'bout it Kelly?" he asked, "why don't you have some lunch. You and Roy can have a nice big meal and you'll feel better." Kelly hesitantly got up and walked to where the kitchen gear had been stowed. "There you go," Brad said, trying to urge them along. "Come on Jesse, stoke that fire up a little and let's eat together. If we can just keep up our routine and vigilance, this will all turn out just fine."

"What are you talking about?" Roy asked in a provoking tone. "Look at this place – I don't think it could get much worse."

"Come on Roy," Brad pleaded, "aren't you in the least bit excited by all this activity? Most people don't even think that bigfoot exists and here we are a clear shot away from the goal."

"Wait a minute," Roy interrupted. "Whose goal? What goal? I don't know what it is driving you to stay out here, but it sure doesn't interest me." Roy was seething at this point. "And we haven't really seen anything that would change *my* mind – it could be a bunch of crazy hillbillies out there tossing rocks at us for all we know."

At this point, Mark was tired of listening to the back-and-forth between Roy and Brad. He tried to stand up, but in doing so, twisted his bruised leg while trying to keep weight off of it. He shouted with pain and slumped back into his chair, grabbing at his leg and moaning.

Jesse stood up and whispered to Brad, "We've got to shut him up. If these creatures are out there in the woods watching and listening to us, we don't want to send them a written invitation to come on in and mess with us right now."

"I don't know," Brad said as he mulled over that idea. "If Mark's noise-making does lure them in, that might accomplish…"

Jesse cut him off. "Just get him something now. If it doesn't draw in a curious bigfoot it's at least going to drive us all crazy listening."

Brad gave in and brought some strong sedatives from his personal first aid kit that he sometimes relied on to get sleep when dealing with his persistent nightmares. "These should do it," he said to Jesse before giving the pills to Mark. The medication did its job quickly, as Mark visibly relaxed within minutes. Soon his eyes glazed over and he slumped further into his chair. After a quick discussion, Jesse and Brad hoisted Mark from his chair and took him to the tent, where they laid him on his sleeping bag to rest.

As the day passed without incident, Jesse loosened up a little. He let his guard down briefly, though he continued to keep an eye on the surrounding woods from time to time. Mark stayed in the tent most of the afternoon, recovering from the pain and painkillers. Roy, Jesse, Kelly, and Brad took turns rebuilding the fire, patrolling the campsite, and lounging in the camp chairs. As evening approached, they stoked the fire up with wood gathered during the bright, sunny afternoon. Jesse began cooking a pot of beef stew, using a pouch of dehydrated foodstuffs and beef bouillon cubes to start with. The aroma wafting up from the pot, mixed with the light and warmth from the fire relaxed everyone sitting around it.

Suddenly, though, they heard something rustling through the woods several yards deep in the forest. The footsteps sounded bipedal. Brad rushed to his pack to grab his rifle and the infrared scope. Though it was evening, it was still warm enough to make distinguishing temperatures through the scope somewhat difficult. However, through the cooler blues and greens of the forest, the scope picked out a warmer area represented by yellows and oranges.

"There's definitely an animal out there all right," Brad said. "It's hard to tell with this scope, but it looks upright, and it seems to be coming our way."

Brad set the infrared device down and shouldered his bolt-action rifle. The rifle had a light-enhancing scope mounted on it. Brad squinted into the scope as he tried to reacquire the object he had been looking at through the infrared device. "As soon as this sucker steps through that next to last row of trees, he'll be dead meat."

Through the rifle scope, Brad could barely make out a blob moving behind the thick row of trees beyond the campsite clearing. From its movements, he was sure it was the same creature he had been watching through the infrared scope. His impatience caught up to him and he squeezed the trigger. The recoil of the gun caused him to momentarily lose sight of his target. Brad quickly scanned the woods with his scope only to see that whatever creature had been heading toward their camp was no longer in sight. He fired one more round in the general direction of the animal he had seen walking through the trees near the camp.

When the gunshot echo subsided, they all became aware of a different noise emanating from much farther back in the forest than the animal Brad had just fired at. Brad strained to hear what sounded strangely like an engine approaching the camp.

Brad turned wide-eyed to Jesse, who was equally shocked. Even Roy and Kelly, who had not been paying attention before the gunshot, were now transfixed on the source of what they could all clearly tell was a vehicular sound. Jesse reached over and grabbed the rifle from Brad. He adjusted the scope to more clearly see in the darkness, but that very darkness was soon illuminated by high- powered beams shining through the trees.

"Headlights?" Brad asked incredulously.

Soon the distinct roar of an all-terrain vehicle reached their ears. Jesse put down the rifle and pointed the big spotlight in that direction. The beam lit up the area and illuminated a red four-wheeler heading towards them with a sole rider at the helm.

"What in the world?" Brad questioned, still in disbelief.

The rider hopped off the ATV some distance from the camp and held up a hand to block the blinding spotlight Jesse was still shining.

A female voice yelled out from under a helmet, "Don't shoot. Don't shoot."

Brad was now at a complete loss for words. Jesse jumped up from his chair when he saw that it was Laura Calhoun after she took off her helmet. "What the hell are you doing here?" Jesse shouted. "Come on over here."

Laura stood up and hurried across the clearing to Jesse. They stared at each other, in mutual disbelief. "Sorry about the spotlight," Jesse apologized. "We thought you were someone else."

Laura was still confused, and shaken from having heard the recent gunshots. Jesse continued to look her over, as if he was still unsure of her presence. Finally, she spoke up. "Jesus Christ, what was that shooting just now? Were y'all shooting at me?"

Before Jesse could answer, Laura had quickly looked around at the campsite. She continued with more questions. "Just what is going on here anyway? I saw your truck at grandpa's farm last night."

Jesse still had a blank expression on his face.

"I thought I would just ride out here for the day and see how things were going. I didn't think I'd get shot at."

"Well, we didn't know you were back there in the woods," Brad responded. "And we certainly weren't shooting at you, by the way."

"What exactly were you shooting *at*?" Laura asked quickly. "You know that hunting elk out of season is illegal, don't you?"

"Look, it's a long story," Jesse offered.

"Well, I'm certainly intrigued. I've never seen so many high-tech gadgets around a campsite."

Neither Jesse nor Brad felt like explaining their expedition at the time, so they questioned Laura further about how she had found them. She explained how, despite her grandfather's best efforts to stop her, she had borrowed one of his four-wheelers and some supplies and had set off earlier in the day. Steve Akers knew which route they had taken into the woods so that was the trail she had started out on. Eventually Laura had found herself on a cleared trail and decided to follow it further into the woods. She had driven in what seemed like circles trying to locate them.

She had gotten increasingly worried until she could see the faint light of the campsite lanterns through the woods. "I knew y'all would be the only ones fool enough to be camping out here in the middle of nowhere, so I headed this direction. I heard that gunshot when I got close, and hoped it was y'all and not some moonshiners or pot growers out here protecting their terrain."

After Laura finished telling of her adventures during the day she was immediately peppered with questions from the group asking her about the goings-on of civilization, as if they had been on a three-month expedition instead of three days. Jesse watched her as she answered their questions. He was certainly happy to see her. Her long, brown hair was done up in a ponytail, which was tucked through the back of a red baseball cap. Jesse found it amazing that, even in a time of such trouble and danger, the instant he saw an attractive female he could only think of one thing.

Jesse smiled briefly as he thought about this, but his mood quickly soured. He was glad to see Laura – her presence was a reminder of more pleasant things. However, he did not like the idea that she was out here in the woods with them because that meant she was in as much danger as they were. That meant one person he actually cared about that he would have to see to safety.

"Why did you come out here?" he asked her.

Laura kicked the dirt at her feet, then looked up at Jesse. "I know this might sound silly, but I just came to see what y'all were doing. I didn't get a chance to see you before you left, and when I found out you'd stopped by grandpa's house, I thought it'd be nice to come say hi."

"You just came to see me?" Jesse asked.

Laura answered with a broad grin and leaned in toward Jesse. "I got the 'good-bye' note you left me at the lodge," she whispered. "Actually, I got both – one of the maids found your rough draft in your room's trash can and passed that along to me too."

Jesse's face immediately turned crimson red and Laura blushed in return, still grinning. However, her smile faded a little as she began looking around the campsite. "I never figured you'd be so hard to find out here," she said loud enough for the rest of the group to hear. "Y'all must've picked the most out-of-the-way spot in these hills. I mean, it's not that far from the farm as the crow flies, but it sure took me a while on the ATV."

"You know," she continued, "this is probably the first time I've been out this way. I didn't like to come out to these woods when I was a kid." She laughed and her smile came back, "And of course, grandpa used to try and tell us all kinds of ghost stories, I think he just got a kick out of trying to scare us."

Brad finally spoke up, "It seems like I remember from a conversation or two back at the lodge that you didn't believe in all those legends."

"I don't believe half of what folks tell, and lord knows my dad used to scold me when I would repeat some of my grandpa's stories. But, you know, you live in a town like this long enough and some of that junk can't help but sink in."

She then turned to face Brad directly, "But to answer your question, I certainly don't think there's any ghosts, goblins, or witches in these woods."

Brad continued his interrogation, "I'm still not following you. You just came out here to pay us a friendly visit? That's it?"

"Well," Laura began, "Like I said - you're not too far from the farm. Maybe a couple of miles. I did get turned around two or three times in the woods or I would've been here sooner. My plan was to get here earlier and head on back to the farm this afternoon." She looked at Jesse. "If I could ever re-navigate that crazy twisted trail I followed, I could probably take a rider with me on the ATV if anybody needs a break from camping for a while."

"And what would make you think any of us would need a break?" Brad asked again.

"From the looks of the camp you got here, and what's-his-name's busted leg over there, things aren't going so hot out here."

Mark had hobbled out of the tent and was sitting in a chair, still nursing his bruised and swollen leg. "She's got a good point," he said groggily. "Not a whole lot's been going right the past couple of days."

"Oh, this is all bullshit," Brad shouted, gesturing wildly with his arms. "We're so close, so close. We can't just pull up our stakes and quit now." He then pointed at Laura. "And you – you need to go back to that little hick town of yours and leave us alone. We don't need help out here, especially not from you."

"Hold on a minute," Jesse spoke up after Brad's tirade, "I might go back to that hick town too. Think about it – Mark's hurt pretty bad, some of the equipment is damaged, and the creatures seem to be getting bolder each night. We're outmanned and should seriously think about cutting our losses. Think of this as a test run and we can come back with a better idea of what to expect. But staying now just seems like a really, really bad idea."

"Creatures?" Laura asked.

Roy, who had been tending to Mark, took this opportunity to voice his own opinion and did not allow anyone to address Laura's confusion. "He's right Brad. I mean, we didn't even think these things existed, let alone that they'd display the amount of smarts and strategy that we've seen. For you to keep us all out here just to fulfill some goal of yours – well it's a goddamn shitty thing to do if you ask me."

Brad's face grew increasingly red as his temper rose. His authority was being directly challenged and his whole expedition seemed to be coming apart at the seams.

"This is all your fault," he screamed at Laura, while picking up the gun he had fired earlier. He did not point it at her, but his temper and the threat of the firearm in his grasp were evident. "Nobody's going anywhere – got it?"

"Whoa, settle down Brad," Jesse said as he positioned himself between Brad and Laura. "Get a hold of yourself." Jesse was taken aback by Brad's flaring temper as yet another sign of the strange unevenness of his moods in the past few days. He tried to calm Brad down, "You're right about us sticking around tonight. It doesn't make any sense to set off into the woods this late in the evening anyway. We can all hang around tonight and just reassess the situation in the morning – how's that sound?"

Brad liked feeling that he was in charge again. He enjoyed being the decision-maker. "That's fine," he said, as he set the gun back down. "We'll make a nice, big fire tonight and everyone'll feel better about this. You won't even want to go in the morning."

Jesse agreed for the group. He took the opportunity to volunteer gathering firewood from the campsite perimeter and suggested that Laura come with him. Brad authorized this and delegated the duties of dinner preparation to Roy and Kelly. Mark needed another pain pill so he decided to lie down for a while in his tent.

Jesse was glad to have a chance to be alone with Laura. As they gathered loose sticks and pine cones, they attempted a whispered conversation. Jesse first thanked Laura for the gesture of coming out to see him, but also admitted that he was still caught off guard that Laura had made her way through the woods to the campsite by herself, and had actually found it.

He then surprised her with his admission that he did believe in bigfoot creatures, and in fact believed that the group had been harassed by these very creatures over the past few days. Laura knew the legends from the area, but had always resisted giving them any credence.

Jesse could tell that Laura was struggling with what he had told her. So, he put down his firewood bundle, grabbed her by the hand, and walked a few yards into the woods. "You probably didn't notice these on the way in," he said, "but there's freakin' tracks everywhere."

He shined his flashlight on a worn, eroded footprint that merely resembled a long, oval depression. Laura could not tell what it was, so Jesse hunted for a fresher track. He found one – so fresh that the blades of grass and groundcover that had been stepped on were still in the process of springing back to shape.

"Jesus Christ," Jesse stammered, "this can't be more than a half hour old."

Laura was confused and upset by what Jesse was showing and telling her. She had merely come into the woods to pay him a quick visit and see if he would like to ride back to the farm with her for a day or two. She had been looking forward to spending some more time with him. Laura was trying to grasp the strange turn her decision had led to.

She looked down at the ground and the strange prints at their feet. "You know," she said, "I've seen tracks like that before on my grandpa's farm. I always figured somebody was trying to have fun at our expense."

Jesse bent down to get a closer look at the footprint. "I've got news for you, Ms. Calhoun. There's nobody in these woods but you and me and those folks back at the camp, and none of us wears a size twenty shoe."

Jesse ran his fingers along the half-inch deep footprint. "I'd say this is most definitely a monster track," he said as he looked up at her, "and it most definitely is not a joke."

*　*　*

As nighttime drew closer, the sky clouded over. The group hurriedly tried to build a roaring campfire. The fire blazed heartily, but soon sizzled and shrank as raindrops started falling from an ever-darkening sky. Despite increased activity in the woods around camp in the past days, no one was willing to stay up and sit watch in the oncoming downpour. Jesse fired up one of the lanterns with enough fuel to last until morning. The glowing light from the lantern would burn all night and at least give the group a slight sense of security.

Brad then climbed in his tent with Kelly. Roy and Mark were already in their tent. Jesse had moved his gear out of that tent and into the tiny emergency tent that had long been stored in the accessory equipment box of Steve Akers' ATV. Laura had not planned to stay the night, so she had not brought any preparations for sleeping. The rain continued and the night cooled dramatically. Soon Jesse and Laura were sharing Jesse's sleeping bag and pillow. They pulled close to each other for warmth. Lying on their sides, Jesse looked at the back of Laura's head. Jesse was amazed at how good her hair smelled. It had been a long while since he had smelled women's shampoo. He smiled as he took another deep breath of the pleasing scent. He closed his eyes and listened to the rain pelting the top of the tent.

"So you got the crumpled note too?" he finally asked, breaking the silence. Jesse could then feel Laura quivering and realized she was quietly giggling.

"Yes, Romeo," she finally replied, "I got them both."

Laura rolled over and faced Jesse in the darkness of the tent. She put her arm around him and pulled him close. "And I liked them both," she said softly.

*　*　*

In the tent shared by Mark and Roy, Roy was huddled in his sleeping bag in the fetal position. Mark, on the other hand, was sprawled out on top of his sleeping bag. He had taken another of Brad's pills after dinner and the drug had almost knocked him out on the spot. Unfortunately, he had fallen asleep before realizing that he was lying under the tear in the tent's roof. Rain dripped continuously onto Mark, mainly on his lower body and legs. Furthermore, his sleeping bag acted like a giant sponge – soaking up the leaking rainwater. The saturated bag kept the rest of the tent dry and Roy never noticed that something was wrong.

*   *   *

Late that night, Jesse awoke from the loud sound of the rain. He tried to go back to sleep but could not ignore the constant splatter of the raindrops hitting the tent fabric above his head. He realized he was wide awake and decided to glance outside to check on the camp. Jesse slowly and quietly got up so as not to wake Laura. He leaned forward and reached for the zippered D-shaped door. Jesse began unzipping the door. He poked his head out and stopped suddenly. He could see Brad outside, draped in a poncho and sitting in one of the camp chairs in the rain.

"What is it?" Laura asked groggily.

"Brad's just sitting there in the rain," Jesse whispered in reply.

"What is he doing? I thought everyone agreed to just stay in their tents."

Jesse studied him for a while, then silently zipped the door flap closed. "It looks like he's crying," he said as he slid back into the sleeping bag.

"Are you sure?" Laura questioned. "The tough guy who was bossing everyone around earlier and yelling about everything?"

"Yeah, that's him." Jesse was quiet for a moment as he situated himself close to Laura. "I think he's got some serious problems."

Laura stifled a worried laugh. "Jesse, that's gotta be the understatement of the year."

Jesse sighed as he realized Laura was exactly right. "Try to go back to sleep," he urged. Unfortunately, he knew that the troubling scene he had just witnessed would make his own sleep even unlikelier now that he had more than just the loud cacophony of rain drops to keep him awake with worry for the rest of the night.

*   *   *

DAY FOUR

As soon as Jesse woke up the next morning, his mind was already focused on preparing to leave. He gently nudged Laura until she opened her eyes. Despite both being awake, they scooted even closer and lay in the sleeping bag for a few minutes, not wanting to brave the cool, damp morning air. In the next tent over, Roy awakened to find Mark shivering and groaning in his soaked sleeping bag. Roy discovered the tear in the tent's roof above Mark and realized that Mark had been under a constant drip of rainwater during the night. He could not wake Mark at first, but after several shoves finally got Mark to at least open his eyes and mutter something incomprehensible.

Brad was the first out of his tent and investigating the campsite. A loud "goddammit" got Jesse out of his sleeping bag and tent quickly. Roy, Kelly, and Laura soon followed, but Mark did not stir.

"What's going on?" Jesse asked as he approached Brad.

"We left the infrared scope out all night. It's totally soaked," Brad answered. "And of course those perimeters sensors are now completely useless. So now all we've got is the night vision equipment, unless that's out here somewhere too."

"That's not the only thing that happened last night," Laura spoke up as she shuddered in the chilly weather. "It looks like we had some visitors."

They all gathered around Laura and soon saw exactly what had caught her attention. Scattered throughout the campsite were large footprints in the soft, wet ground. Some of the tracks criss-crossed each other, even leading to the tent area. Jesse measured them and announced that they seemed to be the exact same size and shape footprints as the two pairs they had found around the perimeter of the camp. One trail circled behind Mark and Roy's tent.

"I could've sworn I heard something last night," Roy said, shaking his head. "But, you know, with the rain and everything and Mark making so much noise, I just wasn't sure."

When Mark's name was mentioned, the question arose as to his whereabouts. Roy explained the leaking tent and Mark's situation. Jesse and Laura went to the tent and peered in at him. Mark's face was very pale in color and his knee was still badly swollen. Laura crouched into the tent and felt Mark's head. She said that his forehead was hot, but the rest of his body felt very cold. Mark shivered at the touch and woke up with a sneeze.

"We've got to get him out of here," she whispered to Jesse, who was still standing in the tent doorway.

"We all need to get out of here," Jesse replied. "Those things were in the camp last night. Who knows what they'll do next."

"I don't want to be here to find out," Laura concurred.

Brad paced anxiously outside the tent. He was annoyed at Mark's health condition, fearing that it would interfere with the expedition or prompt the others to reach a consensus on leaving. While everyone else tended to Mark, Brad plopped down on one of the wet camp chairs. In his agitated state, he did not even notice the dampness soaking through his pants. What he did notice, though, was one of the plastic storage boxes sitting next to his chair. Two massive footprints were imbedded in the ground right in front of the box, as if something had stood at its edge. The lid to the box was barely resting on top, not fastened shut as it should have been.

Brad lifted the lid to discover that some of the ammunition was gone. The shiny brass bullets had been scattered all over the inside of the box. Brad organized them and put them back in their individual bullet cases. On doing so, he counted them and realized that at least ten or eleven bullets were missing. As he looked up from the box in disbelief and confusion, he saw a shiny metallic object lying on the ground several yards ahead. He walked over to it and realized it was one of the missing bullets. In front of it lay another large footprint, heading in the direction of the woods.

Brad turned toward the camp and yelled at Jesse, "Jesse, get over here. I need you to look at something."

When Jesse got near enough, Brad grabbed him by the shirt collar and pulled him up close. "Are these things smart enough to know what bullets are?" Brad asked in a menacing whisper. He showed the muddy bullet to Jesse and explained that several were missing and likely out in the woods somewhere.

"No, I don't think so," Jesse answered after a long pause. "Hell, I'm not really sure of anything right now. But it's more likely that they were snooping around and found some bright, shiny objects to collect. That'd be my best guess."

"Best guess, huh? Your fucking best guess just took off with a magazine's worth of ammo. When are you gonna start giving me some answers with a little sureness to them?"

"Answers?" Jesse replied incredulously. "Answers? All I've got is questions." He leaned into Brad and continued, "Like what were you doing out here last night? I saw you sitting out here in the rain. Where were you when all this was going on?"

"I was only out here for a few minutes. I couldn't sleep," he stammered as his face grew red. "I didn't know anybody saw me."

Jesse decided he did not want to press that line of questioning any further. "OK Brad, you want some facts?" he asked. "How 'bout this – we've had at least two animals with giant feet leaving footprints all over the place, even right up to our tents. They can obviously move around and do whatever they want without us catching on. Hell, they could've ransacked the whole camp last night, or worse. But they didn't."

Jesse looked around the campsite for a second then turned back to Brad. "That's the facts. As bad as it's been, I'd say we've been lucky so far. We're all still alive and still have most of our gear – enough gear to get us out of here anyway. And I'm pretty sure I speak for the rest of the gang when I say that it would be in our best interest to get out of here now, while we still can."

Brad's face had developed into a deep crimson as he contemplated a reply. He was embarrassed that Jesse had seen him crying the night before. He was scared by the points Jesse had just raised. But more than anything, Brad was worried that his expedition seemed to be coming unglued right in front of him.

"Look," he finally said, "The last time I checked this was still my expedition and that still puts me in charge so what I say goes. And what I say is that each day we're out here brings those animals closer and closer in. I think we can definitely all agree on that fact. All it's gonna take is one clear shot. Then we can leave."

He looked Jesse directly in the eyes. "Jesse, I know what you've been through the past couple of years. You've seen one of these things up close and suffered because of it. You need this, man – not just for personal satisfaction, but to show the whole world. I could see it in your eyes when I first mentioned the idea months ago. I think you need the closure just as much as I do."

Jesse paused, making sure Brad was finished. "Brad, proving that a bigfoot exists means more to me than you can imagine. It means more to me than it ever could to you. I understand that something happened when you were a kid and it seems to have scarred you permanently. I have a feeling that's what drives a person to be sitting out in the rain crying in the middle of the night.

"But you've still had a good, successful life. My experience has completely ruined my life. That's why I'm out here. And personally, I think you're in danger of ruining your own life at this point."

Jesse looked down at the ground for a minute, then continued, "Think about it. We're up against the unknown here and so far we've come through with just some bumps and bruises. But that luck won't last the longer we stay out here. And if I stay and someone gets hurt, or worse, then I've defeated the whole purpose for being here. And, if that worst-case scenario happens, you'd be living the type of life I've been trying to escape from for years. Don't do that to yourself – it's already making you unbearable to be around."

"That's bullshit Jesse. You're making this out to be much worse than it is. We haven't even seen one of these creatures face-to-face. Mark's got a busted leg and maybe a cold and we've lost a few dollars worth of equipment. That's hardly enough to call off this mission."

Jesse could tell that there was no point in discussing it any further with Brad. He suggested that they clean up the campsite and get all the gear in order. That way, were they to leave, it would be a quick getaway. If they stayed, the camp would at least be in good shape for the time being. Brad agreed that they should get organized. He delegated that duty to Jesse since Jesse had mentioned it. Brad also checked on Laura and Roy who were still attending to the bed-ridden Mark. Brad decided to patrol the perimeter of camp and called Kelly over to accompany him.

Kelly talked with Brad for a while as they walked around the campsite clearing. Roy left Mark's tent to come out and talk to Brad too. Kelly did not want to stick around and listen to their discussion, so she wandered over to Jesse, who was stacking firewood. At first, Kelly was quiet and pensive. Then, she opened up to Jesse about her relationship discussion with Brad.

"There he goes again," she said. "I think he must know when I'm on the edge of leaving and can sense it. That's when he promises me the moon."

"Has he ever delivered on that kind of promise?" Jesse asked as he gathered some kindling.

"Well, yes and no. He's given me just about everything I could've ever wanted – everything except forward motion in this relationship. We've stalled out and this trip in particular is killing it. I told him I was willing to stick with him through the end of this bizarre camping trip out of some misplaced loyalty. Then, I was going to leave him and start dating Roy."

Jesse dropped his load of firewood, surprised both by Kelly's statement and by her willingness to reveal such a secret. "You told him you were leaving him?"

"Yes I did. I'm not sure why I'm telling you all this, but I guess it was just such a relief – to finally have my decision clear and to just get it off my chest."

"So you said you would stay out here with him for the time being? Do you think that was a good idea?"

"Well, I think he's right to a degree. We haven't actually seen anything that would cause a sophisticated grown adult to get so worked up. Trust me, I've been on much more miserable hunting trips with Brad. This one time, in Ecuador ..."

Jesse looked up from his crouched position as he stacked the last piece of firewood on a pile. He interrupted Kelly. "Kelly, this isn't Ecuador. We're dealing with unknown creatures here. And notice I said *creatures*, plural. There's at least two, maybe more. That's what worries me, and it should worry you too. You can see the footprints all over the camp. How long are we gonna stay here until something worse happens? After all, these are wild animals, we're in their territory, and nobody really knows that much about them. They could be testing us, just waiting for an opportunity to *make* us leave. I'd rather leave on my own – in one piece."

"There you go talking about leaving us again," Kelly responded, with a hint of fear in her voice. "I guess I don't really want to stay if you guys are leaving for real."

Jesse was getting ready to respond when Kelly gasped and cut him off. Speechless, she grabbed Jesse's arm and pointed to where Brad and Roy now stood. In the woods behind them, several yards back through the trees, a large creature rocked back and forth. Kelly tried to speak again, but could not. Jesse watched too, amazed that a large male bigfoot had shown himself out in the broad daylight.

Roy and Brad, now busy arguing, had not seen the creature. It was standing on two legs behind a large rhododendron bush and partially obscured by a tree trunk. Jesse could clearly see its shoulders and massive head. The bigfoot's head was elliptical in shape, covered in cinnamon-colored hair, and seemed to be sitting right on top of its shoulders. The hair on top of its head brushed against an overhanging branch when it swayed back and forth. Jesse estimated that this animal was easily seven and a half feet tall.

The creature's huge eyes were focused on Roy and Brad, who were arguing loudly. Jesse and Kelly were initially frozen with fear. Jesse watched as the bigfoot behind Roy and Brad lowered its massive frame into a crouching position behind the rhododendron. The cinnamon-colored creature virtually disappeared behind the bush, perfectly camouflaged in the dappled sunlight of the forest.

"Holy mother of Christ," Jesse stammered in amazement as he finally found his voice. "I can't even see him anymore."

Kelly's lips were trembling and she finally found her voice. She screamed at Roy and Brad, but they did not listen. The shouting match between Roy and Brad had gotten even louder and Roy shoved Brad backwards. Brad countered with a swinging right hook at Roy, which Roy was barely able to dodge. Kelly continued to shriek their names from the campsite.

"Is that all you've got?" Roy yelled at Brad.

"Oh, I've got something for you," Brad responded, walking towards where a shotgun rested next to one of the tents.

Roy saw where Brad was heading and reacted by running into the woods.

Kelly was nearly hysterical as she watched Roy heading in the direction of the hidden bigfoot. "Where's he going?" as she cried in alarm. Jesse was already running toward the edge of camp to alert Roy and Brad. Then, a loud roar burst through the silence from behind Brad. Brad ducked instinctively at the same instant covering his head from the blast of noise. The roaring scream had so much bass and volume that Jesse could feel the ground vibrate and felt his insides tremble from the explosion of sound.

Simultaneously, Jesse could also feel the heavy thudding of feet thundering through the woods. In a mere second's time, Jesse watched as trees and branches flew out of the path of something barreling through the woods, straight in Roy's direction. Roy let out a brief scream, which was cut quickly short by the animal. Jesse heard the impact of the collision, a crisp, loud "crack," then silence. A few moments later, the creature had moved stealthily back deep into the woods without making a sound. An eerie hushed quiet ensued, then the normal noises of the forest resumed.

As the midday crickets began to chirp again and bird calls recommenced, Jesse shouted out to Brad, "Brad, get over here, quick."

Brad rushed over to join Jesse and Kelly. Laura had also come out of the tent where she had been attending to Mark. She had heard the commotion, the roar, and the loud snap. Jesse and Brad armed the women and gave them instructions to fire at anything besides them. Brad shouldered his Romanian SAR-1, checked to make sure the magazine was full, then handed Jesse one of the handguns to holster and a shotgun to carry.

The two set off into the woods in the direction Roy had headed before being intercepted by the hiding bigfoot. The underbrush slowed their progress until they got to a point that almost resembled a tunnel through the thicket. Bushes and ground plants were flattened into the soil and branches and tree limbs on either side of the path were broken and flung in various directions. "It looks like a freight train came through here," Brad muttered in awe.

Jesse looked to the right, down the path in one direction, then turned to face the end of the path. To the left, the tunnel ended at the base of a giant red oak tree. The massive trunk dwarfed a broken rag doll of a body – Roy. Brad raced over to him with Jesse following. Roy's body was mangled in an unnatural way. He appeared to be in a sitting position with his back flush against the tree trunk, but his legs and feet pointed skyward and pressed against his stomach. It was as if he had been thrown against the tree with enough for to fold him in half – with toes to shoulders. The collision or impact with the beast and then the tree had also sent Roy's head careening against the trunk and splitting open. The vertical crack in the back of his head had already leaked blood and bits of brain matter all over the trunk, roots, and ground beneath Roy's lifeless body.

Jesse and Brad stared at Roy's remains for a few moments before being able to muster some words. "What do we do with him?" Brad asked coldly.

Jesse could tell Brad was struggling to keep some emotions hidden, but he was not sure if Brad was feeling guilt, anger, or fear, or all three.

"We can leave him here, which is inhumane and will likely freak out the girls," Jesse responded, "or we can take him back to the camp which will also likely freak out the girls."

"I'd almost rather just leave him out here," Brad responded to himself. "But I guess he deserves to be back at the camp with us," he said a little louder.

"Well, I can drag if you can shoot," Jesse said.

Brad took both guns from Jesse and pointed the shotgun and automatic rifle into the woods. Jesse pried Roy from the tree trunk after having to forcefully tug on Roy's shirt, which seemed imbedded and stuck to the bark of the tree. Then after much exertion, Jesse straightened out the crumpled body. He grabbed Roy's feet and began to pull him back to camp. "Jesus, Joseph and Mary," Jesse gasped in a whisper, "it's like dragging a bag full of jello. I bet there's not an unbroken bone in his body."

Brad turned around to see what Jesse was talking about.

"Whatever sent him into that tree did so with the force of a car crash," Jesse continued. "I mean, he's shattered, pulverized."

"Knock off the commentary. Let's just get him back to camp."

Jesse quieted down for the next dozen or so yards they had to fight through the thick bushes and tree limbs. As they emerged into the clearing, Brad walked ahead to distract Kelly and Laura while Jesse pulled the body to the side of the campsite and covered it with Roy's own sleeping bag. He did not want either Kelly or Laura to see the gruesome sight he had just dragged from the forest, though it was obvious what had just happened. Kelly glanced back from talking to Brad to see the sleeping bag-covered mass laying on the outskirts of the campsite clearing. She put her hand to her face and began sobbing.

Kelly walked slowly over to Roy's body and collapsed next to it. On her knees, she bent over and rested her head on the sleeping bag-covered body. She knew that Brad would not forget the conversation that she had recently had with him. With Roy gone, she now had no one to turn to. Kelly's sobbing grew louder and more hysterical. She cried just as much for Roy as she did for herself.

Laura ran up to Jesse. "We need to get going right now," she said in a very business-like tone and with enough volume to talk over Kelly's wailing. Laura was obviously trying not to look at, or think about, the dead body laying a few feet away. "I'm packing my little bit of gear now, then heading back to my grandpa's place on the ATV. I'd like you to come with me."

"Well shit," Jesse replied, "of course I'm going to come with you. You're the only sane person out here. And if you're saying it's best to go, I'm with you."

"Whoa, whoa, whoa," Brad said as he walked over to them, gesturing with his hands. He was still holding the shotgun in one hand and now had the handgun in his other. "What's all this talk about leaving?" he asked with a frenzied look in his eyes. "You guys saw what happens when we go off into the woods. We'd get picked off one by one." Brad was still waving the gun around as he talked. "No, we're much safer here together. We've still got plenty of food and water, and guns and bullets. We need to stay here and take these fuckers out, not surrender ourselves to them in the forest." Brad looked over his companions. "Come on people," he urged, "we just saw what happens when we split up."

Jesse shook his head in disgust. "That's your friend lying over there, Brad. Do you still not get it? No 'mission' is worth seeing your friends get hurt or even killed over. You've got to let go of this one."

"Are you wimping out on me too?" Brad asked, angry at both the suggestion of leaving and the unsaid accusation of being responsible for Roy's death.

"He's just being realistic," Laura chimed in. "And using a little common sense," she added. "Roy's dead, Mark should be in a hospital right now, and the longer we stay out here, the more the rest of us are likely to end up in the same situation."

"Oh, so now you're the expert," Brad said in a sarcastic tone.

"Well," Laura began, trying to stay calm, "I never wanted to believe these things existed, but I did grow up around here after all. The stories people tell – the stories my Grandpa still tells – if they're true then y'all haven't seen the worst of it."

"What's that supposed to mean?" Brad asked.

"Yeah, what *does* that mean?" questioned Kelly in between sobs as she wiped her face of tears. She had left Roy's body, but was still weeping.

"It means," Laura explained, "and this is just from what I've heard, that the critters running around here throwing rocks and toying with y'all are like teenagers just showing off. While unfortunately it's cost this group dearly, we've been lucky I think."

"How can you say that?" Kelly asked, fighting back more tears.

"Grandpa always talked about these things, calling them 'monkeys' or 'apes,' and always with disdain or disgust in his voice. But there was one he had a special name for. He called it the gray or 'silver' one, and whenever he was talking about that specific one, he would get real quiet and serious and speak with tones of awe and fear. Silver's been around a long time as far as I could tell from the stories. If it's still around, we should be glad that so far we've been victims of teenage pranksters and not the rage one of the big fellas can unleash."

"You're talking like you know a lot about these creatures," Brad said, still cynically.

Laura responded, "I don't really know squat about them for sure. Probably nobody does. I'm just telling you the stuff I've heard for all my life. I've always wanted to just write it off, but that doesn't mean it didn't sink in on some level."

"So these things that have been attacking us, that killed Roy – they're what your granddad would consider monkeys?" Kelly asked, trying to sort it all out. "How can we be sure that this Silver thing isn't one of them?"

Laura paused for a moment, then replied, "Well, I guess probably because the rest of us are still alive having this discussion right now."

Brad was getting ready to criticize Laura's theories when they all heard a groan from the tent. Mark had moved around some and was waking up. The conversation ended as Jesse and Laura decided to check on Mark. They hoped he would be well enough to get up and out of the tent and ultimately be able to accompany them out of the woods.

Meanwhile, Brad had pulled Kelly aside and the two were engrossed in a hushed conversation. Jesse watched them through the mesh screening in the tent. He felt sure that Brad was trying to convince Kelly to stay. Kelly was still crying, though, and it was obvious that Roy's death had affected her more than anyone. Jesse turned to Laura, who was laying a wet cloth on Mark's head.

"I think he's doing a little better," she said, "but I doubt he can travel today."

"Well, we might be stuck here anyway," Jesse admitted. "Even if we could get our gear together and leave in the next thirty minutes to an hour, it would be a close call getting back before dark. As much as I'd hate to stay here another night, I'd rather not be picking my way through the woods without some daylight – even on an ATV. You saw yourself what a convoluted route it is just to get back." Jesse paused and sighed. "Plus, I think it's going to take some work to get those two on board." He nodded in the direction of Brad and Kelly.

"I bet Kelly will go, as much as she's shook up over Roy," Laura answered.

"But you know what? Forget them, Jesse. If they're crazy enough to stay out here – that's their decision."

"I know," Jesse said as he stared up at the ceiling of the tent, "but I feel somewhat responsible for them being out here in the first place. After all, I'm the one who convinced Brad that a bigfoot was a real creature and not just a tabloid hoax."

Deep down, though, Jesse was recalling the searing pangs of guilt he had always felt for leaving his friend Donny Walker in a terrifying situation in the woods of the Shawnee Forest. He had felt like a coward and had consistently imagined that his desertion of his friend in the creek bottom had directly led to Donny's death. Jesse did not want to compound that grief with more from the scenario that seemed to be developing now.

Laura was getting frustrated with the situation. "Look, Jesse. They came out here on their own free will. You didn't force them. And we've mentioned several times wanting to leave. It's not like we're abandoning them."

It was then Laura's turn to shift her gaze away from eye contact with Jesse. "I didn't come out here out of concern for them, Jesse. I came because of you. I didn't want you to have left without getting to say goodbye. And I'm not going to leave you out here either." She then looked him straight in the eyes.

An awkward moment passed as Jesse was unsure how to respond. His spirits were lifted by what Laura had just revealed, and her assertion that they were not abandoning Brad and Kelly had been just what he needed to hear. "I thought I was just a tourist, passing through," he said as he forced a smile.

"Well, I'd say it's a little bit more involved than that right now," Laura quickly countered. Then, she grinned slightly. "We'll worry about the details when we get back to Grandpa's farm."

Jesse's forced smile broadened into a genuine one. "Oh, we can worry about some details all right," he said, nodding his head up and down.

"This is no time to bring up something like that," Laura responded in as serious a tone as she could muster in reply to Jesse's insinuations.

At this point, Mark rolled over in his sleeping bag to face away from his current tent mates. "You know, I'm lying right here. I can hear everything you guys are saying. I think you've got your own tent if things are going to get out of hand."

After they apologized to Mark and left the tent, Jesse suggested to Laura that she approach Kelly and try to gauge where she stood on the matter of leaving. Jesse admitted that he had not had much luck talking to Kelly in past attempts. As they split up, Jesse tried to get Brad to help him sort through the gear and do an inventory check. This allowed Kelly and Laura to have some time alone to converse.

"Don't even try," Kelly said before Laura had even spoken. "I know you're going to try to talk me into leaving."

Laura was caught off guard. "Umm, OK, look – I know you must've had something with Roy. I could tell by how you two carried on with each other. I think it was probably obvious to anyone who was around y'all. I'm sorry about what happened."

Kelly started crying again, but Laura did not let this stop her. "You've got to pull yourself together and think straight for a minute. We all need to get out of here and the sooner we get a group consensus, the better."

"I can't leave Brad now," Kelly sobbed as she wiped away her runny nose with the back of her hand. "He's all I've got."

"Well you're going to lose him too if you can't talk him into giving up this nonsense."

"It's all he's wanted for years," Kelly offered, no longer listening to Laura's reasoning. "The nightmares, the cold sweats, the therapy sessions."

"Look, I don't have a clue what you're talking about, but if Brad had some issues before he came out into these god-forsaken woods, what do you think is gonna happen if he stays out here anymore. Come on Kelly, think about it."

Kelly did not want to think about it, however. Without saying another word, she simply walked away from Laura and plopped down in one of the camp chairs sitting by the now fully-extinguished campfire.

Laura came back and reported the conversation to Jesse. "She's lost it for sure," he responded.

"Either way," Laura advised, "you've got to realize that you're no longer accountable for what happens to them. Brad's got this idea that he can still win this battle, and get something out of it. And somehow he's talked Kelly into staying. I don't know if it's out of guilt or fear that she keeps agreeing with him. I have a feeling they're going to keep at it until they've completed his task."

"Yeah," Jesse agreed, "or die trying."

* * *

That evening, they all sat around the campfire, sharing a tense and quiet meal. They passed around a pot of re-hydrated beef stew. Mark had finally made it out of the tent and the hearty meal was bringing back a healthy color to his cheeks. Brad sat next to Kelly, mainly mumbling to himself from time to time. He had slowly come to realize that his fellow crewmembers were anxious to get out of the forest as soon as possible. This signaled an inevitable end to his expedition. Yet, Brad was apparently already hatching plans for a return to the area. The next time, though, he would bring a bigger team, more equipment, better supplies and so on. Brad continued to devise his future scheme for almost ten or fifteen minutes while the others ate.

Finally Jesse could no longer sit by and listen to him. "You still don't get it do you Brad?" he asked as he set down his bowl and spoon. "A bigfoot is not a deer or bear or a elk. They think. They understand things to a certain degree. You show up with an army of men and equipment and they'll just melt into the woods. You'll spend a month here and never even see a footprint."

Jesse poked around in the fire for a minute. "It took them a couple of days to size up our strengths and now they're dismantling our group one by one. They're not going to participate in some pitched battle against a mob. In fact, they probably wouldn't even get within miles of any group that size. Now, you bring a smaller, more vulnerable outfit out here and you're much more likely to have some encounters. And get picked off, one at a time. Just like now."

Brad merely waved off Jesse's warning with a gesture of his soup bowl. He kept on plotting his next expedition until long after everyone else had finished their meals. As darkness drew in all around them, blanketing the forest, the small group huddled even closer to the campfire. As evening turned to night, they sized up the firewood stack and realized that it might not be enough to last the night. There were no volunteers to walk the perimeter in search for good dry wood that had been passed by on earlier collecting missions. They finally decided that, since this was likely the last night for most of them, they would keep a healthy fire burning as long as the wood lasted and then switch to the backpacking lanterns for the rest of the night.

Jesse and Brad decided to keep watch. Both would sit by the fire and alternate sleeping times. Mark, Laura, and Kelly would all sleep in one tent for warmth and at least a slight sense of security. Jesse told Brad to get some sleep first. He wanted Brad to get some rest and hopefully awaken with a slightly clearer mindset. Besides, Jesse's fear level was rising with the darkening of the forest and he thought he would not be able to sleep.

* * *

Jesse woke up with a jerk. He leaned forward in the camp chair as he squinted his eyes to see in the pitch darkness of the thick Kentucky woods. Other than an occasional crackle from the dying campfire coals, the night was silent. Jesse then realized that perhaps it was the silence that woke him. Not even an owl or scurrying squirrel dared to make noise. The silence hung in the air like a fog. Jesse did not like this sinister feeling one bit. He nudged Brad, who groggily emerged from his own slumber. Brad wiped the sleep from his eyes and absently rubbed the stubble on his face. He finally looked over at Jesse, who put his finger to his lip, signaling Brad to maintain the quiet stillness permeating the forest.

As the two sat there in the clearing, now alert and on guard, it was Brad who first noticed the strange sound. It was extremely faint at first. He had to strain to pick out the noise. Soon, though, both he and Jesse were well aware of a peculiar whimpering sound coming from the woods. What started as a faint sob grew louder. It sounded like a human baby crying.

Brad instinctually reached for his shotgun and the powerful spotlight. He turned to Jesse with alarm and confusion showing in his expression. "Why would there be a baby this far out in the forest?"

As they continued to listen, though, it became apparent that they were not hearing an infant crying, but an animal making a similar noise.

"Sounds like a wounded animal really, when you concentrate on it," Jesse observed. "But man does it also sound like a baby crying."

"You know," Brad replied as they listened to the noise continuing, "I've done some predator hunting in the past. Especially for coyotes we often make calls that sound like a wounded rabbit squealing, or like some small animal caught in a trap, crying. Those suckers can't resist that call – coyotes will come in from a mile away to investigate. Looking for an easy meal."

Jesse understood what Brad was implying. "I'll have to admit, that shit makes me curious. Kind of makes me want to get up and see what the hell a little baby is doing way out here in the woods crying."

"You think a bigfoot's smart enough to think of trick like that?" Brad asked with concern, still clutching the shotgun.

"Well, they might've done just like you – used it in a hunting situation before to lure in some type of curious forest animal. But I bet that might be their wounded animal call like you were talking about. I can't imagine they know what a human baby sounds like to mimic."

Brad did not respond and Jesse sat silently for a while. The two listened to the unnerving crying noise for several minutes more.

"I can't stand it anymore - that's freaking me out," Brad finally said. He turned on the high-powered spotlight and blasted the beam into the woods. Immediately the noise ceased. Brad turned to Jesse with an amazed look on his face. They attempted to stay awake as long as they could, straining to hear the noise-maker leave its hiding spot. Jesse never heard anything and eventually turned to Brad to say something, only to find him already asleep. Before he could spend much time thinking about this, Jesse himself surrendered to drooping eyes and an exhausted mind.

*   *   *

At 2:15 AM, Jesse awoke again. This time, though, it was from being nudged by Brad who had woken up first. "Did I dream that a few hours ago?" Jesse asked, feeling confused.

"If you're talking about that god-awful baby crying sound then, no. I heard it too." Brad replied. "But forget about crazy noises," Brad continued in a whisper, "you're about to *see* something that's a good bit scarier. I think the silver one Laura was talking about is in the neighborhood."

Brad leaned over and handed Jesse the only remaining pair of infrared goggles. Jesse pulled the goggles over his head and panned across the woods in front of the campsite. He stopped on a thick oak tree. Behind the tree, the blue colors of numerous rhododendron branches and leaves obscured something very large and very orange in the infrared lenses. This massive, heat-producing object could only barely be seen behind the bushes and tree trunk. Jesse realized that the entity would be totally invisible to even a night-vision device, let alone to a naked eyeball.

He increased the intensity of the infrared device's focus. At the same time, a long arm extended from the mass. The arm was bathed in brilliant oranges, reds, and yellows in contrast with the cool colors of the forest backdrop. The arm wrapped around the tree trunk and pulled up the rest of the body. Jesse then realized he had been looking at a crouching bigfoot, which had just hoisted itself up into a standing position behind the oak tree. Despite the width of the massive tree trunk, the creature's shoulders were easily visible through the goggles.

Jesse estimated the shoulders to be about four feet wide. When the head poked out from behind the tree, Jesse could see its shape. The warm colors gave it away, except for cooler, darker colors in the deep eye sockets of the face. Jesse then sized up the creature from head to feet and decided that it was nearly nine feet tall, if not more.

He handed the goggles back to Brad, who gasped in amazement when he finally focused in on the creature.

"That's got to be the silver one, doesn't it?" Brad asked excitedly.

"I don't know who else it might be," Jesse answered. "What's your guess on height and weight."

Brad paused a moment as he sized up the animal through the goggles. "Height I would say eight and a half to nine feet, though without measuring that tree trunk I can't say for sure. Weight – with those shoulders and that height that thing's about the size of an elk. I don't know – 800 pounds, 1,000? Tough to say. But it makes an NFL lineman look like a horse jockey."

As they were discussing the creature's size, a soft murmuring sound came from its direction. A hoot responded from the left of the campsite, then one from the right. Brad and Jesse looked at each other after hearing the noises and simultaneously realized that they were surrounded. Jesse told Brad to take off the infrared goggles as he grabbed one of the spotlights. Jesse blazed the powerful beam ahead. He caught a brief glimpse of a massive silver-haired creature ducking back into squatting position, where it remained out of sight.

A twig crunched on the forest floor to their left. Brad swung his SAR-I in that direction and fired indiscriminately. He then began spraying bullets to all sides of the campsite, eventually emptying a thirty-round magazine. The sound of branches, bark, leaves, and other debris knocked loose from the gunshot barrage and falling to the ground could be heard for a few minutes afterward. Laura and Kelly peeked out of their tent to see what the commotion was. Jesse turned around and waved them back into the tent. He scanned the forest with the spotlight, then with the infrared goggles. He saw nothing.

"Maybe we hit one of them," Brad suggested. "Even if not, maybe that'll keep them away for a while."

"I doubt it," Jesse answered. "Look, I want Laura to stay in the tent. I doubt it's really any safer, but it makes me feel better anyway. I don't think Mark or Kelly are in any condition to be out here being useful. So it's going to be up to the two of us to stay awake and keep these things at bay."

Brad agreed and, after refilling the magazine for his gun, insisted that he could stay alert for the rest of the night.

*   *   *

Jesse shivered in his sleep, then jerked awake as he almost fell out of his camp chair. Jesse decided his nerves were simply shot and the exhaustion had to be preventing him from fending off sleep. He had heard something snorting while in a state of semi-sleep, but turned to see Brad snoring away in his chair. Then, the snort came again and its origin was deep in the woods, not from Brad. It sounded loud and deep, like a bull. As his eyes adjusted to the light, Jesse swore he could see leaves quiver from the rush of air expelled from the next grunt.

Jesse punched Brad in the shoulder to wake him and grabbed for the spotlight. Just as he turned the beam on and focused it ahead of them he saw a huge grey shape dart behind a tree and then go crashing through the woods out of sight. The massive, lumbering size of the silver bigfoot did not seem to fit with its impressive speed and agility as it had swiftly sprung from a crouched, hiding position into a full-blown sprint.

As that creature disappeared into the forest, Jesse heard movement from behind as well. He swung around in his chair and spotlighted the campsite. As if in slow motion, another of the animals stood up from behind the tent occupied by Laura, Kelly, and Mark. It curled its lips back and bared its broad, flat teeth in an intimidating grimace, dropped down to all four limbs and bolted into the darkness.

Brad had shifted in his chair to see the bigfoot creature escaping to the nearby woods. He had just enough time to fire a single shot in its direction. Jesse quickly scolded him, pointing out that an errant shot might hit the tent.

"These guys are getting closer each time," Brad said with a mixture of fear and anger.

"Yeah, and bolder," Jesse agreed.

"You and I have *got* to stay awake, man. I don't care how exhausted we might be. If we could just get a clear shot next time," Brad said as he checked his weapon, "we could wrap this whole thing up by morning."

Jesse stared at Brad in amazement, incredulous that Brad's main concern was still accomplishing some misguided goal of killing one of these creatures. Jesse's thoughts had long ago turned to just surviving the ordeal. He did know that, regardless of motivation, they needed to stay up until dawn.

* * *

Almost forty-five minutes had passed since the last incident. Jesse drowsily checked his watch, which read 5:30 AM. The period of inactivity was lulling him toward sleep again. He fought it as hard as he could, occasionally whispering to Brad to make sure he was staying awake too. Jesse got up from his seat to adjust the two propane lanterns. With just over an hour and a half left before dawn, he decided to blaze them at their highest setting. With the lanterns burning brightly, their light illuminated the campsite and actually reached beyond the first row of trees and a few feet into the dark forest.

When Jesse sat down, something stung him on his forehead. He turned to Brad, who was looking straight up in the sky. "Is it raining?" Brad asked in confusion as he stared at the clear, starry pre-dawn sky. A small shower of tiny pebbles then descended on them, bouncing off the chairs and plinking off the metal tops of the lanterns.

"They're throwing rocks at the dadgum lanterns," Jesse said.

Frightened at the prospect of losing their lanterns and being swallowed up by the darkness, Brad fired several rounds into the forest. Far to the left of his shot placement, the woods erupted as something violently shook pine saplings and other small trees and whacked a hollow log against a thick tree trunk. Jesse yelled out, "it's just intimidation behavior," as Brad rapidly fired at the area.

With the noise of the gunshots and their attention focused on the display ahead, neither Jesse nor Brad initially noticed what was going on behind them. The same bigfoot that had been behind the tents earlier in the night hurtled through the camp with incredible speed and the thundering heaviness of a draft horse. As Brad spun around to fire at it, the creature veered off course and ran right into, and over, the inhabited tent – tearing fabric and breaking the tent's aluminum poles as it went. The impact seemed to squeeze the girls out of the tent, as they leapt through the torn tent door and out into the open.

Jesse found a full magazine in Brad's ammo bag and handed it to him, with instructions to keep an eye on the intimidator in front and the intruder to the rear. Jesse ran over to Kelly and Laura who, though shaken, were unharmed by the incident. Kelly said that thought she had heard a wheezing noise from Mark when the tent was run over. Jesse sent them to stand beside Brad while he checked on Mark.

Mark still lay in his sleeping bag. "What the hell just happened?" he asked feebly as Jesse uncovered him from the tent fabric. "My chest is killing me. It kind of hurts to breathe and I'm not sure I can move my right arm."

"I think you got stepped on," Jesse answered.

"By what, an elephant?" Mark coughed. He clutched his chest with his still-working right arm.

"Yeah, something like that," Jesse muttered. He clicked on his headlamp for a better view. He helped Mark remove his shirt, though it was apparent this caused Mark excruciating pain. Mark's shoulder, chest and right arm already looked red and slightly swollen. Jesse looked up to say something, only to realize that Mark's eyes were closed and he did not appear to be breathing. Jesse grabbed a nearby canteen and poured some water on Mark's forehead and gently slapped him on the cheek.

"Lemme get some of that water," Mark said, coming to again.

Jesse sat with him for a few more minutes to make sure Mark was not going to slip into shock. Jesse tugged the sleeping bag and mat into the center of the tent so that the torn, dewy fabric would not be resting on Mark. He then pulled the sleeping bag around Mark and helped him drink some water. After a while, Mark looked as if he had awakened and come out of his daze.

"He's not looking too hot," he said to Laura as she approached.

"Well, neither is anybody else," Laura complained in a state of near-panic. After talking for a few minutes, everyone settled down a little. Jesse tried to stoke up what was left of the campfire embers, adding some paper and cardboard pieces he scrounged from their gear. While Mark rested up in the tent, the rest pulled seats up to the barely-lit fire. As they huddled close to each other, Jesse looked up to the sky just in time to see a shooting star streak from one horizon to the other. He thought about how, under any other circumstances, he would be enjoying the early morning night sky, sitting around a campfire, taking in the invigorating sights, sounds, and smells of the forest before dawn. All he felt now, though, was fear, and an intense longing for sunrise like he had never sensed before.

The sky itself was beginning to lighten, though the surface of the earth still remained as dark as night. Brad laid his automatic weapon down so he could get some other firearms and distribute them to the group. As he left the campfire circle, a screaming roar burst out from above the camp. There, on the ridge shadowing the campsite, silhouetted against the faint glow of the pre-dawn sky, stood the silver-haired giant.

They could not make out his features, but as the creature was just on the steep ridge behind the camp, they could easily tell this was the largest animal they had seen yet. His fiendish howl stretched for many seconds before it tapered off into a deep growl. Its volume and intensity surprised them, even in light of all they had experienced over the past few days. Kelly began to sob before the roar had even finished. Brad stopped in his tracks, frozen in fear and astonishment, and unable to move or retrieve his gun. The powerful undulating bass underlying the howl buffeted them, and Jesse swore he could feel vibrations from it, even in his stomach. Laura started crying as well, as she leaned over, holding her abdomen. Jesse felt sick, too, but the vibrations ceased when the animal stopped its call. The most disturbing aspect of the grey bigfoot's appearance was the manner in which it left the ridge. It did not crouch and hide or sprint off the ridge, but stood there for a few seconds looking down at them. It turned slowly and casually walked off in long, unhurried strides.

"That thing doesn't fear us at all," Jesse said simply, "not one bit."

DAY FIVE

For forty-five minutes after the sighting of what they only could guess to be a silverback male, Brad and Jesse took turns firing off a round or two into the surrounding forest. They had figured the regular gunfire might give them some protection until dawn. Laura and Kelly helped move Mark from the torn tent to one of the unoccupied ones and tried to make him as comfortable as possible.

As the day broke, they all found themselves exhausted from a night of little-to-no sleep and frequent alarming interludes from the trio of bigfoot creatures antagonizing the camp. Besides sleep deprivation, they were also facing shortages of food, water, and now ammunition. The constant barrages of indiscriminate gunfire had dwindled the ammo supply into a small fraction of what it had been five days earlier.

Assessing the situation and his own degraded state, Jesse spoke up. "We definitely can't stay here any longer," he announced. "It's out of the question. No room for debate."

Brad responded defensively, "Come on man, now we know their tactics – their strengths and weaknesses."

"Were you even here last night, Brad?" Jesse asked in disbelief. "What 'weaknesses' are you talking about? They've just been toying with us the whole time – testing *our* strengths and weaknesses. And our strengths keep getting smaller and smaller every hour with the less sleep, food, and ammo we have."

"Yeah," Laura added, "and what do you plan to do with Mark? He really shouldn't spend another night out here. He should probably be in a hospital getting his chest x-rayed."

Jesse stood up and gazed around the campsite. "I'm sorry Brad. I feel like I'm responsible for everybody being in this mess. But my guilt about this situation ends now because I'm going and taking whoever wants to go. If you stay, that's your own free choice."

Brad's face had been growing redder and more tensed as Jesse and Laura spoke. He felt that it was foolish to give up when his goal was so close. When Kelly admitted that she wanted to leave too, Brad erupted. He shouted angrily, "We've spotted three different creatures in just a couple of days. Most people have never even *seen* one of these animals. We keep waiting, and sooner or later we'll get a clear shot. The odds are in our favor!"

At the end of Brad's ranting, Jesse simply shook his head and walked off. He went to the perimeter of the campsite to relieve himself and get away from Brad's ever-increasing megalomania. When he returned to the group, Kelly and Laura were sitting silently and Brad was pouring over hours of footage and photographs from the trail cameras. "Nothing useful," he kept muttering, "blurs and fuzzy, underexposed pictures. These cameras are worthless at nighttime."

Jesse ignored Brad, knowing that the poor photographic and video evidence would only feed his desire to obtain a physical specimen. Jesse leaned back in his chair for a much-needed stretch. The early morning sun bathed the clearing in a soft, cheerful light. Its warmth felt good to Jesse, and his spirits were also lifting with the thought of leaving soon. A few songbirds whistled back and forth at the edge of the clearing. Their singing made Jesse feel better, and he stood up with gusto, ready to pack his gear and hit the trail immediately.

As Jesse stood up, though, he heard something rustling in the forest. Brad, Laura, and Kelly also looked up in fearful anticipation. Brad aimed his rifle at the area the sound seemed to be coming from and Jesse leaned over to grab his gun too. Their fears quickly subsided when an enormous ten-point buck appeared. The deer's massive antlers were still covered in the velvet-like skin and blood vessels that nourish the antlers as they grow. The forked branches even sported a few twigs that had been lodged in the antlers while the buck had apparently been trying to scrape off the velvet.

The group watched in awe as the old buck paused in the clearing and then nonchalantly trotted away. He was followed a few seconds later by a doe. She did not stop at the campsite but kept up an easy pace on her way after the buck.

"There goes two lovebirds," Laura remarked.

The scenario worried Jessie, though. He had only limited hunting experience, but had always heard that the rut, or mating season, started later in the fall. Also, it seemed to him that the buck usually pursued the doe, not the other way around.

As he thought about this, Brad took advantage of Laura's comment to cover up the gravity of the situation he had created. "You see," he said, "this place isn't so bad. The sun's out, the birds are singing, and the deer are out cavorting around. I know things have been tough but I really think things are starting to swing in our favor."

The songbirds took off in flight, though, as something else was moving through the woods. Another doe poked its head out of the forest thicket and entered the clearing.

"See, here comes another one," Brad confidently announced. "This place is a nature-lover's paradise, not a…"

Brad stopped as they all watched the small doe make its way into the clearing. It hobbled on three legs, dragging its back right leg limply behind. Despite its obvious pain and struggle just to walk, it moved in a determined manner. Then it stopped in front of the group.

"Why'd it stop?" Kelly asked

"What the hell's wrong with her leg?" Laura wondered.

Jesse tried to shoo the deer away with some arm gestures. The doe simply stood still, then actually took a few tortured steps in their direction. "This just doesn't make sense," Jesse said. "I would think deer would show much more fear of humans than they are."

Yet, the deer wobbled toward them some more, then abruptly stopped. The doe's ears twitched nervously as it sniffed the air and its white tail shot up in alarm. Suddenly, a monstrous, earth-shaking roar boomed out from close within the forest. The doe bolted, as best it could, along the same path the others had taken. As it reentered the woods, Jesse, Laura, Kelly, and Brad could see leaves and branches flying as something moved to intercept it. They heard a sickening thud, a muffled deer bleat, then the loud cracking of bones.

Mimicked owl noises and hooting soon filled the air. The group caught a glimpse of a shadowy brown figure moving through the woods from where it had just bellowed its roar to where something else had apparently trapped the crippled doe. They stood stunned, silently listening to more bones popping and the sound of flesh and hide being torn. Laura grew sick listening to the two bigfoot creatures taking apart the deer. She leaned forward and threw up on the ground.

Jesse's mind registered the frightening significance of what had just taken place, but he also realized that it signified the intelligence of the forest giants.

"Son of a bitch," Brad muttered to himself. "That was the most effective deer drive I've ever seen."

Jesse responded, "What's going to stop them from doing the exact same to us? One screams and chases us while the other hides behind a tree waiting to snap us in half. I mean, think about what happened to Roy."

At this point, Jesse gestured to where they had laid Roy behind the tents and out of sight. However, they all noticed that the sleeping bag covering Roy's body had been pulled into the surrounding forest at some point during the night. A small corner of the material was still visible. More disturbingly, Roy's body was no longer where Jesse and Brad had placed it the previous day.

Kelly ran over to the spot, looking desperately for Roy. She began screaming when she saw the marks in the ground where Roy's body had been dragged into the woods. She thrashed about through the bushes trying to find him.

"Calm down, Kelly," Brad said as he came over to her, "we'll all go look for him as soon as we can."

"As soon as we can?" she shouted. She crumpled to the ground and her sobbing grew louder. Brad tried to put his arm around her but she tossed it off. "I'm going to find him now," Kelly declared.

"We need to stay here and fight," Brad countered. "They'll pick us off one by one unless we stick together. This is the best place to make a stand or we'll all end up like Roy."

"Back off Brad," Kelly said stoically. She had a far-off look in her eyes as she stared into the forest. "You don't care about me at all, do you? All you care about is yourself – getting over your stupid childish nightmares that any normal person would've put past them at age twelve."

She slapped Brad in the face and walked away from him. She marched over to her tent and grabbed a small day pack from the gear. "I'm going to find him now," she said again.

"Kelly, stop," Jesse protested. "Brad's right that we should stick together. We should all head back to the farm now and get some help to find Roy." Again, Jesse's years-old guilt had crept up and he could not allow someone in his party to go off into the woods unprotected. Despite Kelly's completely irrational behavior and mannerism, Jesse just could not shake his feeling of responsibility.

Jesse had grabbed Kelly's wrist to restrain her, but after staring into the woods quietly, she whipped around with a strange look in her eyes. She yanked her arm out of Jesse's grasp and dashed into the forest. Jesse was about to run after her in pursuit, but this time it was he who was held back.

"There's nothing you can do now," Laura pleaded. Though Jesse was tense and ready to dash into the woods, he finally let his body relax and melted into the clutching arms of Laura.

* * *

Kelly tromped through the woods with abandon. It was not long before she realized that she had no idea where she was. The woods surrounding her seemed unfamiliar and dark, as the sun barely penetrated through the thick overhead canopy. Kelly's throat was scratchy and dry and her eyes hurt from crying. She did not take a break, though, but kept walking. She no longer cared where she was going or what would happen to her. She put one foot in front of the other mindlessly, occasionally tripping over an exposed root or bumping into a low-hanging branch.

Suddenly, a tremendous roar burst through the woods and shook Kelly free from her melancholy. She was instantly alert and looking around. The horrific scream sliced through the forest again. The noise itself was so loud that Kelly's ears hurt and her insides seemed to throb with vibrations from the thunderous blast of noise.

Kelly clamped her hands over her ears and started crying. She reflexively bent over and tucked herself into a protective ball as she sobbed. After an impossibly long duration, the creature's howl decreased and trailed off into a series of grunts and growls.

Those sounds seemed to be getting closer and Kelly's fight or flight instincts kicked in. She jumped up from her crouched position and took off in a sudden sprint. The trees and bushes behind her parted quickly as one of the younger bigfoot creatures bounded from the woods. The massive, eight foot tall animal loped through the forest with incredible speed, smashing branches and small trees in its path.

Kelly fled down the closest thing resembling a cleared path that she could find. She had heard the creature run into a thick branch that snapped with a loud cracking. She hoped that this collision might have given her a few more seconds' head start. She sprinted down the path but soon could hear and feel the heavy thudding of feet pursuing her. At one bend in the trail, she ducked into the woods and continued running straight through the forest, unconscious of the bushes and tree limbs in her way. In this mindless dash she had no idea what direction she was traveling or what lay ahead.

Soon, though, the rumbling of footsteps had caught up to her. Kelly could feel the creature behind her and made one last desperate dash to outdistance it. She was fleeing towards what seemed to be a clearing, hoping to make better time than running through the cluttered forest understory. When she reached the edge of the clearing, Kelly immediately lost her footing and slid down a steep embankment and straight into one of the bogs dotting the area. She landed thigh-deep in the watery mud of the bog. She tried to move, but her feet and legs were stuck in the swampy muck.

Despite her panic, Kelly had a brief moment of clarity and realized that she would never be able to pull her legs up with her hiking boots on. She reached into her pocket and pulled out a small knife that Brad had given her days ago. She bent over and plunged her hand down through the oozing mud and leaf litter. Her face was almost touching the surface of the bog as she reached for her boots. Going only by feel, she managed to find her left boot's shoestrings and cut them with the knife.

She lifted her foot free as her boot filled with the watery mud. Kelly bent down again to cut off her right boot when she heard a loud splashing thud. The pursuing bigfoot had just jumped into the bog several yards behind her. The creature's enormous weight sent ripples out through the thick mud. Involuntarily, Kelly started crying again. She wiped her eyes, smearing muck on her face, and tried to bend over again to free her other foot.

As the animal waded toward her, she could feel the muddy ripples lapping at the backs of her legs. Kelly was so stuck, though, that she could not turn around to see it advancing. She bent over again and feverishly sliced at her boot. In her panic, she ended up cutting herself more than her shoestrings. Then, she stood straight up. Her arms, chest, and face were black with mud. She could smell the bigfoot right behind her. Its hot breath blasted the top of her head and blew her hair down over her face. The creature's stench was overpowering and, in the midst of crying and gagging, Kelly lost control of her bowels.

The animal paused and simply stood behind her for a moment. Though Kelly could not turn around, she twisted her head enough to see it out of the corner of her eyes. Her vision was filled by the giant hairy torso and wide chest of the creature. It raised its arm, with dingy long hair flowing in the breeze. The animal brought its massive hand down in a swift motion and smashed Kelly on the back of her neck and head with a dreadful thump.

Kelly briefly felt and heard her neck and spine snap from the blow and the force of the strike sent her body face-first into the boggy mud. She was still alive when she hit the surface of the bog and could feel it enveloping her. She could hear the animal exiting the bog and scrambling up the embankment. Her head and ears sunk below the surface and all she could see, hear, and feel at the end was darkness.

* * *

"She's gone mad, absolutely crazy," Brad said a few moments after Kelly had vanished from sight.

"You're the crazy one," Laura shouted, still spitting out the aftermath of having vomited when the deer was attacked near the campsite. "We stay here and we'll die for sure. We make a run for it and we at least have a chance. We can hop on the ATV and get out of here quick. We'll at least be closer to civilization than out here in the middle of nowhere. Your crazy ass can stay here if you want, but as soon as those monsters move off with their breakfast, I'm leaving."

Highly upset, Brad pulled out his handgun and fired a few shots into the woods in the direction of the downed deer. There was no reaction from within the forest.

"See, maybe they're already gone," Brad said. "They're no threat to us in broad daylight. Kelly seems to have been able to just waltz right out of here with no problem."

Laura did not miss a beat in responding. "Good," she replied, "then we better get moving as early as possible since they must be distracted with something." She turned to Jesse. "You coming?"

Jesse nodded his head and walked over to his backpack.

"What about you?" Laura asked Brad, giving him one last chance. Brad simply shook his head and started loading bullets into a spare magazine.

Jesse realized that Brad's fragile mental state was obviously blurring his judgment and making him overlook the loss of Roy and possibly Kelly. Jesse knew that there was no sense continuing this argument. He had been like Brad before – so focused on this mystery that he had purposely avoided letting reality sink in. He shook his head and hoisted his pack onto his shoulders.

"Brad, listen – you've done your best, but if we have any chance to save Kelly and ourselves, you need to go with us now."

"I need closure, Jesse," Brad responded without looking at him. Jesse shook his head again. "Well, I'm afraid you're going to get it."

*   *   *

Laura and Jesse helped Mark out of the tent. His injured leg seemed to have healed a little, at least to a point where he could put some weight on it. Mark's breathing, though, was still labored as his bruised chest ached with each breath. Mark said he was worried about slowing them down as he would have to ride on the ATV, forcing one of them to walk alongside. He instructed them to leave him behind if he became too much of a burden. Either with them or on his own, Mark declared that he was leaving too.

While Jesse tried to find a way to help Mark keep his balance riding on the back of the ATV, Laura finished packing the last of their gear. As she did, Brad approached her from behind. "Don't say anything and don't turn around," he whispered. He leaned over and slid a handgun into Laura's pack and also dumped in a handful of bullets. Laura stood up to say something, but Brad hurriedly walked away.

When Jesse returned, Laura described what had happened to him in a hushed voice. "Surely that shows that he knows how dangerous it is out here," Laura added.

"Or that he's given up," Jesse suggested. "Either way, I'm done trying to figure it out."

Laura and Jesse steadied Mark in between them and the trio was set to leave the campsite. Brad did not look at them as they walked past and arrived at the edge of the clearing where the ATV sat. Despite how appalling Brad's behavior had become, Jesse still did not want to abandon him. In hopes that he might persuade Brad, he turned around and added one last warning. "You know if you stay you're never going to make it out of these woods, don't you?" he pleaded.

"Well we'll just see how you three make out," Brad responded automatically.

*   *   *

By noon Jesse, Laura, and Mark had made slow progress into the forest. Laura was driving the ATV with Mark hanging on the back. Jesse had tried his best to trot alongside. The sun shone brightly overhead, though only dappled, shaded light penetrated through the thick canopy. The early morning humidity had decreased, leaving a cool, dry day for the journey. Despite the pleasant weather, Jesse perspired heavily as they struggled up and down the ridgelines. They stopped frequently to let Jesse catch his breath and take sips of the small water supply they carried.

At one point, Laura revealed to Mark that Brad had given her the handgun.

"That crazy son of a bitch," he exclaimed. "I guess I appreciate the gesture, but we could really use a rocket launcher out here."

Jesse came over and reached into Laura's bag and pulled out six bullets. He fed these into the gun's magazine and slid it into the pistol grip. He holstered the gun in his belt, making sure it was secured tightly. The three travelers had begun to hear something following behind, and were growing worried as the noises steadily caught up to them.

At their next water break, Laura shut off the ATV's engine and they heard something taking an extra step or two. It stopped, but the crunching and snapping of twigs and forest debris had been enough to alert Jesse that one of the bigfoot creatures had followed them from the camp. Jesse pulled out his binoculars and scanned the area behind them. About one hundred yards away, he could clearly see parts of the animal. Its monstrous shoulders stuck out on either side of a mountain laurel bush. Jesse focused the binoculars and he saw the three-inch long brown hair swaying on the animal's arm as it grabbed a nearby tree and hoisted itself up to a standing position.

Then Jesse saw the entire creature from the waist up. Sitting atop its barrel chest and wide shoulders was a rounded, furry head and a leathery face. Its nose was flat, though not as flat as a gorilla's. Its brown, skinny lips were parted, revealing large yellowish teeth. Jesse then looked at the creature's eyes, only to see that it appeared to be looking straight back at him.

"We've got to keep moving, and faster," he said to Laura and Mark. "We've got an escort behind us. It looks like one of the smaller ones."

"It's not the silver one?" Laura worriedly asked.

"I don't think so," Jesse responded. "All the same, so far it seems to just be following us. I don't want to stick around for it to get more aggressive."

* * *

Back at the camp, Brad was adjusting to being all alone. The stoic attitude Brad had presented earlier dissipated almost as soon as Laura, Jesse, and Mark had faded into the woods. Brad mumbled to himself quietly as the silence and loneliness of the empty camp was oppressively crushing. Brad felt as if he was were the last person on earth. He watched as an occasional leaf flittered through the air and landed silently on the ground. He kept involuntarily glancing over at the sleeping bag that once covered Roy's body. He wanted to say something out loud, but lack of an audience and the unnerving quiet and solitude kept him from doing so.

Several minutes of this desolate stillness passed after his companions had left. Brad simply sat in his chair, staring intently ahead. He looked over at the sleeping bag again and was about to say something when an explosion of sound burst forth from the forest and blasted through the clearing. The large silverback had just announced his presence with a screaming howl that cut through the silence and made Brad think the very ground underneath his feet was shaking.

Brad stood up to scan the forest, then stepped backward to grab his rifle. In doing so, he tripped over the chair he had been sitting in and briefly fell to the ground on top of the chair and hit his head on the small stack of firewood logs. Brad rolled over and shook the cobwebs from his head as he caught his breath. He leaned up on his elbows just in time to see the giant silver male enter the clearing. The massive brute was down on all fours, walking on his knuckles.

Brad lunged for his gun, which rested in the dirt nearby. He grabbed it and shot several times at the grizzled bigfoot. His aim was unsteady at best, as he was trying to fire while still somewhat woozy and off-balance. He hit nothing, but the gunfire stopped the monster's advance. With surprising dexterity, it shifted sideways and darted back into the trees in a maneuver whose fluidity did not sync with the creature's size.

Brad barely had time to register his success in fending off the giant when a powerful stench wafted into the clearing. He sat upright then struggled to his feet, turning toward the origin of the putrid smell. There, standing partially behind a tree, was one of the other forest monsters. Brad could see one muddy leg sticking out to the side of the tree and could detect splotches of dark mud, dirt, and even leaves sticking to the animal's hairy exterior. It had just returned from a nearby bog.

The creature had one arm extended, holding onto a sturdy limb above.

It rocked back and forth, hooting and growling at Brad. Brad opened fire directly at it. It screamed a piercing shriek even louder than the gun shots, dropped to all fours and rushed through the woods away from Brad's line of fire. Brad kept firing until his magazine was empty. He quickly released the magazine and fed in another. He was not sure how many bullets it held, but he did not have time to reload the other magazine. He turned to where the silverback had earlier retreated into the woods, but saw nothing. Brad hoped he had hit the giant silver male a few moments ago, but felt that this was optimistic at best.

He listened to the smaller bigfoot crashing through the forest until it stopped. Then he could hear it slowly creeping forward, back to the campsite. Brad kicked the camp chairs out of the way and made sure he had a clear firing lane in all directions. He stood as close to the center of the clearing as possible, anticipating that the increased distance from the woods would give him an extra second or two to aim.

Then, behind a thick oak tree, the smaller brown bigfoot peaked out and stared at Brad. Brad shot twice, hitting the tree. The animal hopped sideways to another tree and Brad shot at it during this movement. Brad fired a few more times, sending up a flurry of flying tree bark and leaves. Finally, the creature stepped out, hunched over, and bellowed a dreadful roar – baring its teeth and exposing the wide expanse of its cavernous mouth. With the clear shot available, Brad instantly flicked the gun to full auto and squeezed the trigger. The campsite and adjacent forest erupted with the deafening sound of gunfire and the smoke and flying bark, tree splinters, and leaves inundated the area.

Everything got quiet for a few moments as Brad waited for the smoke and debris to clear. He felt confident that he had gotten at least one impact shot on the animal, which no longer stood behind the tree. Brad slowly crept toward the area, stalking as stealthily as he could. He saw the animal spread out on the ground several yards into the forest. It was breathing heavily and appeared to have blood on its shoulder.

Brad walked up to it and kicked one of its muddy legs. He was filled with excitement. Lying before him was a physical embodiment of the fears that had haunted him for so many years. He had done it – accomplished what he had set out to do, and felt sure that a rush of relief would be coming to him soon. The hardships of the week melted away as he thought about this. He also realized, with much elation and satisfaction, that his chances for getting out of the forest alive had just increased.

As he took a step closer, though, Brad saw that the bloody shoulder's wound was only from a slight grazing of the animal's hide. He leaned forward to inspect the injury, only to see the bigfoot's giant eyes open. The creature looked up at Brad and snarled. Brad reflexively raised his rifle to finish the creature off. Before Brad could pull the trigger, a swooshing arm sweep from the bigfoot easily knocked the gun out of his grasp and sent it flying into the woods. Brad heard the gun fire a few rounds on full auto when it hit the ground and then go silent. The magazine he had hastily loaded earlier had just been emptied and the last bullet had probably just been fired.

The primate's thin lips parted and the snarl grew into a deep, guttural growl. Brad instantly turned and began running back to the clearing – hoping to find another gun. As he burst through the trees, he saw one of the group's shotguns propped up against a tent. As if in slow motion, Brad could also see the silverback emerging from the forest to his left. The giant charged forward on all fours like a stampeding bull. When it reached the center of the clearing, it sprung up to stand and stretched to its full height of nearly ten feet. The hair-covered beast opened its arms, displaying its broad wingspan, waiting for Brad's arrival.

Upon seeing this, Brad tried to arrest his forward momentum. In trying to stop himself, though, he slipped. He slid several feet on the moist forest floor and came to rest at the feet of the creature. He looked up from his prone position to see its enormous facing looking down at him. Brad felt like he was lying at the bottom of a basketball goal, staring nearly ten feet up into the huge and eerily intelligent eyes of the creature. Brad then also saw the gun he had been trying to get to, just a few feet away. He frantically reached out for it and was able to grab the firearm's stock. Just as he did, though, his arm and wrist were crushed by a colossal, muddy foot. The smaller bigfoot – the same one that had killed Kelly and that Brad had just wounded – now stood over him, rubbing its bloodied shoulder. It shook itself, like a wet dog after a swim, and bits of dried mud and leaf litter showered to the ground and onto Brad.

Brad squirmed, but could not move. The weight of the six hundred pound animal that had crushed Brad's arm caused pain to shoot up into his shoulder as his hand went numb. Brad now realized that death would be coming soon as he blearily gazed up at the two immense creatures standing over him. The forest giants began communicating back and forth with a series of primate noises – hoots, whistles, grunts, and growls. Finally, the silverback let fly an earth-shaking shout that made even the other bigfoot shrink back. Brad's arm was freed when the animal stepped away from the older male in submissiveness. Brad frantically tried to crawl away, but the pain he felt and the use of only one arm kept him from getting far.

The silver bigfoot leaned over and wrapped a massive palm around one of Brad's legs. Hoisting the leg into the air, the creature effortlessly lifted most of Brad's lower body off the ground. It held his leg at its waist level and began walking into the woods, dragging Brad behind. Only the top of Brad's chest and his jaw touched the ground, with his arms following loosely in tow. From this upturned position, blood rapidly flowed to Brad's head, making him even dizzier and less sentient than before. As he tried to concentrate, one of the images that popped into his faint mind was that of the deer ambush he had witnessed at the beginning of the day. The savage attack stuck in his mind and he forced himself to focus on his current situation.

Brad struggled in the creature's grasp and tried to squirm free. He also tried to pull himself loose by frenziedly clawing at the ground. His one arm was shattered and useless, but he fought hard with the other – grabbing and tearing at the passing ground until his fingers were bloodied and shredded. The two giant primates continued their course, nonetheless – unhindered by Brad's feeble attempts to escape. They hiked deep into the woods, dragging Brad behind the whole time.

The first fallen log they stepped over caught Brad on the chin as his face bumped against it. The impact slammed his teeth together and briefly knocked him unconscious. Eventually, Brad regained his wits to discover he was still being carried upside down through the woods. When the creatures easily crossed through a creek that was only shin-deep to them, it almost drowned Brad. His whole head was under water for several seconds as his captors forded the stream. Brad coughed and sputtered to expel the water he had swallowed. The dry, rocky streamed further worsened his state as his head and chest bashed into many exposed boulders on the bank. This knocked him out again and he did not regain consciousness for several minutes.

Later, when Brad finally came to, he wished that the animals had simply put him out of his misery long ago. His mind was dim and he struggled to keep his eyes open. The pain from his bloody, exposed chin and his shattered arm were only worsened by the extended period he had been carried upside down. He could vaguely hear the smaller bigfoot making chattering noises and then the two creatures stopped. The bigger male relaxed his grip and let Brad fall to the ground. Through his hazy, stunned vision, Brad could barely make out his surroundings. Before he slipped back into unconsciousness, he saw that he was lying at the bottom of three rickety old wooden steps. The steps looked familiar, but Brad's weak mind could not focus long enough to figure out where he had seen this setting before. He strained to lean up off the ground for a better look, but this last bit of exertion drained his body and it shut down, leaving him lying limp at the foot of the two monstrous beings.

* * *

By early afternoon, Jesse, Laura, and Mark had made decent progress away from the campsite clearing and deep into the forest. Unfortunately, there was no trail to follow back to the farm and they ended up making some of the same time-consuming mistakes Laura had made when she had ventured out several days before. The bigfoot shadowing their route had not attacked, but seemed to prefer keeping a set distance away. Occasionally it called out at them or swayed some smaller trees to let them know it was still there. Its mere presence was enough of an intimidation factor to keep the trio moving as briskly as possible, pushing the ATV to its limits as they forded streams, climbed up steep hillsides, and bushwhacked through the tough terrain. Jesse was doing his best to keep up, but was quickly becoming exhausted. His adrenaline carried him forward and he hoped that the lone bigfoot was content to usher them out of its territory and might not risk attacking the three of them by itself.

Mark was gradually having a harder time hanging onto the back of the ATV. Laura had to frequently stop to pull him back into a better position so that he did not fall off and risk further injury. Ascending the steep ridges and navigating the slopes to get back down wore them all out. As Mark's knee began to stiffen again and his shoulder and chest injuries hampered his breathing, he became so uncomfortable riding on the ATV that he even offered to get off and walk instead. Laura and Jesse forced him to stay on because of the creature following them.

At one point, just as they crested a ridge they hoped would be their last, Mark fell off the back of the vehicle.

"Come on Mark," Laura pleaded, "I feel like we're getting closer to the farm. You can't give up on us now."

"I wonder how Brad and Kelly are doing," Mark said as he gazed absently ahead. "With this guy following us, I guess Brad had a good chance back at the campsite. Maybe Kelly's already made it back to the farm."

"I doubt it," Jesse replied harshly. "These things are pretty smart. They obviously felt comfortable enough to spare that hairy creep following us. Unless my perceptions are all out of whack, I don't think Kelly's much of a woodsman and Brad went off the deep end days ago."

"Jesse," Laura scolded, "stop being so morbid. We've got to keep our spirits up and keep moving."

"I'm trying to motivate us," Jesse explained. "There's only a single bigfoot on our tail right now. By my calculations it won't be long till the other two catch up. If we'd all been hiking on our own legs, I'm sure we wouldn't have made nearly as good of time. Fortunately, this ATV has given us a little head start, but I'd rather be out of the woods before too much longer."

Mark struggled to his feet and brushed the dirt off his pants. "I never really knew Brad or Roy too much," he admitted in response to a question nobody had asked. "I just thought this would be a good opportunity to get in tight with those guys. I guess I was trying to prove something to them. And to myself, I suppose." He paused, staring at his feet. He looked up at his traveling companions. "I guess that was pretty stupid. I never imagined I'd be in a mess like this."

Laura walked over to him and rubbed his back in consoling manner. "Nobody could have expected this, Mark," she said. "You've been a real trouper so far. I can't imagine the pain you're in, but you're doing a good job of not showing it."

Mark lifted his bad leg and tried to flex it back and forth. "My leg's pretty stiff, but manageable. The worst is my chest when I breathe heavy. Going up and down these hills has been tough. I don't know if I have the strength to hold on to the ATV over one more bump or ditch."

As they had been talking, they did not notice the trailing bigfoot move off into the woods. Suddenly, though, a tremendous disturbance broke out just yards away from the group. The bigfoot thrashed trees around, threw rocks, and screamed agitatedly. Soon, a horrible stench crept into the area. The effect at this close of range was like pepper spray. Jesse's eyes watered almost immediately and he fought to suppress gagging. Mark began coughing, and with each cough clutched his injured chest in pain. Doubled over in agony, with watery eyes, Mark lost his footing and tripped. He tumbled forward and rapidly fell down from the ridge crest they had been standing on.

Mark plunged far down the hill – sliding and bumping into rocks and trees the whole way. Jesse and Laura hopped on the ATV and rushed downhill as quickly as they could without duplicating Mark's uncontrolled descent. Mark lay at the foot of the ridge, with his red camping shirt and blue jeans in tatters and scratches and bruises on his body. Somehow, the antagonizing bigfoot had made it down just as quickly, and had already set up a post just out of sight. It hooted frenziedly and shook the surrounding trees. Jesse and Laura could see this commotion as they approached Mark. More disturbingly, Jesse faintly heard a reply call coming from back behind the ridge. As it got louder, Mark and Laura heard it too.

Mark tried to sit up, but the pain kept him on the ground. "Go on guys, get out of here," he urged. "There's no way I'm gonna make it up the next ridge riding on the ATV and I sure can't move on my own legs fast enough to outpace those things. You guys won't even have a chance if you stick around here much longer or try to carry me. If that's the other one and the silver guy wailing away back there, Brad and Kelly must already be gone. I don't want to cause you two to be next."

Laura opposed the idea of leaving him. "Come on Mark," she pleaded, "you don't have anything to prove to us. I'm plenty convinced of your bravery without you trying to pull of some heroic 'last stand' or something."

Mark smiled upon hearing this from Laura. "I'm not sure the terms bravery and heroic have ever been used to describe me before," he said. "Especially not from a cute lady like yourself." He winked at her and then winced from pain as he stood up. "Now I'm serious. You guys need to get going."

It was hard for Jesse and Laura to think clearly with one giant creature howling at them just yards away and two more coming quickly. Finally, Jesse pulled out his handgun and gave it to Mark. Though he knew this would leave him and Laura unprotected, he could not leave Mark so vulnerable. Jesse grabbed Laura's arm and ushered her onto the ATV. With both of them now riding, they sped off down the path, leaving Mark behind. The ATV struggled going up the next ridge, but Jesse and Laura still made faster progress than when they being slowed by Mark's weakness and injuries. When they finally crested the top of a smaller hill, they stopped to check out the surrounding topography.

Jesse turned back and looked through his binoculars. From the elevated position, he could faintly see Mark in the valley below. Mark was propped up on one arm, using the other to fling stones at the encroaching bigfoot. Jesse could not see the other two and did not want to keep watching. He hoped Mark would save the gun and bullets to use as a last resort.

Jesse and Laura took a quick drink of water and pushed forward, soon reaching the bottom of their last hill. The howling and shrieking came from three distinct creatures as the sounds carried throughout the forest. Jesse realized that all three had reunited. He waited a moment more, almost expecting a human scream to follow, but instead heard a gunshot, followed quickly by four more, then silence.

Jesse knew that Mark had bought them a little time and some distance. He also knew how fast the creatures could move through the woods, covering ground at an amazing speed. He was worried that they would catch up quickly. At the bottom of the hill, he and Laura got off the crude path they had been following and plowed through a stream bed and in the stream itself. Though it made for slower going, the ATV managed well in the shallow water and Jesse hoped the water would cover their visible and scent trails.

As they rounded a bend in the stream, they surprised a half dozen wild hogs drinking from the bank. The hogs snorted, then rushed away. Laura had been alarmed when they first saw the boars, but she and Jesse both felt somewhat comforted to see a normal forest animal for a change. They paused for a moment to watch the hogs scurry into the forest, then continued driving through the stream. After another hundred yards, Jesse saw an interesting site overlooking the stream bank. A pine tree had been broken several feet off the ground, with the top still hanging loosely.

"Come on," he said to Laura, "there might be a good trail to follow up there."

Unfortunately, as they tried to drive the ATV up the steep bank, their balance was thrown off by Jesse sitting in the back. The ATV slowed on the incline, tottered slightly, then started pitching backwards. In the meager moment it took for this to happen, Jesse grabbed Laura and pulled her off the vehicle. They landed in the stream just to the side of the ATV as it crashed into the water upside down. After checking to see if Laura was unharmed, Jesse tried to force the ATV upright. In the uneven streambed, Jesse could not get enough leverage to push the vehicle over. After several straining attempts, Jesse looked up at the steep stream bank and realized they were not likely to be able to drive up it even if he did get the ATV right side up.

He grabbed Laura and they dragged their soaking bodies up the bank and back into the woods. Not more than thirty feet away from the broken pine that they were originally trying to reach stood two oak saplings, bent over with tops linked by intertwined branches. Jesse and Laura hurried over to the arch and walked through it. Once through it, the trail widened and then forked at another bent-over sapling. One direction led deeper into the woods, the other headed toward the farm.

Worried, Laura asked, "isn't this one of *their* trails?"

"Most likely is," Jesse quickly replied, "but I bet we can make some serious time on it and at least have a shot at beating them back to the farm."

"This is like an interstate highway system," Laura marveled. "I bet even the park system doesn't have such good trails and markings."

Jesse and Laura hustled down the wide trail, moving as fast as they could in their heavy, soaked clothes. They were only between one-half and one-quarter mile away from the farm, and the open, smooth trail speeded them along to their destination. As the late afternoon waned on, they were even more worried about darkness setting in before they got back. They knew the monsters were not far behind and did not want to spend another night in the woods with such company. Jesse was terrified of being caught out in the woods at night. Though they seemed to be getting closer to the farm, he did not want to try picking their way through the remaining thick forest in the darkness. It seemed that the bigfoot could move just as easily at night and appeared to prefer the cover of darkness, when Jesse and Laura would be even more disadvantaged.

* * *

As the late afternoon slipped into early evening, Jesse and Laura had covered a large portion of the distance to the farm. Just over a hundred yards ahead, Jesse could see where the tree line ended. He could not see past the trees, but could tell where the farmland began because of the lightness of the opening. As it got darker in the canopied forest, the open farmland contrast became more evident. Jesse's hopes rose as they got closer and closer.

Unfortunately, their pursuers had advanced through the woods even quicker. The three monsters had outpaced Jesse and Laura and even passed them up. Jesse could hear their progress as they crashed through the forest off to the side. Suddenly, the silver one stepped out onto the trail. Somehow the giant creature had slipped silently through the woods while the other two made enough racket to distract Jesse and Laura.

Jesse saw him first and threw out an arm to catch Laura from going any farther. The lumbering giant looked down at them from a mere fifteen yards away. It stooped over, spread its arms wide and roared a shrill, shrieking scream that stopped Jesse and Laura in their tracks. With adrenaline flowing, Jesse grabbed Laura's arm and dashed into the woods. He hoped he was heading away from the two unseen pursuers instead of into some sort of ambush.

He had made the right decision, as the other two bigfoot creatures soon met up with their larger counterpart on the trail. Together, the three hairy giants quickly took to the woods in pursuit. Ahead of them, Jesse and Laura hurtled through the forest, banging into tree limbs and fighting just to keep their balance and their forward momentum. They could feel and hear the heavy thudding of three sets of massive feet following them.

Jesse stopped suddenly and turned around just in time to catch Laura. They stood on the rim of a large sinkhole where the ground seemed to open up in a wide, yawning chasm with no quick route around. They had almost fallen into deep gorge in their panicked sprint. Looking at an ancient hickory tree to his left, Jesse saw some thick vines attached to its trunk. He yanked one free and he and Laura used the sturdy vine to help them get safely to the bottom of the sinkhole. The vine eventually pulled free from the tree, though, and the two fell a few feet onto the rocky ground of the depression. Jesse almost twisted his ankle in the fall, but felt it could have been much worse as he looked up at the twenty-five foot tall wall of the sinkhole.

Jesse dusted himself off and helped Laura to her feet. They headed to a narrow slit on the opposite side of the sinkhole. Just as they got to the shallow canyon, they heard the pursuing creatures reach the edge of the sinkhole rim and scream. The scream gave Jesse another adrenaline boost as the eerie shriek put goose bumps on his arms and raised his neck hair in fright. Laura's pace immediately picked up too, and they hurried through the narrow canyon and up the low wall at its end. As Jesse helped Laura to the top and back to ground level, they heard several heavy thumps as the creatures simply jumped to the bottom of the sinkhole.

Though Jesse and Laura had had to detour from the bigfoot trail leading back to the farm, running through the sinkhole and skinny ravine had actually put them closer to one part of the irregularly-shaped cropland that stuck out a ways into the woods. Through the thick trees, they could barely make out the clearing ahead and rushed forward as fast as they could. They burst through the tree line at full speed, with Jesse looking back into the woods with a feeling of having escaped certain doom.

Before Jesse turned all the way around, though, he ran straight into the split rail fence that framed the edge of the farmland. The impact at his midsection stopped him dead still as the hefty fence groaned and creaked a little, but the thick timbers held tight. Jesse slumped to the ground with the air knocked out of him. Laura was frantic and tried to lift him to his feet. Still winded, Jesse could not make it over the fence, so he crawled under its lowest rung. As he dragged his body underneath the fence, he could hear the raucous sound of the creatures blasting through the woods. The old silver male screamed as he stepped into the clearing, and the other two joined in with deafening howls.

Jesse struggled to his feet with Laura's help and dashed toward the rows of corn in front of them. They made their way deep into the corn until they had to stop because of Jesse's injuries. They labored forward a few more feet until Jesse had to stop again. He lay on the ground staring up at the mature corn, which towered over them. In fact, he could only see a few feet in any direction because of the thick, tall corn stalks. Laura wheeled around, trying to figure out where they were.

"I'm not sure which way the house is," she confessed in a panic.

"Shit," Jesse said, still nursing his hip, "we sure don't want to run back toward the woods."

Laura suddenly motioned him to be quiet and then crouched down. Jesse listened and he too could hear something crashing through the corn. They could even hear heavy breathing as the animals got closer. Laura grabbed

Jesse's arm when it sounded like whatever was coming was getting ready to burst through the closest row of corn.

It was not a giant ape-like creature popping out through the stalks, but instead, Steve Akers' two huge German Shepherds. The dogs were ferocious looking and in any other circumstances, Jesse and Laura might have feared the worst. But, in this case, they were overjoyed to see the stalwart companions of Mr. Akers. The dogs recognized Laura and one even ran up and licked her on the face. They seemed to also remember Jesse from days earlier, or at least felt he was not a threat. A moment later, though, they stopped their happy greeting and began sniffing in the air.

"Easy boy," Laura said as she cautiously reached over to pet one of the dogs. They had both changed their demeanor drastically and were standing firm, with ears focused ahead. Their ears twitched and moved like radars trying to fix on something in the cornfield. The older dog suddenly began growling a low, throaty, guttural growl. The other's hackles on his neck and shoulders shot straight up and his tail tucked between his legs. He bared his teeth and started growling too.

Then, they stopped growling, raised their heads simultaneously to sniff the air, and bolted through the corn away from whatever they had just detected. Jesse and Laura glanced at each other and decided to follow in the wake of the fleeing canines. A moment or two after they took off through the corn, a giant gray foot flattened the stalks right at their former position. The silver-haired beast then dropped to all fours and charged through the corn with his two cohorts flanking each side.

Jesse and Laura fled into the stalks, trying to trace the path the dogs had just made. In the low light of dusk, though, the dogs' route was hard to pick up. Laura tripped on a bent-over stalk while she was running, and fell forward. She had tried to grab onto the corn as she fell, but it gave way under her weight. As a result, her hands were not available to catch her fall, and she hit her head on the hard ground. Jesse, who was several paces ahead, heard the fall and ran back to help.

He bent over her and whispered hysterically for her to get up. She sat up groggily, but her eyes suddenly grew very wide. After a moment's pause when nothing came out of her mouth, she let out a scream. Towering above the corn stalks stood the grizzled, grey-haired bigfoot, glaring down at them. At his full height, his massive shoulders and head loomed high above the tops of the stalks. Just as Jesse thought the monstrous creature was getting ready to lunge forward at them, a sharp crack sounded off through the cornfield and a patch of silver shoulder hair went flying and the animal took a step back. He howled in alarm and the scream's thunderous decibels were deafening to Jesse and Laura, just feet away.

The scream was cut short though, when another volley of shot ripped through the corn stalks and forced the animal to duck. Two more shotgun blasts sailed through the air and Jesse finally figured out what direction they were coming from. Jesse could also hear the dogs furiously barking from the same place. Laura was still in a state of panic as she could now see all three creatures crouching and creeping through the corn stalks toward them.

Jesse and Laura hopped to their feet and scrambled away from the animals and searched for the end of the cornrows and hoped-for safety. Jesse looked back occasionally and could tell the monsters were pursuing by the stalks parting and folding in the creatures' path. The shotgun barrage continued, but it was aimed at the top of the corn stalks. It meant that Jesse and Laura were not in danger of getting hit. Unfortunately for them, it also meant that the hulking hairy giants could continue their progress by hugging close to the ground on all fours.

Finally, Jesse and Laura could see where the corn rows stopped and the open farmhouse land began. The gunshots and dogs barking were also sounding closer. They got right to the edge of the corn when a massive hair-covered hand reached through the stalks and snatched Laura's ankle from behind. She screamed and squirmed as she tried to keep from being pulled down and back into the corn. The monster uttered a threatening guttural growl and bared its teeth menacingly. Jesse grabbed a rusty shovel lying nearby and swung heartily at the giant animal's hand.

The shovelhead snapped free from the handle on impact. The creature let go of Laura and with its other arm took a mighty backhand to Jesse's chest. The blow hit Jesse's body square on and lifted him from his feet. The force sent him flying backward a few yards. Jesse landed flat on his back on the dusty ground. This brief commotion lasted just long enough for Laura to scamper away from the monster's grasp. When she did this, her grandfather saw her flailing on the ground away from the cornrow edge. He charged toward her with his shotgun blasting. One of the shots caught the bigfoot closest to Laura on the side of its head and face, shearing it totally bald in these spots.

This creature howled in pain and shock and scuttled back into the corn. To its left, though, the silverback emerged in an attacking manner. Steve Akers swung around just in time to fire two quick shots after reloading. The giant animal ducked out of the way and retreated a few feet into the stalks. Akers ran over to Laura and helped her to her feet while also trying to see into the corn for a target. In the evening twilight, the animals' hair and fur acted as perfect camouflage in the corn rows. Mr. Akers could not see anything to shoot at, so he pulled Laura back toward the farm.

Jesse had struggled to get up and limped over to Laura and her grandfather. The farmhouse was still several dozen yards away, so the trio hunkered down at Mr. Akers' pickup truck. They could hear a weird hooting, grunting and chattering coming from the cornfield. Mr. Akers emptied the shotgun in the general direction, but this only temporarily silenced the creatures for a moment or two. The shotgun shells were proving ineffective with the monsters hidden in the corn as the tiny pellets from each shell did not penetrate far into the thick stalks.

Mr. Akers grabbed a box of shells from the pickup truck bed and began loading them into the gun he had been using. During this period of cease-fire, the grunting animals launched another assault, with the large male leading a head-on charge right at them.

"Grandpa!," Laura yelled frantically.

Mr. Akers saw the movement out of the corner of his eye and instead of finishing his reloading, he dropped that gun and picked up another that lay in the truck bed. He barely had time to turn around and aim from the hip before the animals would be upon them. He pulled the trigger and a magnificent thundering boom rang out through the air. The blast threw him backward from the recoil, but also sent the silver bigfoot reeling as the shot had hit him right in the shoulder. The hair-covered fiends once again retreated to the cornrows, but remained just out of sight.

"I've got this one loaded with three-inch slugs I use for deer hunting," Mr. Akers explained as he regained his composure. "That's one serious chunk of lead coming out compared to the shot shells I've got in this other gun. The slugs pack a punch – on both ends. I know I hit that tall sonuvabitch square on."

The area quieted down for a few moments after the echoes of the gunshots died down and Mr. Akers stopped talking. The dogs had quit barking and were hiding behind the truck – loyal to their master but still frightened of the unknown creatures hiding in the crops. Then, a foul odor crept into the vicinity, emanating from the corn rows. Jesse and Laura had smelled the rotten odor before, but never quite this strong. Jesse's eyes moistened involuntarily, and Laura began to cough. Mr. Akers pulled out a handkerchief and tied it around his nose and mouth.

Though it would seem impossible, the smell got even worse. The strange chattering and grunting picked up again.

"Here," Mr. Akers said to Jesse, "help me load these up before we're overcome by this stench."

He and Jesse quickly loaded each gun with shot shells and deer slugs. Then, something sailed through the dark and landed right next to Laura. She took a step back and looked at the ground, only to see a still-steaming pile of feces. The stink hit them immediately. Another barrage launched from the corn and a chunk of excrement hit the ground next to Mr. Akers, splattering on his trousers. He ripped off his handkerchief just in time to throw up. Laura could not help but do the same. Jesse fought the overwhelming urge, but could feel his stomach and throat reflexively going through the motions. Then, he could last no longer and doubled over in dry heaves.

The creatures took the opportunity to surge forward from the corn. Jesse saw this happen as he was leaning against his shotgun for support while vomiting. He whipped the gun up to fire, but the barrel was clogged with mud from being pushed into the ground when Jesse leaned on it. Jesse squeezed the trigger with one of the smaller bigfoot creatures right in front of him. The barrel exploded under the pressure, sending shot and metal fragments into the face of the monster. The explosion also blinded Jesse with the blast and sent him stumbling backward.

Simultaneously, Mr. Akers had fired a slug round right at the silverback, catching it in the shoulder just inches from the previous wound. The impact of this shot, and the coinciding explosion of Jesse's gun, was enough to halt the bigfoot onslaught. The three creatures dropped to all fours and hurried to the corn stalks. Mr. Akers fired a few shots after them, but in the increasing darkness he was more trying to scare them off with the noise of the gun blasts than trying to accurately hit anything.

Laura bent over Jesse to see if he was all right. He still could not see anything, as his vision had been blinded by the flashing explosion, and his face was covered in blood from the impact of several bits of metal that had cut into his head and face. Laura grabbed his hand and helped him stagger to the pickup truck. Jesse sat down behind it and wiped his face with his shirt. Meanwhile, Laura's grandfather continued to load the last of the ammunition into the one remaining gun. He looked back and asked how Jesse was doing.

"I'm all right Mr. Akers," Jesse responded, "as long as you can hold those brutes off until I can get back on my feet."

"Well, I've got one slug in the chamber and a mixture of shot shells and slugs in the magazine. I've never tried something like that before, but we don't have any other options at the time. I'm just glad that it was the side-by-side that blew up, and not this autoloader."

"Sorry about that," Jesse apologized.

"Save the apologies for later," Mr. Akers said gruffly, "those damn monkeys ain't gone yet."

Against the light green and brown of the corn stalks, Mr. Akers could barely make out the hazy grey outline of the silverback standing up to advance again. He fired two shots in that direction and could hear them passing harmlessly through the corn stalks.

"Down to one more shot shell and two slugs," he fearfully announced.

Growling started to come from the corn rows and the giant male worked himself up to a feverish scream that made the surrounding stalks quiver and tremble in its wake. Suddenly, the cornfield lit up with a brilliant, piercing light. Even Jesse, with his impaired vision, had to shield his eyes. The monsters quieted down in the corn rows and became silent as the light grew stronger.

A full-sized Ford Bronco sped through Mr. Akers' yard, throwing mud and grass out from its sides. The town sheriff was driving the vehicle, and he illuminated his flashing police lights and turned on his siren. He skidded to a halt near Mr. Akers' pickup truck and turned on his door-mounted spotlight. From his higher-up vantage point in the modified SUV, the sheriff could see the situation unfolding in front of him. He saw Laura and her grandfather on one side of the pickup truck and Jesse huddled behind it. In the brilliance of the spotlight, he could also detect three huge objects moving around in the cornrows.

Immediately, the sheriff realized what had been going on. He put the police vehicle in park and focused his spotlight on the cornfield. He stood up in the door frame, leaned over the top of the vehicle and started firing out at the field. He paused firing only long enough to lean down and hand Mr. Akers a police-issue handgun. Akers handed it to his granddaughter, who pointed it at the corn stalks and rapidly emptied the magazine. Mr. Akers shot his last two slugs and set his shotgun down.

While the sheriff continued to fire at the now-fleeing creatures, Mr. Akers leaned into the vehicle and started honking the horn. The spotlight, headlights, flashing police lights, wailing siren, honking horn, rifle shots, shotgun blasts, and handgun firing created such a commotion that the bigfoot group moved quickly toward the far corner of the field. When the sheriff ran out of bullets for his rifle, he reached behind his seat and pulled out a tactical shotgun. He knew the animals were far out of range, but he fired repeatedly, stopping only to pump the gun in between shots. The combination of all these activities drove the three hulking creatures all the way to edge of the field.

The sheriff panned his spotlight across the tops of the cornstalks and illuminated each bigfoot as they stepped easily over the three and a half foot tall split rail fence. He lost sight of them when they entered the tree line and disappeared into the woods. He left the spotlight pointing in that direction and kept his vehicle running so the headlights could continue to shine on the field. The sheriff set his still-smoking shotgun on the hood and reached inside to turn off the sirens.

"Steve, what the hell is going on out here?" he barked in an upset manner.

"Well, Harmon," Mr. Akers replied, "the kids here got into some trouble. I think that's plain to see. I think the boy here needs a doctor. Why don't we tend to that before you start your lectures?"

The sheriff helped Jesse up and they all escorted him into the farmhouse. Laura stayed with him to take care of his facial wounds. Steve Akers and Harmon Willoughby walked back to the police vehicle. Sheriff Willoughby radioed his dispatcher and told her to send a doctor to the Akers farm. He then explained to Mr. Akers that he had received a call about all the shooting from the next farm up the road. The neighbor knew that Mr. Akers had not been hunting in years and certainly would not be taking that many rapid shots in a non-emergency situation.

"I knew this was going to happen," the sheriff said. "I told those goddamned kids not to try a stunt like this." He paused and looked around. "Where's the rest of 'em?"

Mr. Akers slowly nodded his head in the direction of the woods beyond his cropland. "I guess they're still up in those woods, Sheriff." Mr. Akers then stared down at his feet and then rubbed his hands together. "I'm sorry Harmon, I shouldn't have allowed them to use my property to do something like this."

"Apologies aren't going to help anyone out right now, Steve. I will need your help with that SUV you've got parked by the house. If we don't find the owner in the next couple of days, I'm making it your responsibility to get rid of that vehicle. I don't care if you have to drive it down the deepest, darkest ravine you can find or drive across state lines – just make sure it disappears."

Sheriff Willoughby took a deep breath. "Look, don't beat yourself up over all this, Steve," he said after calming down. "You know those kids woulda just gone somewhere else and done the exact same thing. As long as you got your granddaughter back, that's really the main thing. How'd she get involved in all this anyway?"

Mr. Akers gestured towards the house where Laura had just helped Jesse inside to await medical attention. "I think she's taken with the boy, there. She wanted to go see him and his friends out in the woods. I warned her not to, but she never did listen to me on that subject."

Sheriff Willoughby shook his head. He grabbed his shotgun and rifle and put them back behind his seat. Mr. Akers handed him the handgun Laura had briefly used. The sheriff checked the empty magazine and shook his head again. "We'll tidy all this up tomorrow, Steve. I just hope those big ol' apes got enough of a taste of lead to keep them away for a while. Last thing we need around here is a bunch of little battles like we saw tonight."

The sheriff holstered his pistol and finally reached in the vehicle to turn off the spotlight and headlights. "They've always just kept to the woods mostly," he said, staring out at the dark forest beyond the field. "Goddamn kids."

* * *

The next day, Sheriff Willoughby managed to arrange a helicopter flyover of the Akers farm and surrounding forest. Willoughby had not wanted to pursue the normal channels of requesting a helicopter from the state police. Instead, he had phoned a friend of his from a neighboring county search and rescue department who owed him a favor and was able to loan a rescue helicopter and pilot for the day with very few questions asked. The small crew set off that morning and, despite the surface injuries to his face, Jesse was along to help point out places where his missing travel companions might be.

As they flew over the Akers farm, Jesse looked down at the cornfield. He saw massive stretches of flattened-down stalks and wide trails crisscrossing the cornfield, illustrating the giant creatures' movements from the night before. Passing beyond the field, they flew over the woods. Jesse tried to pick out landmarks to point them in the right direction. He saw a high, clear bald and realized that was the spot they had camped at the first night. The helicopter circled around this area, with them all looking to the forest floor below.

In an adjacent valley, the pilot spotted something red on the ground near a stream. The opening created by the stream and its banks meant that the helicopter above had a clear view down to the ground. They circled back and passed over the shallow valley. Sure enough, this time they could all see a body facing up from the ground. Jesse realized that it was Mark, wearing his red long-sleeve shirt. The pilot positioned the helicopter so that a lifeline could be dropped down to Mark.

Sheriff Willoughby climbed in a harness and lowered himself to the ground. Through his radio, he announced that Mark was still alive, but barely conscious. The sheriff then fastened Mark to the rigging and had his limp body hoisted up to the aircraft. Jesse helped pull him inside and propped him up behind the cockpit. Soon the sheriff was lifted back up as well.

After a short consultation with the sheriff, Jesse admitted that it was very unlikely that there were any other survivors. He was amazed, in fact, that Mark had made it through the night. The sheriff determined that, with the possibility of finding other survivors doubtful, and with Mark's critical condition, it would be best to fly to the nearest hospital to take care of Mark first. He noted that he would return to check the forest the next time he could get the helicopter and pilot on loan.

The helicopter spun around to head on toward the nearest city with a hospital capable of treating Mark's grave condition. As they sped over the woods, the crew inside gave complete concentration to making Mark comfortable as best they could. They were not paying attention to the passing forest below. Nobody had even caught the quick view of a tiny, dilapidated cabin when the helicopter rapidly buzzed by.

Someone in the cabin noticed, though. Inside the small, dark structure, littered with leaves and twigs and smelling heavy with musk and rot, a beaten and disfigured face looked up as the helicopter flew overhead. Brad opened his mouth and screamed in vain when he heard the swooshing rotors of the helicopter flying past. The scream was short, and not very loud as Brad was in too much pain to do more. His legs and arms were broken, and his face and chest were scraped almost free of skin from being dragged through the woods by his giant captors.

The creatures had left him in the cabin when they took off through the forest to pursue Mark, Jesse, and Laura. Brad thought they might have forgotten about him and that if he could only regain some strength, he might still make it out of the woods. The sound of the passing helicopter gave him even more hope, as he was sure they were out looking for him. He tried to scream again, but his hoarse, feeble voice did not carry far beyond the walls of the shack.

His scream did, however, elicit a response from outside the cabin. The monsters had returned, and all three stood at the door. The old silver male bigfoot stepped up on the creaking steps, stooped down and turned sideways to fit its massive frame through the doorway. The silverback stood back up once inside and his lofty head pushed the warped ceiling upward. Brad could see a bloody patch on the animal's shoulder and a few tufts of hair missing from its scalp.

He locked eyes with a creature that had been a shadowy presence in his dreams and nightmares since childhood. Yet, the crippling fear that had troubled him for so long was not present this time as Brad experienced a fleeting moment of peace. He knew that relief from his years of torment would be coming soon. Then, a mighty roar rocked the cabin, shaking its flimsy walls and rattling the windows. Brad closed his eyes and prepared himself for the end.

* * *

EPILOGUE

Harmon Willoughby raced up the steep incline on his forest green sheriff's department ATV. He was followed by two trusted deputies on their own vehicles. The three officers had just left Steve Akers' farm a day after having rescued Mark Dunston and flown him to the hospital. They were heading into the dark Kentucky woods along nearly the same path used by Jesse and his companions days earlier. Sheriff Willoughby and his men were each armed with shotguns and sidearms and carried evidence packs on their ATVs. They were not looking for more survivors. They were venturing into the woods for one purpose – cleanup.

Sheriff Willoughby trusted the men following him. They were locals. They had either done something like this before or at least heard of it from older officers on the force. It did not take long to find the campground at the base of Devil's Ridge. Torn tents and wrecked camping equipment were strewn about the clearing. Willoughby assigned one man as look out and the other deputy to help him collect and bag the evidence. Willoughby started picking up spent rifle and pistol cartridges and a large amount of shotgun shells. The assisting deputy began boxing up some of the camera equipment and electronic devices and then moved on to the tattered tents and miscellaneous clothing, sleeping bags, and discarded personal items.

They had started early in the morning and worked until well past noon, but eventually had the campsite picked clean and loaded into boxes and bags strapped to the ATVs or loaded into the small utility trailer that Sheriff Willoughby towed. The Sheriff slid his assault shotgun into a scabbard strapped to the side of the ATV and looked around with satisfaction.

"With a little weather," he said as he put on his helmet, "you'd have no idea that anyone ever stepped foot around here."

* * *

Back at his office, Sheriff Willoughby grabbed a legal pad from his desk and headed to the warehouse at the back of the building. He locked the door behind him, flicked on the lights, and stared at the pile of items in front of him. As he pulled on some white latex gloves, he reached into the first box and pulled out a torn, blood-stained sleeping bag. He wrote a brief description on his legal pad and stuffed the item into a large paper bag. He continued this procedure, methodically going through the items he and his deputies had found out in the forest. He stopped when he got to the camera equipment.

Sheriff Willoughby turned on one of the digital cameras and began skimming through the pictures captured on it. There were many of the campsite and surrounding forest, a few blurry ones of nothing in particular, and then one that truly caught his attention. An involuntary smile of amazement crept across his face.

"Haven't seen that clear and close of a picture in a long, long time," he mused to himself. "That's the type of picture that could take a man from unknown to famous in no time flat." Sheriff Willoughby's smile then faded. "Of course, there'd be a lot of people out there that would view this as if there was a UFO and Elvis in the background. I think I'd rather stay unknown than be 'famous' in that sense. Humiliation and ridicule's not the kind of attention we need around here."

The sheriff powered down the camera and tossed it into another paper bag. After adding a few more items, he carefully folded the bag top over and stapled it closed. He slid the bag over next to several others just like it containing all of the items that he and his deputies had recovered. After taking off his white latex gloves, Sheriff Willoughby put a small blue tarp over all of the bags and a handwritten note on top of that, which read, "TO BURN" in bold black letters.

* * *

Sheriff Willoughby had already accompanied Mark Dunston to the hospital and impressed upon him the importance of dropping the subject of mysterious forest creatures. Mark promised he would not mention a word of it. "I'm a CPA," he offered. "Can you imagine even bringing up 'monsters' around the water cooler at my accounting firm?" He shook his head. "Not a chance. I wouldn't have a job after that."

Mark insisted that he had been concocting a story to give his fiancée as explanation for his injuries. "I'm a novice at camping," he had stated. "She knows I'm no outdoorsman. I think she'd probably be surprised if I showed up having mastered the wilderness without a scratch."

Sheriff Willoughby was worried that Mark's fiancée would be more than casually suspicious when he returned from the wilderness without his traveling companions. Mark thought about Vanessa for a while, particularly about her zealous desire to be considered successful in social and economic terms. Though he did not particularly like this side of her at times, he knew that this trait would give her the capacity to deal with the current situation appropriately. "I may have to tell her a lot of what really happened out here," he decided. "But if keeping that information quiet will keep us out of trouble, that is one thing I know Vanessa will be able to do."

* * *

The sheriff also had a cautionary conversation with Laura and Jesse. Jesse had spent years searching for evidence of bigfoot, but he realized that every clue he and his companions had gathered would soon vanish at the hands of the sheriff. Jesse was initially surprised that this did not bother him. His original encounter with the creature years ago had stoked his desire to reveal these animals to the world. The disastrous expedition he had just barely survived had had the opposite effect. Though he now had personal knowledge of their existence beyond a shadow of doubt, he also knew that this information would be received with skepticism and disbelief without a specimen to back up his claims.

More importantly, Jesse did not want to waste any more of his life or put anyone else's safety in danger to get the proof needed to successfully expose this creature. He had found something in his budding relationship with Laura that had been missing for many years in his life. He did not want to risk losing that by obsessing further over the bigfoot mystery. He could now see that such a pursuit would only have one outcome and that would create pain and loss to everyone involved.

Something Laura had said also helped shape his decision. She had reminded him of her grandfather's attitude on the subject. Jesse recalled what Steve Akers had said, that the bigfoot were just as much a part of the surrounding mountains as coal.

"Maybe they have more of a right to be in those woods than we did," Laura offered. "Besides, think about the people in this town. They probably know more about those creatures than we ever could and it seems like they just accept them, or tolerate them." She had then suggested to Jesse, "Maybe we could do that too. Just let the whole thing go."

Jesse and Laura left together from the hospital and had seemed not too worse for wear to the Sheriff. Trying to augment the scant information hesitantly given by Mark, Sheriff Willoughby had pressed Jesse to provide any additional details possible on the three party members still unaccounted for. He knew that eventually their absences would be noticed and they might get tracked to his town.

Sheriff Willoughby began typing,

"Dear Sir or Madam,

I am writing in regard to your inquiry into the absence of _____. Your letter/phone call indicated that you thought he/she might have spent some time in this area. Rest assured that this office takes all such missing persons requests very seriously. If _____ had come to this area for outdoor activities as your query noted, then I will immediately contact associated wildlife guides and tourism professionals to see if their services were used by _____.

There is also the possibility that _____ ventured into the surrounding mountains on his/her own. In which case, this office can mount a search, though it will be inherently impeded by rough terrain, weather conditions, and manpower constraints. Furthermore, the amount of time _____ has been missing lessens the likelihood of a successful search. Regardless, we will pursue such a search with due diligence as long as reasonably possible."

Sheriff Willoughby quit typing for a moment and leaned back in his chair. After saving the document, he felt satisfied that he had tied up as many loose ends as possible. He could finish the remaining paragraphs of the letter later, in which he would offer alternatives for the whereabouts of the person in question. He knew now it would just be a matter of waiting, and filling in blanks.

* * *